# FIRESTORM
## RECOMPENSE

GLEN E. DERICKSON

WestBow Press books may be ordered through booksellers or by contacting:

WestBow Press
A Division of Thomas Nelson & Zondervan
1663 Liberty Drive
Bloomington, IN 47403
www.westbowpress.com
1 (866) 928-1240



ISBN: 978-1-9736-1346-6 (sc)
ISBN: 978-1-9736-1347-3 (e)

Print information available on the last page.

WestBow Press rev. date: 01/10/2018

# TABLE OF CONTENTS

# INTRODUCTION

I am a professing Christian. I am not a bible scholar. However, I believe I do have a significant understanding of much of what the bible teaches.

I suspect the end times spoken of in the bible, is soon upon us and Jesus Christ is returning to rule the world for a thousand years.

God's wrath is coming upon the world. The matter is not if, but when. Signs indicate the coming is close if not imminent. God has somewhat against the peoples of the earth who have rejected and reviled Him and His Son, Jesus Christ. "Vengeance is mine, I will repay, saith the Lord."

If the bible is true, and I know it is, unimaginable catastrophe shall come upon the earth between now and then. Ten, twenty, thirty, forty or more years from now? Only God knows. Proverbs 27:1 states: "Boast not thyself of tomorrow; For thou knowest not what a day may bring forth."

Why am I writing this story? If I were to see an unaware person standing on a railroad track with a train coming, I would be compelled to warn them.

People must get their heart right with God or they are going to hell.

A judgment of God happened at the time of the flood. A judgment of God shall happen again.

Take heed folks. Time is short.

As American Christians, I think a lot of us believe that we are especially protected by God and many believe that regardless of what happens in the future, God will save us and protect us from physical duress, persecution, starvation, etc. Many believe that Jesus Christ will come in the clouds and take all Christians out of the world before really bad times come. (The Rapture).

We pride ourselves in being a special nation and as a people should receive a special dispensation of protection and privilege from God. I do not believe the United States of America will be spared a harsh judgment. We sinned away our day of grace.

Yes, America WAS a great nation founded on Judeo-Christian principles. God has blessed us greatly. However, each generation and each time period is accountable for their own actions.

When prayer was taken out of the schools in the 1950's, it was a deliberate movement away from Christianity, Judeo-Christian morals and beliefs, the constitution, laws, and societal civility. It began the destruction of the very fabric of the nation. The movement away from Christian beliefs and principles has accelerated since then.

And God said in Romans 1:28, "And even as they did not like to retain God in their knowledge, God gave them over to a reprobate mind, to do those things which are not convenient;"

This is where we are today. It is probably too late for true repentance.

From the beginning, God established the family as the basic building block of society. The anti-God, anti-Christian folks who promote Liberalism, Secularism, and anti-Americanism have made the family, the sanctity of marriage, and sexual purity as their number one target for destruction. (kinda like in the days of Noah?) They have changed terminology to make everything wrong sound right. Their "political correctness police" work night and day to sell their poison.

A boy and a girl "moving in together" used to be called "shacking up". It was frowned upon by society. A child born out of wedlock was looked down upon by society. Since prayer was taken out of school, these practices have increased manifold.

"Woman's choice" of having an abortion, was, and is, the murder of a child. The murder of children in the womb should torture our very souls!

There are many signs that God is moving the world toward the end time and the end of this age. A spiritual battle rages between God and Satan for the hearts, minds and souls of people. WE know that God is victorious in the end but there is a countless number of victims who end up in hell who could have been saved.

God offers an eternity in heaven. Satan offers people the opportunity to be their own god and do their own thing. However, their reward is hell. Where will you spend eternity?

This same battle was fought before the flood. The end result? Eight people were saved and millions, or billions, were drowned. They were warned. They did not believe. They died.

Trying to understand what is taking place in a worldly/spiritual realm, we need to take a look at the makeup of a person. Each person is a descendent of Adam whom God created from the dust of the earth. Of course, God made Eve from Adam and thus gave Adam a wife.

Each of us has an earthly body which some day, if we die, will return to dust. Each of us has a spirit given to us by God. When the person dies and returns to dust, the spirit returns to God who gave it.

The spirit of a person is the critical element in our makeup. There is the unregenerate spirit we are given at conception. There is the regenerated spirit we possess after being born again by accepting Jesus Christ as our savior and Lord. There is the lost, unregenerate spirit that resided in a person who died without accepting Jesus Christ as savior.

The New Testament teaches that during the time Christ walked the earth "unclean spirits" were numerous. Our dictionaries refer to them as "demons". From watching news on TV and seeing the hatred spewed forth by anti-God, anti-Christian, anti-American politicians and others, I believe I can spot many who I believe are demon possessed! (I won't name any names).

What about all the other religions? What about the Buddhists, Muslims, Hindus, Mormons, Jehovah's Witness, Seventh Day Adventists, etc?

Bottom line, if they haven't accepted Jesus Christ as Lord and Savior, they are doomed to hell. The bible is very clear on that. Whether people think God is fair, unfair, or whatever, God makes the rules.

We know the rapture is coming! Probably sooner than later! We know that Jesus Christ, the Lamb of God who takes away the sins of the world is coming back as the Lion of Judah and will rule the world with a rod of iron the millennium!

Where do you think we are in all that? Jesus told us to watch for signs. I keep watching for signs. I believe I'm seeing signs.

A lot of Christians believe that the bride of Christ, the church, will be "raptured" and will be taken out of the world before the trouble starts. I don't believe it. I believe the trouble has already started. I believe the first seal has been opened and the rider of the white horse is riding. I believe the second seal could be opened at any time.

Spiritual discernment comes from God. The vast majority of the people in this nation and in the world lack spiritual discernment. The vast majority of our national leaders and world leaders lack spiritual discernment. Without this discernment, our nation and the world is on the verge of being blindsided by Almighty God!

Surely, man has the potential of wreaking a considerable amount of havoc among ourselves. However, since I profess to be a Christian, I believe what the bible teaches and that God IS in control. He will carry out His divine plan in bringing the world to and through the spilling out of God's terrible wrath during "The Day of the Lord."

God does not need man's help but will undoubtedly manipulate humans and nations in the process of accomplishing His will as He has done in history past.

Not being a bible scholar, I claim literary license if you believe I am straying from strict scriptural interpretations. I encourage you to study the bible and works of scholars if you seek more accurate biblical information on the subject.

In studying the bible, one thing I have noted. When God sets an event in motion, it does not stop until completed. Examples: The flood, Exodus from Egypt, Coming of Jesus

Christ, Establishment of the Church, etc. I believe end times are in motion.

Isaiah 14:9 states: "Hell from beneath is moved for thee to meet thee at thy coming: . . ."

Although this is a work of fiction, I truly believe horrendous events, similar but worse than is depicted here, is coming to this world in the not too distant future. I believe that billions will die in a cataclysmic series of events which will devastate this planet and the peoples on it.

I also believe that, by far, most of those who die will go to hell and reside there through eternity.

Mankind was created with a free will. Each of us is given a choice between heaven and hell. Most will choose hell. It is as simple as that. Any argument against that is as futile as trying to count the number of angels who can stand on the head of a pin.

The purpose of this book is to provoke thought about potential serious events coming to the world affecting your lives, probably very soon. The story includes the fictional Bailey family who attempts to cope with and survive unfolding events. Without being specific, I'm placing the fictional time frame sometime between 2020 and 2040.

# CHAPTER I
# NIGHTMARES

Middle aged John and Ellen Bailey went to bed in their suburban home with no more worries on their minds than the average American family. This was about to change as God began working in the heart and mind of John, urging him to prepare for that which was to come.

The gigantic backfire bomber flew at tree top level, pushed hard against the sound barrier, jinked from side to side, jerked and shuddered from turbulent vapor clouds building in front of the wings. John, standing in the midst of bursting bombs and fire, continued shooting until the plane roared just above his head and then zoomed back into the sky. John screamed and screamed and screamed again, shattering the calm and quiet of his home at 3:00 a.m. He threshed in the dark like a person possessed.

Ellen, waking in terror from a deep sleep, not realizing for some moments the source of the soul rending, unearthly screeches, blended her screams with his until she realized they were coming from him. Ellen groped wildly for the bed lamp, almost knocking it off the night stand. She turned on the light and saw John sitting upright in bed, staring sightlessly, his eyes protruding.

Ellen finally regained control of her voice. "John!" she cried, grabbing his arm and shaking him. "John! John! Wake up! Honey! What's wrong?" She sobbed, continuing to shake him.

John screamed again but less convincing, his senses dragged back to reality by Ellen's voice and her hand on his arm. Finally, he awoke enough to realize where he was. He shook uncontrollably, his face ashen. Although the night air was only slightly cool, he pulled the sheet up to quell the deathly chill that mingled large bumps with the profusion of black hair on his chest.

John continued shuddering, his speech almost incoherent, "What a horrible, horrible nightmare! I've never had one this bad before. It was so real I can't shake it from my mind." His eyes darted wildly about the room; his mind continued having flashbacks.

Light glinted from the liberal sprinkling of gray in John's dark, brown hair. Although forty-three, he was a virile, handsome man who carried his six foot, 160 pound frame lightly, normally appearing at least ten years younger.

Ellen partially regained her composure and embraced him to get him to settle down; the acrid odor of fear-induced sweat assailed her nostrils. She reached for her robe and stepped out of bed. "Lie back down and rest. I'll fix some hot tea and then you can tell me what happened."

John, finally coming back to reality, followed Ellen with his eyes as she walked lightly through the bedroom door and into the hall. In his mind's eye, he saw the same slim and trim five foot-two girl he had married twenty-four years ago and could detect only a slight hint of thickness through her waist to account for the bearing of four sons. Although deeply troubled by the nightmare, the sight stirred his intense and abiding love for Ellen.

After she left the room, John sat on the edge of the bed with his head in his hands, still trembling. "What does it mean? Why have I had this terrible dream?"

Ellen returned with the tea and noticed that although John's agitation had subsided, his hands were still shaking so badly the cup and saucer rattled; he held them with both hands. Ellen walked over to the bed, sat down, and placed her arms about him. "Honey, tell me about it."

"I'm sorry Ellen, I can't. Not now. It was horrible. It probably relates to my war experiences." John shivered. "You go back to bed; I'm going to the study and read awhile and see if I can settle down enough to get sleepy again."

Ellen wanted to remain with John and offer comfort. However, through years of experience she knew there were times he wished to be alone; she reluctantly went back to bed.

John went to the study, eased his body into an overstuffed chair and shuddered again, as he recalled the nightmare, including the realistic dream of a fiery hell engulfing him and multitudes of people. His previous bad dreams usually resulted from actual memories of incoming artillery rounds or supersonic planes at tree top level, strafing and bombing, but this dream especially disturbed him since it didn't relate to any actual event.

*Peace and safety,* he thought. *One of our men ran, screaming and shouting those words over and over in torment.* I'm sure I've heard that expression used before.

"Seems to me that's a biblical passage," John reflected, removing his Bible from the shelf and thumbing through the concordance. "Oh, here it is! 1Thessalonians 5:3." John began reading the passage aloud. "For when they shall say, Peace and safety; then sudden destruction cometh upon them, as travail upon a woman with child; and they shall not escape."

John sat trance-like, his face wearing a puzzled frown, as he pondered the passage. With head in hands he wondered; *Why have I dreamed such a dream?*

When day finally came, John went to the bedroom and woke Ellen. "Six o'clock dear." He walked on down the hall and knocked on the door to Mark's room. "Mark, time to get up." John turned to the door on the opposite side and knocked again. "Tim, time to get up." Shortly, the house teemed with activity while John shaved, Ellen cooked breakfast and the boys dressed.

Soon, the door to Mark's room opened and the handsome teenager appeared. Then he strolled down the hall and took his place at the table. Although he had become seventeen on February 10, his frame, a fraction of an inch short of six feet, supported a solid 160 pounds. His build resembled that of his father; his light hair, light complexion and features were undoubtedly bequeathed by his mother.

Mark's aura of gentleness caused some people to ignore his physique and more than one aspiring bully found out to his sorrow that looks could be deceiving. Mark carefully avoided trouble but quickly dispatched troublemakers who insisted on testing his prowess. He played football, basketball, volleyball, and any other sports he could work in on his perpetually full schedule. Surprisingly, even with all the athletic events, his scholastic standing remained high. He ranked fifth in the senior class at Breton High. Although extremely shy, he attracted girls, and vice versa.

Ellen picked up a small, leather-covered mallet from the

top of the refrigerator and then struck the brass Japanese gong four times. After the muted musical tone subsided, she announced, "Tim, Mark, John, breakfast is ready."

John walked over to the head of the table, pulled out the chair and sat down. Ellen sat opposite John with Mark and Tim at the sides. As if by one accord, the four bowed their heads and John said grace. "Our gracious heavenly Father, we thank Thee for the food, for good health, and for all Thy blessings. Amen."

For a few moments, only the clinking of silverware against china, and china against china sounded while the Bailey family ate breakfast.

John picked at his food in preoccupied silence; his mind insistently returned to the nightmare.

Ellen cast an occasional worried look at him and wondered, for she intuitively sensed that something of major portent foreshadowed their future. The unsettling jangle of raw nerves throughout her body left her feeling frustrated and helpless.

"Pass the butter Tim," Mark said, breaking the silence. Tim rose slightly from his seat, picked up the butter and passed it across to Mark.

"Thank you."

Tim, when compared to Mark, produced quite a contrast. At fifteen, Tim was plump and stocky, standing five-foot four-inches tall, and weighing 140 pounds. His chubby, pleasant face gave him a cheerful, roly-poly appearance. He also loved sports, as long as he sat in the bleachers, in front of the television, or at one end of a chess board. Tim wasn't necessarily lazy; he could see the games much better from that viewpoint.

Tim, the most tolerant and patient member of the Bailey family, saw goodness in everybody and didn't have any enemies. In addition to his sincere concern for people, stray animals, including cats, dogs, and birds, received his bountiful and loving attention. Scholastically, Tim wasn't doing well at all for his roving mind flitted from thought to thought, never staying in one place long enough for anything to sink in. John and Ellen sometimes became exasperated because of his bad study habits but, after each lecture session, they could only fall back on the one hope-that the "Good Lord" would help him turn out okay. Even in troublous times, a short visit with Tim somehow made a person's problems fade into the background and disappear.

After breakfast, John noticed Ellen's troubled, faraway expression and deduced their other sons were occupying her mind. He cast a compassionate look and said, "Ellen, call Bob and Jesse today and find out how they're doing."

Ellen looked up with a start. "Oh, I believe I will."

"Time to go to work." John arose from the table. "Bye dear, have a good day." He stooped and kissed her.

"Good-bye hon. Be careful."

"Bye Dad," Tim added.

John went through the kitchen and across the yard. Ellen got up from the table, started clearing away the dishes, and heard the garage door open. John started the car, backed out into the graveled turnabout between two oaks, shifted gears, and drove slowly down the drive underneath a canopy of trees.

John looked about him and felt a deep contentment. They had been fortunate ten years earlier when this property, which consisted of five acres, with a nice house nestled among several large shade trees, became available and they bought it. The drive led from the house and down to a lane that changed into a graveled road. Two miles beyond, the graveled road connected to a blacktop highway that proceeded on toward civilization, the small city of Breton, Kentucky, which was ten miles to the south.

Breton, a new city with a population of ten thousand, sprang up almost overnight following the Greater Lexington industrialization. The city provided homes for many of the people who manned the machines in Lexington industries. A bedroom community, it contained all the supporting department stores, supermarkets, and services expected in a city of its size. A commuter airport gave them quick access to the rest of the world and Breton had a fine restaurant which attracted large crowds from all over Kentucky.

John drove on toward Breton and work, his thoughts turning to his oldest son Robert, or Bob, who became twenty-three last November. A year ago, Bob married Ruth, a beautiful, blue-eyed, winsome girl of twenty whom he met at Breton High six years ago during his Junior year, when she was a Freshman.

Ruth recently gave birth to a daughter whom they named Sabrina. When Bob, Ruth and baby visited to celebrate Sabrina's three months birth date, she became the focus of all activity, possibly a spoiled child in the making. John smiled, recalling the decision Bob and Ruth made when they finally agreed that their child would probably be safe with the older Baileys while they went for a stroll.

John, well pleased with the girl Bob chose for his wife, recognized her as intelligent, level headed, and very much in love with Bob. She dropped out of college after two years when she married Bob, who had just gotten his Electrical Engineering degree at the University of Kentucky. Her immediate interests and goals focused around making a home and starting a family, after which, she intended to go back to college and pursue her interest in social work.

John stopped at the traffic light, waited for it to turn green and then, one block farther down, turned right on the street which led to the construction company where he worked.

Ellen finished the dishes and began placing the rest of the house back in order. She sometimes felt that straightening up the house was useless. After John left for work, Tim and Mark walked down the lane to catch the school bus. Following their departure, the house gave the usual appearance of the aftermath of a half-grown tornado.

Ellen felt depressed as she went about the routine of her household tasks. The events of last night intruded upon her thoughts and left her with a sense of foreboding. John's nightmare, his first in several years, presented the only event to disturb the tranquility of their life since Mark broke his leg five years ago.

She chided herself for allowing the thoughts to persist and decided to call Jesse and Karen. She walked over to the telephone and punched in the area code for Detroit and then their number. Detroit, lay about 350 miles to the north, in what was formerly the industrial heartland of the Great Lakes region.

Karen answered the phone.

"Hello Karen, this is Ellen."

"Oh, hello."

"Karen, I thought I would call and see how you and Jesse are doing."

"Oh, just fine. "Karen sounded cold and distant when she made the short, noncommittal remark.

Ellen floundered at the obvious rebuff but quickly regained her composure and continued: "Karen, when are you and Jesse coming to see us?"

"We've been busy and Jesse can't leave his job. He may work during his vacation next month." Karen made it clear she would have nothing to do with Jesse's family.

After more small talk, Ellen said good-bye and replaced the phone on the cradle, sorry she had called. Her conversation with Karen left her feeling more dejected than before.

Ellen went to the kitchen, poured a cup of coffee, took it to her work room, and set it on the sewing machine. She remained in deep thought, pondering the details of Karen and Jesse's elopement, as she slipped into her painting smock and began arranging brushes and paints in front of the easel. Realizing the futility of working in her present state of mind, Ellen retrieved her coffee, sank into her relaxing chair in the work room, and allowed her mind to become totally engulfed in reverie.

Karen and Jesse left three months ago with their elopement and marriage coming in the aftermath of a stormy confrontation between Jesse and his father.

Nineteen-year-old Jesse completed his first year of college and then met Karen. Karen, an only child reared by doting, over indulgent and financially well-to-do parents, although a real beauty, acted strong willed, selfish and possessive. What Karen desired she almost always got, and Karen wanted

Jesse. This in itself seemed odd since Jesse just didn't seem to be her type for she exhibited the outward appearances of the typical jet-set socialite.

Jesse was a handsome young man with a studious and thoughtful disposition. From the narrow and biased viewpoint of his parents, they believed that because of his easy nature, he fell prey to Karen's designs. They also believed, as if through hidden powers, Karen mesmerized him. When Jesse approached John and made his intentions known three weeks after he met her, his speech, attitude, and conduct were completely out of character and John became nonplussed by his behavior. John told Ellen the details of his conversation with Jesse.

"Father, I've met the girl I'm going to marry."

"Fine, Jesse, do I know the lucky girl?" John asked. The thought hadn't occurred to John that the marriage was eminent.

"Her name is Karen Matthews; she's from Detroit and visiting her aunt over in Breton; I met her at Georgia Wallingsford's party." Jesse blurted uncomfortably.

The news shocked John. "That party you attended six weeks ago?"

"Yes," Jesse replied shortly.

"This is rather sudden isn't it, Jesse?"

"Yes sir, it is but we've decided to get married anyway." Jesse avoided his father's eyes.

"Jesse, you aren't doing this because you-have to, are you?" John probed.

Jesse flushed and answered testily, "Dad, it's none of your business but no, that's not the case."

"When is this to take place?" John asked, feeling apprehension as he realized the truth.

"Next week."

The news dumbfounded John and his voice scaled up. "Son, isn't this a rather hasty decision? What about your college? You're right in the middle of this semester! How can you support a wife and continue college?"

Jesse, eyes averted, looked up defiantly. "I'll quit college and go to work. I knew you wouldn't understand." He wheeled suddenly, ran out of the house and to his car.

John followed and called from the porch. "Jesse! Don't leave! We can still . . ."

Jesse didn't wait to hear more. He disappeared down the lane, leaving a pall of dust.

The news appalled Ellen when John told her what happened. They tried several times to contact Jesse at the rooming house where he stayed but the landlady informed them during each call and at each visit that she hadn't seen or heard from him. Finally, they checked his room and discovered his clothing and other personal effects were gone.

Since the next logical step was to contact the people where Karen stayed, Ellen called Georgia Wallingsford and got their name and address. They searched for a telephone number in the directory and not finding one, John and Ellen drove by to see them. The obvious poverty suggested by the run-down, dilapidated house shocked them. The painted fence, neatly mowed yard, flowers, and neatly trimmed walk, contrasted the house, which badly needed paint. Ellen recalled the meeting.

"I'm John Bailey and this is my wife, Ellen," he said, when

an elderly, white-haired woman, dressed in a faded but clean, print dress came to the door.

"Yes, what do you want?" The woman asked suspiciously, giving them the once-over with her piercing blue eyes.

"We have a son that has been missing for three days now. We've searched all over and haven't been able to find him. All we know is that he has been seeing Karen Matthews and that she's staying with you," John explained.

"Yes," the woman admitted grudgingly, "Karen stayed here but she left three days ago, bag and baggage, with a young man that may have been your boy. Is he fairly tall and slender?" She visibly relaxed and slipped into her more natural well-bred mien.

"That sounds like it could be him," John conceded. "Did they say where they were going?"

"She said they were going back to Detroit, where she's from."

John thanked her and he and Ellen walked back to their car and got in. Ellen was crying. "Oh John, what have we done to make him feel this way toward us?"

The events perplexed John. "I don't know Ellen. I know he has always been quiet and reserved but I never dreamed he held any resentment toward us." John and Ellen were more puzzled than before, after visiting the place where Karen lived.

It took several letters and phone calls before they finally made contact with Jesse. He talked reservedly on trifling matters but when they broached the subject of his leaving, he quickly excused himself and hung up.

Jesse's actions left Ellen feeling hurt and bewildered. She loved their son along with the rest of their family. It pained

Ellen as she thought of Jesse and Karen. She yearned for the renewal of their close family ties. "Oh, well, there's nothing I can do." Ellen forcibly turned her attention to the oil painting on the easel.

For the rest of the day, John went about his work, remaining withdrawn and thoughtful. As Senior Foreman for the Blanton and Guice Construction Company, his duties were mostly supervisory. He had been with the company for sixteen years and coordinated the activities of all the other foremen which resulted in the construction crews working smoothly. His force was in the process of building a redistribution warehouse complex for an internet firm.

"Come in," John said in answer to a knock.

The door opened and a weather-beaten, rawboned man of fifty-eight walked in.

"Good morning Paul, how are you doing today?" John greeted his pipefitter foreman.

"Fair to middling," Paul replied. "I've come to see what you want done about some fixtures out here. We only installed them two months ago and the paint is beginning to flake off already."

"Uh, what's that again Paul? I'm sorry, my mind was on something else," John apologized.

John listened to him with an unnatural intensity when Paul repeated his statement. "I'll go with you and take a look."

Paul, slightly stooped, led the way as they left the temporary office building and threaded their way through neat piles of construction materials until they came to the warehouse. They entered a door, cut diagonally across, and turned left in through another door to a row of lavatories.

John ran his fingers over one of the faucets; paint flaked away and left a rusty spot. He checked several more with the same results. "What about the commodes and shower heads?"

Paul replied. "They're all pretty much the same. We got them all from the same company."

"I'll go to the office and give them a call. We'll replace the fixtures but it may take a few days to get them." John stated.

"OK John, thanks. I'll get on over to the other side and check with you later in the day."

Paul replied and coming out of the warehouse, he turned to the right and strode along the walk at its side wondering, *what's bugging John today? He sure is acting strange; I wonder if he's sick?*

Occasionally, John caught himself reviewing the nightmare, which kept recurring like a catchy tune, and he forcibly ejected it by thinking of something else. *This is silly of me. Lots of people have nightmares. Why should I let just one bad dream upset me so?*

Although John down-played his fears, he became uneasy each time his thoughts returned to the disturbing dream.

The day seemed endless and although tired, after bathing, John spent the evening in the study reading, reluctant to go to bed for fear the dream would return.

John's eyes showed streaks of red when Ellen came in for the fifth time at one a.m. Ellen walked up behind John, ran her hands down his chest and suggested firmly, "Come on to bed John. Maybe you'll sleep better tonight."

"I may as well. I feel tired enough to sleep all day tomorrow." John, tired and sleepy, went on to bed and, in a short time, snored lightly.

"Blood! Blood! Blood!"

At three a.m., Ellen woke to the blood curdling, soul wrenching screams. "Wake up! Wake up!" she urged shakily, grabbing John by the shoulders.

John, a hideous look of terror on his face, sat upright in bed. His actions terrified Ellen; he may be losing his mind!

She repeatedly entreated John to wake up and her insistent hand on his arm finally calmed him enough to grasp reality. He clutched her arm in his big hand so hard his fingers left bruises that could be seen for days. John was on the verge of nervous collapse and his mind insisted on flicking back and back and back to the horrors of the vision.

"I'll go call the doctor, John," Ellen ventured.

"No, wait," John whispered in a barely audible voice. "I'll be all right in a few minutes."

He shuddered violently. "Why? Why am I having these nightmares?" The despair in his voice reflected inner agony and the aftermath of this dream left him even more shaken than the one of last night.

Peace! Peace! What is happening to my peace? Why do I keep having this horrible dream?

Ellen fluttered about the room, helpless. She placed her arms around John, left him to cross the room, turned, and then came back to place her arms around him again. Ellen wanted to scream; her taut nerves cried for relief. Trembling, she walked over to the door, opened it, and listened for any sounds down the hall. It was quiet.

How did the boys ever sleep through that? She wondered.

Ellen closed the door and firmly insisted: "John, see the doctor today and find out what's wrong. Maybe you've caught a virus or something and it's affecting your nervous system."

John thought: *Explosions and a lake of fire! Am I seeing visions of hell?*

John called his office when morning came and told the secretary he wouldn't be in. He fidgeted away an hour, called Doctor Murray's office and made an appointment for two that afternoon.

Time lay heavy on his hands while he waited and John had opportunity for thinking. He walked through the kitchen and den and onto the screened-in side porch where the morning air felt cool and refreshing on his bare arms. Walking into the rays, he immediately felt the warmth of the bright sun. John sat down in the rocker, leaned back, closed his eyes and relaxed, basked in the morning air, and reminisced.

The state of the nation and the world was very troubling, as usual, on this lovely Wednesday, May the fourth.

John thought back on fairly recent history. Current events, the overall state of the world with 7 billion people, the US with 330 million or so, were enough to create unease in the minds of those who thought about it. Most people though were too busy living their daily lives and trying to make a living to get too concerned.

North Korea, Iran, Syria, Iraq, Palestine, Israel, Radical Islam, Russian aggression in Eastern Europe, Chinese expansion, and all the other pushing and shoving around the world was pretty well accepted as the norm. The uneasy world peace became even more uneasy during the terms of our "Strategic Patience" president. Then the president with the tweets really kept people on the edge of their seats. His heart was definitely in the right place where the welfare of the nation and its people were concerned.

Looking back from 1940 until now, the world has been pretty scary at times, John thought.

World War II, of course, was a nail biter. Essentially, the United States of America was crucial in saving western civilization from the dictatorial rule of the evil axis powers. Never has a generation of people, the American people and their allies, offered a more worthy and selfless sacrifice. President Harry Truman's use of the atomic bomb saved the lives of millions of Americans and Japanese.

Worldwide, the cold war with communism began when WWII ended. General George S. Patton begged our president and military leaders to let him immediately take on the Soviet Union. He told them he could do it in such a way it would appear they started it. At that point in history, it seemed that everybody was tired of war except General George.

Communism began a hard push to dominate the entire world. The Soviet Union immediately occupied and absorbed Eastern Europe, including East Germany. The communist in China overthrew the Chinese Nationalist and forced them to flee to the island of Formosa.

In 1948, an event of supernatural significance and cosmic ramifications occurred. Descendants of Israel were drawn from countries all over the earth and began to populate the newly established state of Israel. The nation of Israel had been reborn as prophesied!

In 1950, the Korean War broke out and in three years, took the lives of another 55,000 brave Americans who helped stem the tide of communism. The Korean peninsula remains divided and is more dangerous than ever with a mentally deranged, satanic leader in power with multiple nuclear warheads in his possession.

The Vietnam War, ill conceived and atrociously managed by liberal, greedy politicians actually was a victory, but surrendered by the political left who were in power at the time and forced an untimely withdrawing of forces.

Although not apparent at the time, the Vietnam War still remained a victory in that it was an extreme burden on the resources and economy of the Soviet Union. Some years later, President Reagan would build on this weakening of the Soviets and bring them to economic meltdown with the "Star Wars" missile defense and other moves which caused the Soviets to overburden their national resources.

John F. Kennedy, who preceded Reagan and Carter, made a run at world affairs and became famous (or infamous?) for the abject failure of the Bay of Pigs debacle, the Cuban Missile Crisis (which came close to a nuclear conflagration) and getting himself shot. During the Cuban missile crisis, it was exciting watching all the convoys of landing craft, troops, artillery, and other weapons of war as they passed through Fort Walton Beach on their way to the southern tip of Florida. President Kennedy backed off on invading Cuba. We will never know if that was a mistake.

Although there was much conjecture and many conspiracy theories about "Who shot John?", there's one I like best. JFK tried at least a half dozen times to have Fidel Castro killed. Lee Harvey Oswald spent a considerable amount of time in Cuba prior to shooting President Kennedy. I suspect Castro succeeded where Kennedy failed.

As for President Carter, many have viewed him for years as our worst president. Since the terms of Barack Obama, many now view President Carter as our second worst president. (More on that later)

After President Reagan forced the Soviet Union to the edge of economic collapse, Gorbachev came on the scene with "Perestroika," and the Soviet Union disintegrated.

World peace was now inevitable. Nations apparently were truly "beating swords into plowshares" through massive disarmament agreements. Destruction of certain classes of nuclear weapons and missiles were already taking place with many more scheduled for the near future.

Russia, in an unprecedented move, vowed she would unilaterally downsize her conventional forces. She intended to move tanks, artillery, and other weaponry into marshalling yards where they would eventually dismantle, melt down and convert them to civilian use. Russia highly publicized events where destruction of nuclear and conventional weaponry took place and the entire free world became euphoric; the menacing Russian "grizzly" began to take on the image of a "teddy."

A huge billboard in Washington, D C, erected by "Peace Lovers International" proclaimed: Peace at Last! Peace at Last! Peace at Last!

The Russians, in the process of implementing a new economic system, a strange blending of communism, socialism, and capitalism, could finally see a glimmer of hope for a better economic future; the system sputtered and faltered for several years and then swept Russia like wildfire. Tens of thousands of Russians, making up thousands of economic delegations, entrenched themselves in every city of any size in the free world; their purpose was to study the free enterprise economic system and set up trade relationships with the free world.

Great things lay in store for the world! Since the breakup of the Soviet Union and the super powers were disarming, the chances of a nuclear holocaust receded. Money not spent on arms could be channeled into much more useful areas. Finally, after years of darkness, a light appeared at the end of the tunnel!

So much for light at the end of the tunnel. Seems we're back in another tunnel.

## CHAPTER II

# THE SWORD OF DAMOCLES

As John sat and pondered, he thought of the Sword of Damocles. The one truism related to the sword, if one is hanging over your head, it is very likely to fall. The perils I see hanging over the head of the world makes the Sword of Damocles look like a pocket knife. Of course, the greatest threat hanging over this world, no doubt, is the divine, righteous wrath of God prophesied in the bible.

However, John reflected, an imminent threat from a world view is the tens of thousands of nuclear weapons in existence. Here where it's all happening, we live, clinging desperately to the skin of this ticking time bomb, wondering. Will it go bang! Shall we all go out in a flash of heat? Will we die a slow agonizing death from the mushroom syndrome, breathing toxic radioactive dust, or will some exotic germ come upon us to make the Bubonic Plague and AIDS seem more like the common cold in comparison?

Do we really live in a time of peace and safety in this new age? Are we on the verge of moving into the era of paradise and plenty, all by our own efforts?

Looking back over events from 1944 until now, considering history and the Bible, common sense screams out warnings. If bombs began falling today, it wouldn't surprise most people at all. Twenty years from now this could be history.

In 1944, mankind loosed the fiery atom on Alamogordo, Hiroshima and Nagasaki and introduced the potential for unlimited destruction.

In 1962, President John F Kennedy stated: "Seventeen years ago, man unleashed the power of the atom. He thereby took into his mortal hands the power of self-extinction . . ." and in July, 1963, he said, "A war today or tomorrow, if it led to a nuclear war, would not be like any war in history. A full-scale nuclear exchange, lasting less than sixty minutes, with the weapons now in existence, would wipe out more than 300 million Americans, Europeans, and Russians, as well as untold numbers elsewhere. And the survivors, as Chairman Krushchev warned the Communist Chinese, the survivors would envy the dead -for they would inherit a world so devastated by explosions and poison and fire that today we cannot even conceive of its horrors."

Total mega tonnage increased a thousand fold in the decades after Kennedy and Kruschchev gave their warnings. Possibly, forty thousand or more atomic devices exist today and many are five hundred times more powerful than the Hiroshima bomb. The nuclear devices on hand could destroy the population of a hundred earths.

Occasionally, men like Gorbachev and Reagan met, tried to tackle the insurmountable problems, and offered slender threads of hope and when the Russian empire disintegrated, the whole world became euphoric. Peace at last! We would hope!

However, there's one problem. Where are the tens of

thousands of nukes worldwide? Whose hands are they in? When and where will they be used? We now have many small nations, some of them extremely unstable and vulnerable to overthrow, with nuclear weapons.

There's Pakistan with maybe hundreds, North Korea probably with 60, Israel with dozens, Iran with no telling how many, and these are just the ones we know.

And keep one thing in mind. God has, in times past, prompted nations and world leaders into wars and actions to accomplish His divine will. This can happen at any time WITHOUT WARNING!

John continued his review of history. Before catching up with the present and the looming cataclysm soon to come upon the world, look back at 1948, at the time of the rebirth of the nation of Israel.

Following the end of World War II, as the US was preoccupied with the occupation of Germany, Italy and Japan, the restoration of their economies and the normalization of the people's lives, there was not a lot of time to pay attention to the Middle East.

After Israel was established as a nation in the Arab/ Muslim heartland so to speak, a lot of apprehension, ire and hostility were directed toward them from their neighbors.

Not long after Israel was proclaimed a nation, Egypt, Jordan and Iraq attacked them militarily. Their armies were inept in comparison to Israel and they were defeated. This set off a series of events and in 1952, King Farouq of Egypt abdicated his throne following a coup. In 1953, coup leader Mohammad Najib became president. In 1954, fellow coup leader, Gamal Abdel Nasser became prime minister.

In 1954 – 1956, the British pulled out as occupiers,

leaving Nasser as president. Nasser ruled until he died in 1970.

In October, 1956, Nasser nationalized the Suez Canal. Britain, France and Israel invaded Egypt. The US objected and did not join them. Israel, France and Britain backed off, leaving Egypt in control. Communist cadres around the world began sabotage attempts at US military bases around the world, as Russia attempted to use the occasion to their advantage.

Gamal Abdel Nasser worked hard at trying to unite the Arab nations. He had some success but it didn't last long. It was named the United Arab Republic.

Anybody working at Cairo International during that time would have seen a host of world leaders, from mostly communist and non-aligned nations, trooping in countless numbers through the airport and being greeted by Nasser. There were heads of state such as Gorbachev and Kosygin from Russia, Tito of Yugoslavia, Sukarno of Indonesia, Chou en Lai of China, King of Saudi Arabia, Revolutionary Ernesto Che Guievarra of Cuba, and even Mohamed Ali of the US.

In the late 1950's and early sixties, the US began courting Egypt and by 1964, we had given Egypt around 4 billion in aid. Egypt, playing the US against the Soviet Union, tried to pressure the US into building the Aswan dam. The US refused. Nasser told the US to "drink the Red Sea" and turned to Russia.

Russia then assumed a leadership role in the Middle East, which remained volatile, a hotbed of unrest and intrigue, ready to explode at any moment. How the Russian premier finally convinced the Arabs, no one would ever know, but many of the Arab countries, including Egypt, accepted Russian advisers within their armies, allegedly to provide stability in the area, which would ultimately lead to peace. This move initially caused quite a stir in the free world nations, especially in the United States, but the integration which took place over several months seemingly was achieving its stated goals. The world finally relaxed following this move and most people forgot the event ever took place.

John's thoughts began to focus more on Israel and the Middle East. As a Christian, John had always had a special place for Israel in his thoughts, mind and heart. Although Israel lost their nation for almost 1900 years following their rejection of and crucifixion of Jesus Christ, their Messiah, God is not through with them yet. Prophecies are full of their participation in the end time events and beyond.

John marveled at the thought of Israel being such a tiny nation geographically and such a tiny nation in population and yet, since 1948, it has remained at the center of the world's attention.

"In fact, I'm not sure it isn't the center of the world, and for that matter, the center of God's creation," John thought.

The road for the new country of Israel has had many bumps. Following Egypt's nationalization, the focus of Arab and Muslim hatred toward Israel has increased.

In 1967, Egypt, Jordan and Syria began an obvious military buildup with the destruction of Israel as their goal. In June of 1967, Israel made a preemptive strike and defeated all three in six days. Egypt then sank ships in the Suez Canal, blocking it until 1975, the year Nasser died.

In 1973, Israel was again attacked by its Arab neighbors,

this time Egypt and Syria. In 1977, Egypt and Jordan made a peace treaty with Israel.

1979 marked a turning point in Mideast affairs as the Shah of Iran was deposed by Muslim forces and Iran became a religious versus a secular state. A few months later, Iran radicals overran the American Embassy and took our diplomatic personnel hostage and kept them imprisoned for 444 days. (The debacle of Iran, the giving away of the Panama Canal and the revealing of the names of dozens of our foreign spies, and hyper inflation, was probably the Carter administration's most noted achievements.)

Radical Islamic Terrorism! --- Brand new. --- Right? --- Wrong! When Islam came into being, their self proclaimed prophet, Mohammad, became the first leader of Radical Islamic Terrorism. Study the history. Down through the centuries, the impact of Islam rose and fell as history played itself out. When weak, Islamic forces laid back and patiently waited. When overpoweringly strong, they struck and conquered. The 1979-81 events that took place in Iran is nothing more than the resurgence of Radical Islam in a modern day form.

Iran is no doubt a key player in current events in the Middle East. They have provided the heart, mind, soul, and much of the material brawn, for terrorism, anti-western, anti-Israeli, anti - US activity in the Middle East and some of the rest of the world. Iran is far more dangerous than Iraq ever was to the Middle East and world stability. Iran is probably the powder and Israel the spark that will set off the big one.

Iran's finger is in the pie of Syria, Iraq, Lebanon, Palestine, Yemen, North Korea and no telling where else. In addition, they receive support either directly or indirectly from Russia, China, and many of the other Mideast countries.

Iran, no doubt, is heavily involved in the cyber warfare against all the western nations. Iran is also a very close collaborator with North Korea in weaponry of all kinds. This is particularly significant in their mutual assistance in nuclear and missile technology. If North Korea has nuclear weapons and ICBMs (which they have) then Iran may have them as well.

Barack Obama, the former (thank the Lord) president of the United States, was a great facilitator in giving Iran 300 million dollar in cash, 1.7 billion in financial relief, removing sanctions and clearing the way for them to obtain nuclear weapons. Just what was he thinking? Although it's immaterial at this time in history, Barack Obama was probably the greatest accelerator this nation has ever had toward moral ruin and decay. He was indirectly the greatest facilitator of radical Islam since Osama Bin Laden.

Iran will likely be annihilated during the end time war preceding the great tribulation, and then obliterated during the battle of Armageddon.

The Muslim Brotherhood, which was founded in Egypt in 1928, is seen by many as responsible for the spread of militant Islam throughout the Middle East. Periodically, Egypt would try to purge the country of the brotherhood resulting in their spread to many other countries in the Middle East. Barack Obama courted and supported Mohamed Morsi and the Muslim Brotherhood following the Arab Spring uprisings.

"Well, time for my doctor's appointment, John thought.

"May I help you?" she asked in a low, modulated voice.

"My name is John Bailey and I have an appointment with Doctor Murray."

She looked down the entries on the appointment sheet. "Oh yes, Mr. Bailey. Have a seat. Doctor Murray will see you shortly."

John walked over, selected a magazine from the rack and sat down.

Fifteen minutes later, the receptionist called his name. "Go through that door and in the first door on your left. Have a seat and the doctor will be with you in a few minutes."

John entered the exam room and sat down.

"Hello John. I haven't seen you in a long, long time." Doctor Murray, short, stocky, and energetic, greeted heartily.

John grinned. "You're right. I wouldn't be here now if I could have avoided it."

The doctor, unobtrusively scanning John's features, noted the pale and drawn features. "What seems to be your problem John?"

In a strained voice, John nervously related the events of the past two nights.

"Undress and let me check you over,"

John stripped to his shorts. The cool room and his tension made his hands feel clammy with perspiration. Doctor Murray fitted the stethoscope to John's chest, listened to his heart, and after several minutes, completed the examination.

"Go ahead and get dressed John," the doctor walked over to the table, sat, and began writing on some forms while he talked.

"John, I didn't find a thing wrong with you. Your blood pressure is up a little, which I attribute to your unsettled nerves. I'm going to do some lab work and make sure we aren't overlooking anything. Have you changed your exercise habits lately?"

"No, I can't think of anything different in my routine. I felt fine up to the time of the first dream."

"I'm going to give you prescriptions for sleeping pills and tranquilizers. Take them for a week; take things easy and see if you straighten out. I'll call you later today and give you the results of the tests."

John finished dressing. "Thank you Doctor Murray. I appreciate your help. If these dreams come back, I'll let you know."

John went next to the lab. Shortly, John emerged from the lab, went back through the lobby and out the door. The bright sunshine looked good and felt good.

John almost forgot the milk, but in passing Burkharts grocery, a handy place to stop only a half mile toward Breton from Earl Townsend's service station, Ellen's request flashed through his mind.

John glanced at the rearview mirror, braked the car, turned into a drive, backed out, and minutes later, he parked at the store.

"Hello Gary," John greeted.

"Hello John," He answered in his slow, deliberate speech. Gary, slowest speaker John had ever heard, stuttered when young. Most people didn't know his slow speech resulted from therapy. John liked doing business with him. He was honest, fair, and a good man.

Twenty minutes later, John arrived back home. With time on his hands, he felt fidgety waiting for the call from the doctor, halfway hoping something would turn up in the lab tests accounting for his dreams. John puttered around while he waited.

"Ellen," John called, peering in the door of her work room.

"Yes?" Ellen turned from her easel with a questioning look.

"You have some paint on your cheek."

Ellen took a tissue and began to wipe.

"A little higher. Got it."

"If Doctor Murray calls, I'm out back."

"OK," Ellen responded and went back to her work.

John went down the back steps and met Marge Kline. "Good afternoon, Marge, come on in."

"Well hello John. I didn't expect to see you here. I thought you would be at work."

"I'm a little under the weather and decided to stay home today." He replied.

"Well, take care." Marge said cheerfully, tripping up the steps and into the house.

Marge and Ed Kline, their closest neighbors and best friends, lived two miles beyond the turnoff to the Bailey's house with sixteen year old Kathy, their only child. Mark and Kathy, friends since early childhood, spent much of their time together and Ellen felt comfortable, seeing Mark interested in her. Kathy, sweet, gentle, and kind, metamorphosed before their eyes into a beautiful young lady.

Marge and Ellen schemed in the way of all mothers to make a match but, unknown to them, nature already fueled the process.

Mark and Kathy became friends and playmates at an early age, and growing up, their relationship remained platonic, mostly good buddies, as they practiced basketball, romped and ran in the fields, fished and hiked and spent most of their waking hours together. Recently, the strange tugging of sexual awareness developed a shy feeling in them toward each other that they had never known. The casual handclasps of the past, while running through the woods, helping one another through fences and across creeks, and playing, were no longer to be ignored and the electrifying tingles they now felt during contact left them faintly disturbed. Their feelings toward each other remained undefined and unspoken as they groped their way along the unknown and untraveled path. Kathy and Mark were unusually innocent for their age.

Kathy, almost physically mature, five foot four inches, her slender waist accentuating the soft, flowing curves of bust and hips, had thick, shoulder-length black hair which framed her flushed face. A slight tan accentuated the spattering of freckles across her nose and cheek. Although not all that small, she appeared dainty standing beside seventeen year old Mark's almost six foot, 160 pound frame.

John walked around the house and stopped beside the air conditioning unit where his eyes took in the landscape behind his house. John could see his property line on the left but beyond the fence, solid forest, with an impenetrable undergrowth, met his eyes. The rear two acres of their five acre tract, covered heavily with trees and the underbrush cleared, appeared cool and inviting.

Closer to the house, the ground opened up except for some young fruit trees on the right, and a garden spot on the left. The earth there had been turned recently, laid off, and planted. As yet, no signs of life broke the surface. A small chicken house nestled in the center, back next to the trees.

Tim's pig pen, with four piglets, set all the way back and out of sight on the right.

Croquet wickets and posts, set up among the fruit trees, provided hours of relaxation and entertainment on Sunday afternoons. Grape vines ran along the fence on the right while flowers, coming up all along the side of the house, and some of the roses climbing the trellis by the bedroom windows, already bloomed. John, feeling much calmer and more relaxed, gazed over the sights of nature which he loved.

Ellen called from the house. "John, telephone!"

John walked hurriedly through the house to the living room and picked up the telephone and spoke. "John Bailey speaking."

"This is Doctor Murray, John. Your tests all turned out negative. Let me know though if you have any more problems."

John thanked him and replaced the telephone on its cradle. The call left him feeling uneasy and slightly apprehensive, facing the unknown.

Following the doctor visit, John had a reprieve for a week, followed by another horrible nightmare.

The Bailey household returned to normal from all outward appearances but Ellen could tell something still bothered John. However, since he had improved, she decided not to pursue it.

The next night, John dreamed again of the rushing fire and salvation through the opening. He kept hearing an insistent voice saying over and over like a broken record, "Hurry! Hurry! Hurry!

He went to work Tuesday morning but his heart wasn't

in it. He made a conscious effort all day long, trying to keep his mind on his tasks. The day dragged interminably.

When John returned home, Ellen accosted him. "OK John, tell me what's going on."

He grinned sheepishly. "Ellen, I'll confess, I've dreamed the past two nights. They're different from the others but are upsetting nevertheless."

He related the details of his latest visions.

"John, what in the world are you going to do? Have you called for another appointment with the doctor?"

"No, I haven't yet but I may later on today, depending on how I feel."

Tuesday night, John dreamed a third time of the rushing fire and the beckoning opening. He grew evasive when Ellen questioned him the next morning and left for work without relating any of the details.

After work, John went by the library and browsed through articles and papers covering the past two years. This refresher triggered his memory and vast numbers of information pieces welled into his consciousness. He began developing a shadowy picture, almost like lying in bed, asleep and dreaming, but almost knowing.

Following the review in the library, John went to the park, occupied the same bench as before, and reviewed all six dreams in minute detail, trying to extract some reason from them and, time after time, giving up in nervous frustration. Finally, he wrote down all the points brought out in the dreams.

(1) He envisioned tremendous explosions and fire.

(3) Massive destruction included cities, forests and even the countryside.

(4) Their family, to escape, found haven in a hole in the ground.

(5) And then, there was the repetition of the "Hurry! Hurry! Hurry!"

(6) His family would survive for he saw them emerging from the hole after the fire.

(7) Then there were the Bible passages.

John carefully studied them again. Could it be the end of the world? No, for we survived, he decided.

Realization suddenly dawned on him! His subconscious accepted the reality several days ago but his conscious refused to believe anything so terrible!

The massive destruction must be the result of a nuclear holocaust! The rushing fire represented the danger to his family! The hole, was it a haven of some sort? Was it an underground shelter to escape destruction? Of course!

The message came to him in terrible clarity! His mind continued fighting and refusing the horrible truth, a nuclear war with massive destruction! His visions were a forewarning! Just then, the words echoed in his mind. "Hurry! Hurry! Hurry!"

John thought, whoa! Before I get carried away with this and tell Ellen, I need to spend some time in prayer, thought, and study on this. Could this be the beginning of the end times? I know for sure that Jesus told his disciples that nobody, not the angels, but only God in heaven knew the day or the hour when these events would take place and Jesus would return. However, Jesus went on to say that we should watch for certain signs as the time drew near, for we would recognize them and understand.

At one time, John had gone through the bible and

worked up a time line, understanding the results were in general, since several factors would affect the accuracy, such as differences in lengths of years in Old Testament times, etc.

John looked at a 7,000 year time period from the creation until the end of the thousand year reign of Christ. His calculations indicated it was around 2,000 years from the creation until Abraham offered Isaac as a sacrifice to God when Isaac was 16 years old. He calculated it was around 2,000 years from Isaac being offered until Jesus was crucified. It has been close to another 2,000 years from the crucifixion of Jesus until now, in possibly another 16 or 17 years.

John continued his thoughts. I don't know if there's any significance to that but it makes me wonder. I could guess that the time frame could have a bearing in God's plans.

I believe the end times events leading up to the millennium will consist of a series of events, which are outlined beginning in chapter six of the book of Revelation. When God sets these in motion, and I believe they are already in motion, I don't think they will stop until the end of the thousand year reign of Jesus Christ.

We hear and think a lot about the seven years of tribulation preceding the millennium. I believe the end time events include several years preceding the 7 years. In fact, I suspect we are probably well into the end time events.

John reviewed Matthew chapter 24. In the last half of verse 3, Jesus' disciples asked him when shall these things be and what will be the sign of your coming? In the following verses of Matthew, Jesus gave them a general description of what was to come. In verses 32 and 33 Jesus told them, "Now learn a parable of the fig tree; When his branch is yet tender, and putteth forth leaves, ye know that summer is nigh; So likewise ye, when ye shall see all these things, know that it is near, even at the doors."

John turned to Revelation chapter 6 and reviewed the words of the first six seals. "I really think this is where we are in history. Generally, I believe we are on the verge of entering into some really bad times. Forget the details. I believe it is urgent that I do what I can to prepare for myself and my family to survive as long as we can. We will just have to depend upon God to see us through it."

"I need to talk to Ellen."

John arrived home Friday afternoon barely able to suppress his excitement. He rushed into the house and located Ellen. She stood in front of an almost-complete oil painting. John kissed Ellen hungrily, holding her in a fierce embrace.

Ellen laughed when John released her. "Careful, you may get paint on you; and another thing, don't start something unless you're prepared to finish it."

John grinned momentarily but then turned grave. "At another time you can be sure I would finish but right now, I have something to discuss with you."

Ellen looked at him strangely. "What is it, John?"

"I finally understand my dreams. For some reason, I've received a message, why or where from, I don't know for sure but I think it's from God."

"Just what is this message?" Ellen began to feel dread.

"Maybe you should sit down," John advised, leading her to a seat in the study.

While John gave his translation of the dreams, Ellen's face reflected horror and revulsion. She thought, John must be mad! What can I possibly do to help him?

John finished his story and stopped. Tension ran high between them and Ellen sat silently, afraid to trust her voice.

"Well, Ellen, why don't you say something?" John asked nervously.

Her face a sickly yellow hue, she finally answered shakily. "John, do you realize . . . ?"

"Honey, I know what you're thinking; you think I'm crazy. I assure you, I've never been more sane in my life and I hope you'll believe me for we have to act right away. There isn't a moment to lose," John responded tensely.

John left Ellen sitting rigidly, almost in a state of shock, walked hurriedly to the telephone and dialed Bob in Cincinnati. Ruth answered the phone.

"Hello Ruth, this is John. Is Bob there?"

"Yes he is. Just a minute and I'll get him for you."

"Hello father."

"Hello Bob." John didn't waste time on small talk. "How soon can you come down? I must see you at once."

"It depends on the urgency. I could start now."

"Bob, it's plenty serious; I can't explain too well over the telephone but it's a case of life or death."

"Is mother or one of the boys sick? Or hurt?"

"No Bob, nothing like that, but it's very serious."

"Then we'll be there later tonight,"

"I'll be looking for you. Don't break the speed limit."

John broke the connection with Bob and then punched in Jesse's number in Detroit.

"Hello Jesse, this is your father. I need to see you right away and I want to know if you can come home?"

"What is this about?" Jesse asked.

"It's too complicated to explain over the phone."

"I'm sorry father but I can't afford the trip and I can't leave my work."

"Jesse, this is a matter of life and death. I'll send you the money. Don't worry about the job for, under the circumstances, it isn't important and you can live with us."

"I'm sorry father, I couldn't do that." Jesse remained resolute.

John finally saw he couldn't convince Jesse and reluctantly said good-bye.

Ellen had walked into the living room and heard John's conversation with Bob and Jesse.

"John, what in the world has come over you? What are you doing?"

"Ellen, my dreams have convinced me that, for some reason, I've received warnings of coming destruction. I intend to prepare shelter for our family."

Ellen could see John's obsession with the idea and visualized difficult times ahead. She didn't say anything else but thought, when Bob comes tonight, maybe he can reason with him.

Mark sat in the den watching television and Tim played outside with Trixie, a brown and white mongrel stray that Tim took in two months before. The dog weighed fifteen pounds and ate like a horse. Ellen wasn't too happy with it but held her thoughts since Trixie replaced Pal, Tim's Collie, that died a few weeks ago.

John opened the door. "Tim, come in the den for a few minutes."

"Be right there, father."

After Tim entered, John turned the TV off. "Boys, we have a serious matter to discuss."

Mark and Tim perked up and listened. John was unusually tense and they had never seen him this serious before.

John spent an hour explaining the dreams, his analysis of them, and his plans for survival. "I've been reviewing past events and the world situation, trying to tie it all together. I see a lot of disquieting factors on the world scene but it's all too complicated for me to analyze them and come up with clear answers. Later, when we have time, I'll try to explain it to you. I know I'm basing my decision on intuition more than anything else, and to the rest of the world, this would appear wholly irrational. However, I've made up my mind and I'll stick with it." John continued. He fielded their questions, many of which he couldn't answer.

"Tim, you and Mark have only one more week until school is out, don't you?"

"Yes dad. We get out on Friday, May the twentieth."

"Boys, I consider the matter serious and if your school were more than another week, I would take you out. I'll expect you to work hard in the evenings and on weekends."

The boys were skeptical but respectful and didn't question his decisions. They raised eyebrows at each other and sat in stunned silence. Mark and Tim both started asking questions.

John held up his hand until they became silent. "Tim, you go first."

"What about my pigs and dog?"

"You picked a good one Tim. There are many questions to answer and many tough decisions to make in the next few days and this is one of them, for right now, I just don't know."

John nodded to Mark.

"What about our neighbors and friends, father? What about the Klines? What about Kathy?"

"Mark, I'll do my best to warn and convince people of what's coming, but, unless there are definite signs, I doubt if many will listen."

"May I tell Kathy?" Mark asked.

"I'd rather you waited until after I've talked to Ed."

Mark lapsed into silence, subdued and bewildered, his mind whirling from the threat to his well-ordered world.

"Do you have any other questions?"

"Not now," they both conceded.

John sat in the study reading until Bob pulled into the drive a little past midnight. John walked out to their car and opened the door on Ruth's side. Bob climbed out from under the steering wheel; Ruth handed Sabrina to John.

"Don't worry about waking her; she's wide awake."

Three month old Sabrina looked more like a doll than a baby, wearing a pink bonnet, pink frilly dress, pink-laced panties, white socks, and tiny black shoes.

Ellen arrived and John handed her Sabrina. "I'll take care of this young lady." Ellen grasped Sabrina firmly and clasped her to her breast.

Ruth rummaged around in the car and brought out diaper bag, purse and a box. "I'll have Bob bring the rest of the things a little later."

"We'll take them in now and let you and Ellen get settled for the night," Bob stated as he walked around to the trunk, opened it and removed their luggage.

John took one suitcase and the box from Ruth and led the procession to the house while Bob brought up the rear with the other baggage. They went to the guest room and deposited their burdens.

John and Bob left Ellen and Ruth talking animatedly and went to the living room. "We may as well get comfortable; this will take some time," John advised.

"Dad, my curiosity is killing me. Everything here looks normal but you sounded so mysterious. What is there that's so urgent?"

Bob, we'll call all the family together so I can explain everything to everyone at once."

After Bob and Ruth got settled in, John got Ellen, Tim and Mark to join them in the living room.

John related his experiences in minute detail, knowing he must convince Bob. He sounded almost apologetic as if the disturbing foretold events were his fault.

Bob listened carefully and heard the entire story before asking any questions. He couldn't keep skepticism from his voice. "Dad, how can you completely abandon an entire way of life on such flimsy evidence? Before you take such drastic steps, don't you think you should wait a month or two and see if your doctor can help you? He may have a perfectly reasonable explanation."

In a more positive tone, John answered. "Bob, there isn't time. I'm not sure that we aren't too late already."

"Dad, there's absolutely nothing on the world scene or in the United States remotely suggesting such a thing."

"I disagree with you, Bob. I see many danger signs which point to this possibility." John related national and international conditions he had been mulling over the past few days. John continued voicing his thoughts in a taut, controlled voice. "Since I've finally opened my eyes, I'm scared. It's almost like sleep walking and suddenly waking up outside, naked, and believe you me, we are naked. We're kinda like the frog in the pan of water with the temperature rising gradually over several hours. The water boiled the frog and it never realized there was a problem."

"Bob, we've sublimated the events of the past several years and now our goose is practically cooked." As John continued the dissertation, he loosened up and resumed a normal tone. "I'm going to explain the key element in my interpretation, and incidentally, there's nothing mystical; it's basically common sense.

"We need to look at the overall world makeup from a political, military and religious perspective. Most of the world is hostile toward the United States. Some of it is political, some of it is ideology; some of it is pure old jealousy. A few nations will stand with us if things go bad. Most won't. Militarily, we are dangerously weak. Weakness invites aggression."

"Look at Israel, A tiny nation in the middle of a hotbed of hostility. If there is any nation in the world more hated than the United States, it is Israel."

Look at the rise of Militant Islam. Look at the Radical Islamic Terrorism. Here in the United States, look at the rise in right wing nationalism, the left wing nationalism, the sense that we are on the verge of anarchy at all times. Look at the influx of radical Islamic terrorists into this country. Look at what some call the Deep State, the hidden government of left wing, progressive, anti-God, anti-Christian, anti-American cells."

"The nation and the world are ripe for the picking."

"In the day of the flood, who set it in motion? God. At

the time of the Exodus of the Israelites from Egypt, who set it in motion? God. At the coming of Jesus Christ, who set those events is motion? God. At the events preceding the Day of The Lord, who shall set them in motion? God."

"Well family, I hate to break it to you, I believe that time is here."

Bob, who had been concentrating on John's words with almost hypnotic intensity, still wasn't convinced. "We can discuss it again tomorrow after I've slept on it, Dad."

Bob lay awake a long time, trying to absorb and fathom all his father told him. He finally drifted off into fitful sleep, disturbed by horrible dreams.

John drove to Breton the next morning and bought tools. Among other things, he obtained picks, shovels and gloves for the project. He purposely went alone and allowed the family time to discuss his plans out of his presence.

The car was no more than out of sight before Bob, Ellen, Ruth, Tim and Mark gathered in the den.

Ellen spoke first, sounding distressed. "I really don't know what we should do. John may be losing his mind."

Ruth defended. "He doesn't act like somebody out of his mind. He's tense and nervous but entirely rational."

"He's more normal now than when he was having the nightmares," Mark added in support.

Tim retorted, "There's one thing for sure. He will build the shelter and I don't believe anybody can stop him."

After a silence Ellen spoke. "We really have only two choices. We can cooperate with him or have him committed for observation. His mind is made up and there's no way we'll talk him out of it."

Complete silence prevailed; each of them considering the dilemma.

Bob finally broke the quiet. "I, for one, am in favor of backing Dad even though I think he's wrong and making a big mistake. Since it will only cost us time and money, I think we should humor him. If he is wrong, maybe he'll come to his senses."

Ellen sobbed with relief when they unanimously approved and the crisis passed.

"Ruth, would you like to take a walk?" Bob asked, walking over and offering his hand.

"Yes, if mother will keep Sabrina," Ruth accepted, grasping his hand and rising. "I'll be glad to."

Bob and Ruth always enjoyed walking around the small farm, pleasant and cool under the green trees and among the flowering shrubbery. Walking arm in arm, they were a striking couple. Bob stood six feet tall with broad shoulders, slender hips, dark brown hair, brown eyes and well tanned features. Ruth's head came to the top of his shoulder. She looked small at his side, well proportioned and dainty. Her black, natural curly hair formed ringlets at the temples at the slightest dampness. Childbearing made little difference in the appearance of this lovely, winsome girl. Bob and Ruth bowled, played tennis, and it wasn't uncommon to see them in their back yard playing croquet.

When John returned at noon, Bob met him at the door.

"Let's go into the study Bob."

Bob closed the door and asked, "How was your trip?"

"Fine, but let's get on with it." John spoke with a trace of sharpness. They both acted stilted and unnatural.

Bob smiled sheepishly. "Father, I'll be frank. I don't

consider this the time for soft soap or politeness. We discussed your dreams, your intentions, and all the effects it will have on our lives and we explored the possibility that you may be mentally unbalanced. We even considered the advisability of having you examined and, if necessary, committed, for we all believe right now that what you're doing is a bad mistake. However, our final decision is that, regardless of the outcome, you get the benefit of every doubt and we'll stand with you. We are totally committed."

Bob smiled and moderated his voice. "If you're wrong, our time, money and efforts will have built the most expensive storm cellar in history." Solemnly, he continued, "If you're right, well, you will have saved all our lives."

John grinned and relaxed. He realized how sticky the situation could have become if they had taken a different stand. This cleared the way for fast action. "Bob, I hope I'm wrong. I'm convinced though I'm right and our only hope for survival lies in careful preparation. Bob, would you get Tim and Mark?"

They were out behind the house where their imaginations continued soaring over the recent happenings. Mark and Tim came in the house and joined Bob and John.

John immediately began giving orders. "Mark, you and Tim can work with Bob drawing up the preliminary plans. Bob, when you get it roughed out, call in Ellen and Ruth and get their ideas on things we may need. Since it's too late to work today, you can plan and make material lists."

John leaned toward them and continued. "I can't impress upon you too strongly the seriousness and urgency." John got up and walked to the other side of the table. "There are two things I must do. I'm going by the church and speak to

Reverend Burger and then drive out to see Jesse. I'll return by late tomorrow night, hopefully. I have a letter I'm going to give to Reverend Burger and ask him to pass out to the congregation. He may not. If not, then I'd like for all of you to get to the entrances and hand them out. He may not like it but if it's outside the church, I don't see why he would stop you."

"Father, Mark asked, "when will you tell the Klines?"

"It will probably be Monday night before I can see Ed."

Mark seemed disappointed.

"Bob, make arrangements to take your vacation. If nothing happens by the time you've used it, you can try for a leave of absence. I don't want you to quit for that would ruin your future if nothing develops from this."

"Father, Ruth and I will probably drive back home Sunday night and come back Monday night. I'm hoping the company will give me the time off."

"It would probably be a good idea if you and Ruth brought back all the clothing you'll need for a few months."

Ellen waited for John in the kitchen where she had prepared a food hamper and quart thermos of coffee. "John, be careful. I love you." Ellen went into his arms. John kissed her, picked up the food hamper and thermos and with a husky good-bye, went out the door. He harbored mixed feelings, embarked on a mission wholly alien to his past life.

Sunday night, John went to bed at 10:00 p.m., no longer fearful. He slept peacefully until 3:00 a.m. He tossed and mumbled and, after ten minutes, awoke.

John dreamed again, but this time with a difference and strangely, he felt great peace and tranquility. An overwhelming lassitude came over him and after a few minutes, he went back to sleep and didn't wake up again until morning.

Ellen was exuberant. "Oh John, I'm so glad you aren't having any more of those horrible dreams. I worried about you."

John kept quiet about last night for he didn't wish to spoil her hopes. He finished breakfast and went off to work.

That evening when he came home he went to the study and took down his Bible, for something from his latest dream puzzled him. A Bible passage kept running through his mind. He remembered where to find this one, verses he knew well and loved dearly, Psalms 23:4 "Yea, though I walk through the valley of the shadow of death, I will fear no evil; for thou art with me; Thy rod and thy staff they comfort me...."

John tried hard to relate this to the vision in his dreams. He and his family ran desperately, trying to outrun a fire rushing toward them and when it appeared they would perish, a hole appeared in the ground and they ran into it headlong. The fire swept over them and, crackling and burning, fiercely, receded into the distance. After a time, they cautiously came out and walked away. John felt frustrated and pondering the vision gave him a headache.

## CHAPTER III
# THE FIRST SEAL IS OPEN

Revelation 6:1, 2: "And I saw when the Lamb opened one of the seals, and I heard, as it were the noise of thunder, one of the four beasts saying, Come and see. And I saw, and behold, a white horse: and he that sat on him had a bow; and a crown was given unto him: and he went forth conquering, and to conquer."

John went to his study and with his head bowed, petitioned God for understanding. Later, as he sat meditating, he began to take notes as thoughts came into his mind.

From the end of World War II an uneasy peace settled upon the world, broken by the Korean War, Vietnam War, Cold War with MAD (Mutual Assured Destruction) hanging over us, Bosnian conflict, Israel's 1967 and '73 wars with her Arab neighbors, Yemen's Civil War, Iraq War, 911, 2nd Iraq War, Afghanistan, Syria, Yemen, ISIS, etc.

The United Nations, meanwhile, did its thing in the world and only God knows if it was a plus or a minus in the scheme of things. Of course, it has made a good platform for nations of the world to pick at the US.

We had a push around 1990 for World Government and a new world order voiced by President George HW Bush.

An attempt was made by world leaders to get the UN more involved, transfer our parks over to the UN, etc. The most significant thing apparent was speed signs in Natural Bridge State Park in Kentucky changed from miles to kilometers. Oh well.

Anyhow, on the peace issue, we come down to one of our recent presidents who ran partly on the promise of peace in the world. Even before he signed his first executive order, he had been awarded the Nobel Peace Prize in advance for bringing peace to the world. No wonder one of our illustrious news people felt a warm feeling down his leg!

This same president made an apology tour in many parts of the world telling folks how mediocre his country was and how sorry he was we had thought ourselves exceptional. No doubt, he hoped to bring peace and unity to the world.

Some folks say he wasn't an American citizen. Some say he was a Muslim. John thought, "Whether he was or wasn't either of these, its immaterial. I believe this. He never had the mindset or the heart of the type American most ordinary American patriotic citizens believe in. He may or may not have been a professing Muslim. He certainly appeared to be a Muslim sympathizer. His actions did not indicate he was a Christian sympathizer."

This particular president systematically and totally destabilized the Middle East. Pulling our troops out of Iraq apparently led to the rise of ISIS. He could not have done a better job of placing that part of the world in turmoil if he had planned it. He certainly was not a friend of Israel.

God gave this president to the US. God is in control of who does and does not become president. God does not always give a nation the president they need but the president they deserve.

Much evil has befallen this nation since prayer was taken out of school, legalized murder of babies by abortion, promotion of homosexuality and unfettered sexual perversion.

We have seen a lot of anti-God, anti-Christian, anti-American actions in previous administrations. However, in my view, we seem to see more evil decisions coming from our government than ever before. The administration of our peace president is the most evil yet to come upon the scene. Over the past few decades, all three branches of our government have fallen short where the moral integrity of their decisions has been concerned. Unfortunately, we, the people are responsible to a large extent. We have allowed it. As a people, I'm afraid we got what we voted for, asked for, and deserved. We have sown to the wind. We shall reap the whirlwind!

John continued his meditation and suddenly, a stark realization came upon him! For the past several years, we have had attempt after attempt at trying to bring peace to the world through small wars, attempts at nation building, and talk, talk, talk.

***The Rider of the White Horse has been riding, riding, riding!***

*Jesus Christ, the Holy Lamb of God who came to take away the sins of the world by the shedding of His blood, has opened the first seal!*

This explains everything! It is clear the end times are upon us! Looking back, I believe the first seal has been open for some time, probably years.

Looking ahead, what is next? *The second seal! The Red Horse! War, destruction, starvation and pestilence!*

Lord, what do I do now? John prayed. I need to explain all this to my family. I need to explain it to friends. I need to explain it to the pastor and the church.

What about the country? Whatever I say or do will be met with total disbelief and hostility.

John made his first stop in Breton. He turned into his pastor's drive, stopped the car and got out. He walked across the lawn, hesitated a moment before pressing the bell, took a deep breath, and pushed. He could hear the chimes inside. Ten p.m. seemed a little late but the urgency warranted it.

Reverend Burger came to the door. "I'm sorry to disturb you so late but I need to see you about a very urgent matter, Reverend Burger."

"Come on in John. I'm available to you any time, day or night, if you need me." Reverend Burger led the way to his study. "Have a seat and tell me what's upsetting you."

John's appearance, nervous and excited, gave him away.

"Reverend Burger, I have a story to tell you that will try your very soul and I must convince you of its truth for I know that only you will be able to make our church members believe and save their lives."

John took a deep breath and blurted. "Reverend Burger, a nuclear war is coming soon, very soon, and fallout shelters offer the only hope for survival. We must warn people and convince them or they will all die. The fallout danger will remain for many days even after the war is over."

Reverend Burger looked at John in amazement. "John, is . . . is this a joke? What do you mean by this?"

"It's no joke. Hear me out and see if you don't change your mind."

Reverend Burger's face registered shock and disbelief as the story unfolded.

John talked for an hour and related all the events about the dreams. He told him he thought the first seal had been opened. Reverend Burger's face told John long before he finished he was wasting his time. John continued detailing his beliefs. His feelings of love for his fellow man wouldn't allow him to stop until he finished.

By the time John concluded, Reverend Burger had regained his poise. "John, have you sought medical treatment for these delusions?"

John's face flushed. "Reverend Burger, I did see a doctor about the dreams. However, I'm not suffering from delusions. I know the story sounds crazy but it's true. Time will prove me right. Everybody must act now if they are to survive."

"John, are you and your family Christians? I know you all live and act like Christians but you do realize, don't you, it takes a personal commitment? You were already members here when I came so I just assumed you were all converted."

John's face turned a deeper red. "I believe we're all Christians Reverend Burger. We go to church regularly, say grace at the table and live the best we know how. We try to worship and serve the Lord."

"John, I know you're in a hurry but when you have time, stop by and we'll talk about it some more."

"I'll do that but for now, I'd like to ask a favor."

"What do you expect of me?" Reverend Burger asked, feeling unsettled.

"I have a typewritten copy outlining what I believe will

take place, and why." John reached inside an inner coat pocket and removed a sheaf of folded papers. "I've included plans for a fallout shelter and a list of all the things that families need to do to survive the coming destruction. I also have copies of this which I'm mailing to some newspapers, the governor and the president."

John handed the papers to Reverend Burger. "I'm asking that you make more copies of this and give them to the church. I would do it myself but I don't have the time."

Reverend Burger took the papers and read them.

John fidgeted, in a hurry to leave for Detroit.

Reverend Burger spoke, "I couldn't possibly relate such a story, John. The congregation would think me insane. For one thing, the shelter and all the other equipment would cost a fortune. Less than half our people could afford it, even if they decided to do it."

John became more agitated. Under a terrific strain now for days, his inability to convince his pastor made it even worse. "Reverend Burger, even if you can't believe me, you can include a statement on the same paper that these are entirely my opinions and don't express yours."

Reverend Burger answered defensively, "I won't make you any definite promises that I'll do it John. After praying about it, I'll see if I can do so."

This left John with a complete lack of assurance that anything would be done toward warning his friends. "I hope you pass out the letter," he spoke fervently. "I must leave now for Detroit. It's a long trip."

Reverend Burger followed John to the door. "John, I hope you get to feeling better soon. Come by again when you have time and we'll discuss it further."

"Reverend Burger, I'm not sick!" John retorted in exasperation. He strode hastily to his car, backed into the street, and drove rapidly toward the expressway.

Bob, Mark and Tim had gone to work before their father got out of hearing. Bob took charge for he understood the project requirements much better than his brothers. He explained briefly the life support systems they would need for survival. Bob drew preliminary sketches of a fallout shelter and listed the many details while Tim took notes. By 3:00 a.m. the desk became cluttered with scribbled pages.

I'll make some more coffee," Mark volunteered, pushed up from the chair, stretched with both arms overhead, and yawning, strolled down the hall to the kitchen.

Mark refilled the cups setting on the desk. Bob arose from his chair. Tim stood up also. They all stretched and walked around a few minutes before resuming their seats.

"The excavation comes first," Bob explained. "Once we determine the needed space, we can mark off the area and begin digging. We don't have much choice for the location since it should be fairly close to the water well."

"When will we start digging?" Mark wanted to know.

"Early Monday morning. We may get in two or three hours work before you and Tim go to school."

Tim questioned. "Why don't we start on it tomorrow?"

"Father expects us in church to get people's reaction when Reverend Burger gives them his letter."

John, traveling on toward Detroit, jerked his head erect as the right front wheel left the pavement, corrected the direction of travel, and brought the car back off the shoulder. The incident left him wide awake. He looked at his watch. It was 5:00 a.m. He drove three miles farther down the highway and pulled into a rest area. Within minutes he fell asleep and slept soundly for two hours.

John awakened when a diesel semi passed on the expressway and, after walking up and down the length of the car several times, resumed his journey.

Sunday morning at 10:45, Ellen, Bob, Ruth, Mark, Tim and Sabrina arrived at the church on Miller Street. Reverend Burger approached their car hurriedly, looking worried, as they got out.

"I'm so glad I saw you before church. Are you aware of John's request for me to publicize a letter?"

Ellen answered. "Yes, I'm fully aware of the contents."

"Mrs. Bailey, if I inform the congregation of this they will all think John is deranged and probably question my sanity for giving it to them."

"Reverend Burger, John realized the possible results. Tell the people you are doing it solely at his request."

"Mrs. Bailey, if I were you and your family I would have John placed under psychiatric observation."

"Reverend Burger, we aren't treating this lightly and we considered that option. I know that what he advocates sounds impossible but we're becoming more persuaded he may be right.

Please let the people have the letter," she pleaded.

"Ellen, I can't. It's against my better judgment. I'm not sure how everybody would react but I believe their response would be unfavorable."

"May I have the letters back?" Ellen asked tersely.

"Ellen, they're on my desk in the office. They're yours."

"We'll hand them out after church just outside the sanctuary," she stated.

"I wish you wouldn't but I won't try to stop you." The pastor turned and strode quickly back to the church.

The Baileys left their car and Bob went by the office and picked up the letters. They went into the auditorium and sat in the back. Smiles and greetings were exchanged with those around then during the organ interlude. Ellen relaxed when there was no more opportunity for talk as she felt sure some would wonder why John didn't come.

The services opened with a song and a prayer and then progressed until finally, the choir sang their special. After they sat, Reverend Burger stepped to the pulpit and began delivering his sermon, the delivery stilted and unnatural. The church members who knew him well wondered what affected his usual excellent delivery. Obviously, something was drastically wrong. People sensed the spirit missing which normally pervaded the auditorium and a chill came over them.

Reverend Burger realized the futility of continuing and cut the sermon short. After a slight pause and without preamble, he made the announcement. "Brothers and Sisters, one of our members asked me to deliver a message to you. He made a very unusual request with an even more unusual message. I refused to relay it personally since I totally disbelieve it. However, he and his family insist that you get the letter and they plan to exercise their rights by handing them out as you leave."

Heads came erect all over the auditorium.

Reverend Burger continued: "Keep absolutely in mind that his views do not reflect my views and I have strongly urged him and his family to seek professional help.

Excitement coursed through the auditorium.

Reverend Burger, beginning to perspire, appeared uncomfortable. "Don't judge him too harshly; you will see he is only trying to help you. Be kind and extend a helping hand to him and his family. I'm sure they'll have some trying days ahead."

The preacher stepped to one side of the pulpit and looked down at one of the members. "Brother Tom Jerome, will you please offer the benediction?"

They all bowed their heads. Reverend Burger wiped perspiration from his face and neck and made his way to the exit. The Baileys took up positions at all the doors and passed out copies until they ran out. Most of the people, suspecting trouble, averted their eyes as they took the letters.

"Thank you very much Reverend Burger. I know you're in an awkward position but we appreciate your thoughtfulness for what you said," Ellen spoke gratefully and then moved down the steps.

John arrived at Jesse's house at 7:30 on Sunday morning. They were still in bed when he rang the bell and Jesse came to the door in his housecoat.

"Hello dad. Come in." He welcomed John eagerly, obviously happy to see his father. Jesse led the way to the living room. "Have a seat and I'll go tell Karen you're here."

Jesse went through the door into the bedroom and John heard them discussing his appearance in subdued voices.

Jesse returned. "Father, your coming without notice like this caught us by surprise. I'm trying to get Karen to come out and meet you but I don't know if she will." Jesse walked over to the couch and sat. "What brought you way up here to Detroit?"

"Jesse, what I have to tell you is terribly important. You'll have a difficult time accepting it but I want you to believe and trust me. I would like for Karen to hear what I have to say also since it's a matter of life and death."

Jesse's grey eyes opened wide. He stared at his father without saying anything and his face showed apprehension. Jesse stepped backward, still staring, turned, and went back into the bedroom. John heard them talking. This time the voices were louder and their tone conveyed excitement.

Jesse returned sooner this time. "Karen will be out in a minute. Wild horses couldn't keep her in there now that you have brought up the chance of a mystery." Jesse became more comfortable and relaxed in his father's presence. "Could I bring you a cup of coffee?"

"Yes, with a teaspoon of sugar."

"I'll be right back." Jesse went out to the kitchen.

Karen came in from the bedroom, took one look at John sitting alone, and stopped. She resisted the impulse to flee and, regaining her poise, resumed walking, approached within ten feet and stopped again.

John experienced shock, seeing Karen for the first time. She was beautiful! There was no wonder Jesse wouldn't listen!

Karen, petite and dainty, had an abundance of coppery red hair which hung halfway down her back and like diamond facets, intermittently reflected rays of light as she moved. She stood five foot tall, was light skinned and had delicate features. She was wearing a plain print dress. "I presume you are John Bailey, Jesse's father?" Her soft voice gave the impression of strength and firmness.

"That's correct, Karen, and I'm pleased to meet you." John stood up and his voice conveyed his sincere feelings.

Jesse heard the voices, came in from the kitchen and placed his arm around Karen's slender waist. "I'm sorry I missed the opportunity to introduce you."

"I'll fix some breakfast," Karen said, and suddenly shy, slipped out of Jesse's arm and went out to the kitchen.

"Have a seat father. I'll bring our coffee and we may as well talk until breakfast is ready."

Karen overheard him from the kitchen. "Your coffee will be right out."

"How is mom and all the rest?"

"Just fine Jesse. Everybody is in good health and the only problem concerns the message I have brought you."

"I'll sure be glad to hear what you have to say."

"Time for breakfast," Karen announced.

They seated themselves around the table and Jesse asked hesitantly, "Father, will you say grace?"

John Bailey asked blessings on the food and family and prayed for enlightenment for Jesse and Karen on the message. They ate in thoughtful silence except for the necessary talk connected with passing food.

With the meal over, Jesse and John carried their coffee to the living room while Karen cleared the table and placed the dishes in the sink. She poured in liquid soap, filled the sink with water, then joined the men in the living room.

Jesse and Karen looked at John expectantly.

John began hesitantly. "Jesse, you and Karen should prepare yourself, for what I have to tell you may seem beyond belief."

"Go ahead dad," Jesse invited. "We're ready."

John dropped the bombshell. "In a very short time our

country and the world will be devastated by an atomic war." He stopped and waited for his words to sink in.

Karen gasped.

Jesse stared in wide-eyed, open mouthed amazement and shook his head hard, as if to clear it. "Father," he asked slowly, "do you understand what you're saying?"

John acknowledged, "Yes I do, Jesse. I can't tell you the exact date but it can come soon. I'm here to ask you and Karen to come and live with us in the shelter we're building. We want you with us and could use your help."

Karen's legs became weak and she began trembling. "Mister Bailey, are you trying to scare us?" Karen's blue eyes snapped and her voice registered anger and her face turned white.

The pronouncement dumbfounded Jesse. "Father, just how in the name of goodness do you know this war is coming, and why hasn't the news media broadcast it?"

John spent the next hour detailing the dreams and world conditions.

"I'm sorry father, I don't believe there's a bit of truth in it," Jesse stated flatly.

"Karen, Jesse, I have never been more serious in my life. Please believe me and try to understand; we don't have much time left," John begged.

"Father, I couldn't possibly quit my job and leave on such flimsy evidence. We'll have to stay right here."

"Karen, try to change his mind. This may be your only chance when the war comes." John's eyes pleaded.

The color had returned to her face and she spoke defiantly, eyes flashing, "I'm with Jesse."

John changed his tone. "I know there's no need for me

to say any more. I don't know what the signs will be, but I'm sure certain things will begin taking place."

John spoke clearly, his voice taking on a commanding tone. "Remember, we're preparing a place for you. When you see the signs, come home. Don't wait too long."

John shook Jesse's hand, bowed slightly toward Karen, and said good-bye.

The message John delivered visibly disturbed Karen and Jesse but they remained firm in their resolve.

"Father, why don't you stay and rest? You must be worn out after such a long, hard trip," Jesse urged.

"Jesse, there's much to be done and a short time left."

Jesse followed his father out the door and down to John's car. Both men stood silently for several moments absorbed in their thoughts, and after final good-byes, John left.

John got back home at 10:30 Sunday night, worn out.

Ellen waited for him. "How was your trip, John?" Her voice faltered.

"The drive up and back went OK but I couldn't convince them they should come," John answered dejectedly.

Ellen and John, preparing for bed, remained silent and absorbed in thought. Ellen made sure John slept and then sobbed quietly into her pillow until well after midnight.

Monday morning started hectic. John and Bob went into conference in the study. Fortunately, Bob was able to contact his supervisor on Sunday afternoon and arranged his vacation.

Ellen and Ruth prepared breakfast while Mark and Tim rushed around preparing for school. Ruth carried two cups of steaming coffee to the study and set them on the desk.

"Good morning Ruth," John affectionately embraced his daughter-in-law.

"Good morning Father. How do you feel after such a hard trip?"

"A little tired but I'll get over it in a day or two."

"How were Jesse and Karen?"

"They are well. I'm disappointed though that they wouldn't come."

"Maybe when things start getting bad they'll come," Bob said, sipping his coffee.

Ruth left the room and the two men rearranged their chairs at the desk. Bob shuffled through several papers and brought out one showing a structural layout.

"Father, here is what I came up with in the way of a general plan. It's a start."

John studied the drawing for several minutes. "How deep do you think we should place it underground?"

"I believe we need a minimum of five feet of earth between the shelter and surface."

"Let's see, two foot thick floor, six and a half foot ceiling, and four feet of cement for the roof. With five feet of earth on top, that will make our excavation seventeen and a half feet deep."

John thought for a few minutes, studying the plans. "You don't think we'll hit water at that depth do you?"

"It's not likely father. We're on somewhat of a knoll here and I'm sure the water table will be below us."

"Bob, do you believe we'll need all this space? Fifteen by twenty-four feet seems quite a large area for an emergency shelter."

"By the time we stock it and install all the necessary

equipment we'll need it all. After sixty days or more underground we'll probably wish the room were much larger."

The telephone rang and John answered. "Hello John, this is Tom Morris. I heard you were sick so thought I'd call and see how you're doing."

"Why no, Tom, I'm not sick. By the way, did you get a copy of my letter at the church?"

Tom cleared his throat. "Why yes John, I did. You don't really believe the things you wrote, do you? I figured you must be working too hard and needed a rest."

"No, Tom, I'm not overworked and I'm sorry to say that everything mentioned in the letter will happen. Only those who prepare now for what's coming will survive."

Tom's voice took on a sharper note. "John, you have no right writing things like that and upsetting people. Sometimes I think my wife almost believes you because she has even suggested that maybe we should build a shelter."

Tom's voice became harsh. "Several people have considered suing you. I suggest you keep things like that to yourself in the future."

John's face took on a flush and he prepared an angry retort but Tom broke the connection.

"Was that another crank, father?"

"What do you mean by "another'?" John asked edgily.

"We had so many calls yesterday we finally left the phone off the hook. Many of them were well wishers hoping you have a speedy recovery but a few of them were threats."

"We can expect more of this I guess," John sighed, his anger subsiding. "It's too bad people won't believe, but they didn't believe Noah either, not that I'm a prophet."

The telephone rang again; John snatched the phone up and answered with the edge still in his voice. "Yes?"

"John, I'm Dean Davis. I'm calling about the letter."

"What can I do for you Dean?" he asked warmly.

"I'm interested in what you say and I'd like to hear more. What you have suggested is scary, to say the least."

"Dean, we can talk over the phone or you can bring Hazel and the kids and come on out. That would probably be best if you're serious."

"At this point, I don't know if we're serious or not, but I'm interested enough to hear what else you have to say. Would 7:00 this evening be OK?"

"7:00 is fine with me. We'll see you then."

"Breakfast is ready," Ellen announced.

After breakfast, John and Bob resumed planning. Mark and Tim went to school. Ellen and Ruth sat in the living room, discussed events, and made a few plans of their own. Sabrina lay in the crib on her stomach and slept.

"Bob, we'll dig the hole first. I'll rent a backhoe and get started. Meanwhile, you can run by the Baker and Martin Construction Supply Company and pick up anything else you may need." John tossed the sheaf of work sheets onto the table top and leaned back in his chair, stretching.

"What about the dirt, father? We're going to have one big pile left over."

John considered the question for a few moments. "We don't want the dirt left right here at the shelter. You pick up a bob tailed dump truck at Kyle's Equipment Rentals where I'm getting the backhoe and we'll haul the dirt out back and spread it."

"Don't you think we should complete our plans before we start building?"

"No Bob, I believe we have enough now to start and we can work out the rest while we're digging. We do need a final design though before we pour concrete.

We need to think through and plan for everything, such as power, water, ventilation, communication, light, sanitation, entertainment, etc."

Bob laughed. I doubt if we'll be depending on the internet, cell phones, U tube, Fox news, power grid, and all the other things we seem we can't do without."

John answered grimly, "Bob, we can't imagine the half of it. I'll stop by the library today and see what they have on shelters." John got up, walked to the door and paused. "Since we'll need quite a bit of money for this job I'll stop by the bank and arrange the necessary financing."

John left the house and drove off toward Breton. He stopped at his place of work, went to the personnel clerk and asked for a vacation form. With all the blanks filled out, he took it to pretty, raven-haired Melinda Cruse. "Melinda, would you take this form to Mister Blanton and tell him I wish to see him. I'm John Bailey."

"Certainly Mister Bailey, I'll be glad to." Miss Cruse arose and entered the door to the inner office. She returned moments later. "Mister Blanton will see you now."

John walked past Melinda and entered the office. "Good morning Mister Blanton."

Mr. Blanton, an imposing figure sitting behind the desk, a large man, lantern jawed and beetle browed, slowly and reluctantly laid aside a sheet of paper with columns of figures and looked up. "Good morning John. What gives with the vacation?"

John, running his finger around his shirt collar which suddenly felt too tight, blurted out uncomfortably, "Well sir, to make the story short and not waste your time, I've been having forewarnings of coming danger and I've decided I need to build my family a bomb and radiation proof shelter."

Mister Blanton sat and stared. "John . . ." He started to speak, stopped, and stared some more. "John, are you sure this is what you want? I'm sorry to lose your services for the next five weeks but since you've always been such a faithful employee, I won't question your decision. Come back sooner if you change your mind."

"Mister Blanton, I've alienated a lot of my friends and acquaintances by advising them of a coming war. I feel I owe you a lot and the least I can do is recommend that you prepare for what I am convinced is coming. We don't have much time."

"John, I appreciate your concern and I'll think about what you've told me but I really don't see the necessity." Mister Blanton picked up his paper, signaling dismissal.

Sadly, John left the office thinking, there's nobody that believes me and sometimes I doubt my own decisions.

John stopped at the news stand, bought a Breton Daily News and leafed through it hurriedly, looking for his letter. He wasn't surprised when he didn't find it.

He made his next stop at the Breton Public Library where Mrs. Bolen, a courteous and pleasant lady, helped him locate the Civil Defense file. John browsed through several booklets and finally selected four he considered helpful. He laid them on the counter and presented his library card. John fidgeted while Mrs. Bolen slowly and methodically placed the card in the register and stamped the slips.

John next visited the Sheriff's office.

"May I help you?" A deputy lounging behind the counter offered his help. "I need an explosive permit."

"What type, how much, and what for?"

"I need two cases of forty percent dynamite and fifty blasting caps for stump removal." Telling the lie made John uncomfortable.

The deputy shuffled over to the file cabinet, leafed through the folders of blank forms until he found the right one, and then placed it on the counter. "Fill out two copies and fill in all the blanks." The deputy hitched up his trousers and pistol, tilted his hat back, and leaned on the counter.

John filled out both copies of the form and shoved them down the counter. The deputy took the papers, studied them, walked over to a door that had a frosted glass window with the word SHERIFF written in four inch high letters, entered, and closed the door. John waited apprehensively. The dynamite was crucial.

He looked about the room, whiling away the time. For the most part the office was a bare, drab room with a half dozen chairs lining the wall on his side of the counter. A tobacco juice spattered brass spittoon sat on the left and a cigarette urn stood between the chairs and the door. The floor was dirty, the air musty and smelled strongly of stale tobacco.

The deputy came out of the sheriff's office and approached the counter. John stood and faced him. "The sheriff wants you to understand that the only place you can shoot the dynamite is on your own property. If any of it gets stolen, let us know immediately."

"I'll handle the dynamite properly," John assured. He picked up his copy of the form and feeling relieved, went out the door and crossed the sidewalk to his car.

John went next to the Baker and Martin Supply Company, parked, walked across to the entrance, and went up to the counter where a tall, skinny man stood on the opposite side. His Adam's apple bobbed when he spoke. "May I help you?"

"Yes, I would like two cases of forty percent dynamite and fifty blasting caps."

"Looks like you're getting ready for some fun. Do you have your explosive permit?"

"Yes, here it is." John laid the form on the counter.

The attendant looked it over carefully and filled the order. "Mister Bailey, do you want us to deliver this or will you take it yourself?"

"I'll take it with me."

"Is your truck at the loading ramp?"

"No, I have my car in the parking lot."

"Bring it over to the loading ramp. I'll have this ready by the time you get back."

John moved the car and went back inside.

The salesman asked, "cash or credit?"

"Credit." John removed his wallet from his hip pocket and handed him the credit card.

John signed the credit card slip and then helped the attendant carry the materials outside.

"Put the dynamite in the trunk." John placed the blasting caps gently on the front floorboard. I don't like hauling these in the car with dynamite but I don't have time for two trips. If the caps go, the dynamite will go.

John, uneasy on his way home, watched approaching traffic carefully. Only a minor accident could produce a terrific explosion with a resulting large pile of wreckage. They probably wouldn't find much of me, he realized.

He parked just outside the garage, feeling relief. Bob walked out the front door and met him. "Bob, be careful with these caps. Empty out my small tool chest into the large one and we'll store the caps in it."

Bob, with a questioning look, took them into the garage and John began unloading the other supplies. "Dad, does the dynamite go in the garage?"

"No. Dynamite is relatively safe by itself so we'll store it in my study."

They each carried a case of the explosives to the study. Bob walked over to the corner behind the desk and set the crate down gingerly and John stacked his on top.

"What's the dynamite for dad?"

"We may need it during our shelter building," John answered evasively without looking at Bob. John hesitated and then continued: "Well, actually, I plan on using the dynamite for defense of the shelter."

"I see." Bob replied

John changed the subject. "I stopped by the library and picked up some booklets on fallout shelters that should give us some good ideas. They're in the car."

"I'll get them," Bob responded.

John sat at his desk and shuffled through Bob's sketches and notes, his mind ticking off survival needs and work required. An immediate problem involved dirt removal from the hole once the backhoe dug all it could. The largest backhoe available on such short notice could only reach twelve feet deep which left another five. Five foot of dirt in a twenty by thirty foot hole amounted to a prodigious task.

Bob returned with the booklets. He and John spent the next hour looking through them. John stated, "according to this, we need only six inches of concrete with three feet of dirt on top." Bob advised, "That may be enough but I'll feel better if we go over their recommendation for we can't be sure how intense the radiation will be. They listed a minimum requirement anyhow. The date on the pamphlets range from 1959 to 1970 and, since then, the atomic stockpile and megaton yield has grown tremendously."

"You're right Bob, there's no need to take chances. We'll build extra good and still have too much exposure."

John studied more pages in the pamphlet. "They recommend a two week stay in the shelter with a four week supply of food and water. However, I believe we should prepare for a two-month minimum, and I'm not sure that's long enough. What do you think?"

"I'm in agreement with you, dad. Better too much than not enough."

Ellen came to the door. "Come and eat lunch."

"We'll be right there," John replied.

During lunch, Bob and John discussed their plans while Ruth and Ellen listened. John spoke to Ellen. "Ellen, when you and Ruth find time, read the booklets on my desk. Some of them describe clothing and food needs in shelters."

Bob got up from the table. "Well father, I guess digging comes next."

"You're right," John agreed.

John and Bob went outside and tackled the formidable task, building the shelter. Bob had already marked off the area and stretched strings between the stakes. John climbed aboard the backhoe, turned the key to start, and the engine roared to life. Bob took his seat in the dump truck, started it, and backed into position for loading.

The hoe bit deeply into the ground as John manipulated the controls. He removed a large pile of dirt and then used the loader end of the backhoe to fill the truck. It took an hour for the first truck load. John signaled Bob and then recommenced digging.

Bob put the dump truck in gear, drove slowly to the back of the property, stopped the truck and began raising the bed. At the halfway mark, Bob tripped the tailgate lever and drove off, spreading the dirt.

Shortly after noon, Ellen left the house swiftly, got in the station wagon and left. She returned forty five minutes later and John knew something was wrong for he saw Mark get out and then Tim slowly emerged.

"Bob, come on, let's see what's going on."

They ran over to the garage and were shocked at what they saw. Mark's shirt was in tatters and there was a long, red welt across the rippling muscles on his back. He had some blood on his left cheek and a noticeable knot over his right eye. However, he looked good compared to Tim, who from all appearances had taken quite a pounding. Tim's face was covered all over with black and blue splotches. His nose had been bleeding and his left eye had swollen shut. His shirt was missing and he had welts and scratches over most of his upper torso. John, feeling the rage welling in him, asked in an icily calm voice, "What happened?"

Mark told the story. "Dad, during lunch, one of my friends came and told me that Tim was in a fight. When I got there, these four guys had made a circle and were tossing him around and around, hitting and shoving with their elbows." Mark bared his teeth in a wolfish grin, "I dove in and got a piece of the action." He kept grinning, looking half wild with his short cropped light brown hair sticking straight up all over his head and his normally blue eyes glittering a luminescent emerald. "Don't feel sorry for us. You ought to see what the other guys look like."

"What did the principal have to say?" Bob asked,

Mark turned serious. "He expelled us."

"Did he expel the others?" John asked.

"Not that I am aware of. He claims it was our fault because of the letter you handed out at church."

John's face, already reddening, turned livid. "Bob, let's you and me go talk to a principal."

"Dad, you'd better cool off," Bob warned. "We've got more important things to do besides talking to a principal."

Ellen intervened. "I'll take these two young men in and help them get cleaned up. You two can get back to work."

"You're right," John agreed, but still seething. "Let's get after it!"

By 4:00 p.m., Bob and John could see a significant dent in their excavation. Mark and Tim came back outside dressed in old clothes ready to work. Mark appeared unscathed but Tim's face, although Ellen had applied some makeup, still looked puffed and swollen.

"Father, have you talked to the Klines?" Mark asked.

"Dean Davis and his family are coming tonight at 7:00. If it isn't too late I'll go by and see Ed after that."

John used the backhoe until, with the boom fully extended, he couldn't reach anymore. They bared the water well casing on the north end for future access. He moved over thirty feet to the west and dug the hole for the generator and fifty-five gallon gasoline drum.

Finally, they completed the backhoe work. "It's time to shut down and get ready for our visitors. Let's all go in, eat, clean up a little and Bob, after you eat, go ahead and rig lights and do what you can on the shelter for we need to work late tonight. I'll meet with Dean and Hazel, then I'm going over and talk to Ed." John felt a greater sense of urgency with each passing hour.

When Dean and Hazel arrived, John and Ellen greeted them at the door and showed them into the living room. Dean and Hazel, in their mid-thirties were both short and stocky. They were well matched in their ideals and beliefs but there the resemblance ended.

Dean's light skin, blue eyes, and a rectangular face, accentuated by a thick shock of blond hair cut severely flat on top, had been passed on to him by his mother Eva, who was of fair German descent. Dean worked as a tool and die maker in a precision machine shop in Lexington.

Hazel, on the other hand, had a dark, almost olive complexion, with brown, expressive eyes. She had an abundance of long, straight black hair, framing her smooth features in a pear-shaped portrait, flowing down the front of her shoulders, with the ends reposing on the gentle slopes of her ample bosom. Hazel was dressed in a severe high-necked, blue blouse with long sleeves and a long, flowing skirt which reached almost to her ankles.

"If you like, you can let the children play out in the front yard. It might be a little dangerous for them out back." Ellen explained. "Ruth, come on in here and join us."

"John, what's all this about a nuclear war?" Dean asked.

"Dean, my letter pretty well explains it. I dreamed a series of dreams and thought about the world military and political conditions. That left me certain a war is coming and I'm building a shelter for me and my family. Also, I feel I should warn my fellow man."

Always looking for a religious implication, Hazel also expressed her curiosity. "John, do you think your dream was a vision or a revelation from God?"

John laughed. "Hazel, I don't know for sure if it's a revelation from God but I hope so."

Dean spoke. "John, I've been troubled and uneasy about the direction of our country for a long time. Looking back at history and the makeup of our government, I see very little hope of our future turning out well. The nation and constitution was founded upon God's principles for the most part. Many of the men involved were Christians and statesmen. Bottom line, due to its very makeup, the construct of the foundation of this nation, our constitution, could only exist if supported by its citizens.

"John, I share in your uneasy feelings for the world in general and our nation in particular. As a nation, we are in a rapid decline in morality and everything else that had made this nation strong and a leader in the world."

"The three branch governing framework based upon the constitution and Judeo Christian principles no doubt was God inspired and God led. A Christian should view this as a Christian government structure for a Christian nation."

"In 1950 or thereabouts, a US congressman brought

forth a resolution to declare the USA a Christian nation. It was voted down. The representatives of the American people spoke. Since then, we as a nation, have proved it time after time, we are not a Christian nation."

"I hate to disparage all our congressmen and congresswomen. However, I believe it is becoming very difficult to find very many true statesmen in that body. In seeing some of them on TV and hearing them speak, junk yard dogs come more to mind. In fact, there's one political party I can think of should probably change its name to junk yard dog party. Not naming any party."

"Ultimate responsibility and ultimate blame for where we are rests upon, "We the People." An un-Godly population, becoming more-so every day, lacking Godly spiritual discernment, really can't tell good from bad. Consequently, where our elected congress is concerned, we get what we ask for and they legislate accordingly."

"Another thing that would be funny if it wasn't so serious, these left leaning folks are quick to yell racist, bigot, prejudice, this phobia, that phobia and the other phobia at the drop of a hat. In reality, they are the most bigoted, racist, prejudiced, and phobic people in the world. The father of their lies is Satan."

"If you ever saw a dog acting up the way some of them do, you would swear it was rabid! I challenge them to look in a mirror while they are spouting all that garbage!"

Dean continued, "Most of the people in this nation have lost their moral compass. Without a compass, it is easy to get lost and go the wrong way."

"I heard a preacher one day that said God had removed His hedge of protection from around this nation. I believe it."

"It isn't hard to see we are internally in trouble as a nation from moral decline. At the same time, we have been in steep decline as a leader within the world. As a nation, we are weak in leadership and militarily. Up to five or six decades ago, this nation pretty much led the world in trying to do the right thing in world affairs. We, of course, had our lapses from time to time. Militarily and morally, as a leader in the free world we are in an alarming and rapid decline. If push comes to shove, who will stand with us?"

Dean added, "I'll tell you one thing for sure, if I don't do anything else, I'm going to study my Bible the next few months and see if I can find a connection."

John replied, "There's one problem Dean. I feel the strongest sense of urgency. The coming events won't occur in a matter of years, months or weeks, but days. If you wait until it starts, it'll be too late."

Hazel had been sitting quietly taking it all in. "What you say makes a lot of sense. I don't keep up with the military and political stance of the nations too well but I can see things happening around us that is deeply disturbing."

"For one thing, I see God taunted and mocked in this nation as never before. I just can't see God allowing us to get away with this forever."

"What do you mean?" Ruth asked curiously.

Hazel continued, "for starters, there's the Supreme Court decision banning prayer in public schools. As far as I know, this was the first official, United States Government, slap in God's face. This mocks God, and the Bible clearly teaches in Galatians 6:7, "Be not deceived, God is not mocked; for whatsoever a man soweth, that shall he also reap."

"I never had thought of it that way before," Ellen admitted.

"Another thing," Hazel continued, "take the matter of homosexuals. As long as we officially condemned this perverted action, the disapproval was a deterrent and sent the message to our children that it was wrong. With public approval, the practice is escalating to epidemic proportions. I know a lot of people get upset when some insinuate that AIDS could be God's judgment but who am I to say God isn't getting tired of this taunting, and open rebellion?"

Ruth added, "One of the other flagrant mockeries is the TV programming and the movies constantly chipping away at the family. A large number of Television movies depicts the fun and rightness of illicit sex and infidelity."

"Yes", Hazel agreed. "As the family goes, so goes the nation. Add all this to the murder of children through abortion, use of alcohol and drugs, and the general falling away from God by the people of the United States and it scares the daylights out of me."

"We cringe at the news of ISIS chopping off the heads of a few people, yet abortion doctors crush skulls, chop off limbs, burn with acids, and otherwise brutalize living humans by the tens of millions. Yes, we foolishly have fooled ourselves into believing this is OK. We are not fooling God."

"Paul Hill, the Presbyterian minister who killed the abortion doctor in Pensacola Florida, never admitted that what he did was wrong. Paul Hill declined all opportunities to appeal and was executed relatively soon after his conviction. As a Christian, and a believer in the rule of law, I accept the fact that he committed murder and was punished fairly. However, there's also something within me that wonders if a great monument shouldn't be erected, celebrating all the lives he saved!"

"Hazel is really getting on her soap box now," Dean laughed and then spoke seriously, "I've had alarm bells ringing for quite some time now also. I do believe we live in perilous times and need to take a good look at what's happening."

"Would you like to go outside and see what we've started?" John suggested, rising.

"No, we'll pass on that for now. That might add to the confusion I'm already feeling." Dean answered, getting up, and then helping Hazel to her feet.

After Dean and Hazel left, Ellen and Ruth resumed their chores. John went back outside with Bob, Mark, and Tim. Bob and his two brothers finished stringing lights. "Tim, on the south end here, start digging a shaft four feet in diameter, three feet away from the side of the hole," Bob instructed. "Take it easy at first and make sure you weren't seriously hurt in the fight."

"Ah, I'm OK. What's the hole for?"

"This is the entrance. We'll have a four foot pipe inside the shaft with ladder rungs for going up and down and a connecting tunnel between the shelter and the shaft."

"Why not put the entrance in the top?"

Bob explained. "For one thing, it would be harder to seal and it would also be a weak spot. If marauders found it, they could force their way in. We will build a mock barbecue pit over the top of the shaft and disguise it. Keeping this shelter hidden could mean the difference between life and death."

John poked around the shelter area until Bob finished

explaining. "I'll see you all later. I'm off to visit the Klines. Wish me luck."

"Good luck dad," all three of his sons responded. Mark's response was markedly fervent.

John drove to where the Klines' lane turned off and, after entering the graveled road, another quarter mile brought him to their house. John got out of the car and tall, lanky, easy going Ed came out with a smile on his face to meet him; they shook hands warmly.

"Hi Ed."

"Hello John, how have you been doing the past couple weeks? I wondered what had become of you."

"Ed, this is what I came to see you about. By the way, have you heard anything concerning me?" John probed.

Ed admitted cautiously, "I've heard some things but the stories sound strange, if they're really coming from you. We weren't going to form an opinion until we heard your version. Marge and I were sure you would tell us about it when you had the chance." Ed shifted his feet uneasily.

"I would've been here sooner but some urgent matters got in the way." John apologized. "Ed, could Marge and Kathy hear what I have to say?"

"No, I'd rather hear the entire story myself, and then I can tell them." The smile left his face and the warm friendly atmosphere took on a slight chill.

"I'm ready anytime you are," John declared in a grim voice, tinged with hardness.

Ed detected the change in his neighbor's passion and suggested, "Let's go in the living room. It will be more comfortable there."

As soon as they sat, John began relating his story, using

all the persuasiveness at his command, seeking to impose his beliefs on his good friend.

Although forewarned by the rumors, the unfolding tale coming from John's lips deeply shocked Ed. He listened impassively, squirmed in his chair from time to time, and occasionally interrupted and asked questions.

"John, I'd like to know what's really behind all this. Do you believe this is Bible prophecy coming to pass? I know you and your family go to church and I'm wondering if some of your religious beliefs have brought this about?"

"Ed, it's true I've studied the Bible some. Naturally, some of the areas I've studied related to the end time prophecies. I'm familiar with a lot of the different ideas and opinions concerning that subject but I'm not sure that any of that caused my dreams or influenced them. However, I admit these things could possibly alter my subconscious without my being aware of it."

"Just what does the Bible say on the subject that might have a bearing on your dreams and what you're doing?"

"First, several different events were prophesied such as the rapture of the church, the end time, tribulation, battle of Armageddon, second coming of Christ, the thousand year reign and so forth. There are several schools of thought on all this and a lot of disagreement. Many people believe the end time will come about by an atomic war. I don't know, maybe so. I do believe that if God decides to bring on the end of time, he won't need any help from man."

"What would this have to do with the battle of Armageddon I've heard about?"

John laughed, "Ed, I haven't really thought of my dreams in the context of Bible prophecy but since you're interested,

I'll try to give you a quick overview of what little I think I believe about prophecy. And again, I'll emphasize that this probably doesn't have any connection with my dreams. I'm convinced my dreams are prompted by my mind surveying history and current events and waving a flag of alarm when Russia and communism enters the picture.

"There were three major schools of thought about the end time but I won't confuse you with all the different ideas. A common belief says that at a certain time, Jesus Christ will return to earth and take all Christians back to heaven with him. A seven year tribulation period follows that and the Battle of Armageddon occurs during the latter part of the seven year period."

"Who fights the battle of Armageddon John?"

"I'm not sure exactly but I think that some tremendously large forces from Asia, Africa and possibly Europe all come against Israel and are defeated. Then, at the end of this seven year period and during the battle of Armageddon, Jesus Christ comes again and begins his thousand year reign here on earth."

"Do you believe all that?"

"Well, I don't exactly disbelieve it but I sure don't understand it all either."

John continued relating his story and Ed's face took on an odd look generated by the mixture of several emotions including frustration, anger, fear, compassion, sorrow, impatience and concern. John began having a sinking feeling well before he was through for he could sense the disbelief and resistance building in his neighbor. "Ed, that's the story from beginning to end. I know I'm asking a lot for you to believe but I don't know what else to say. I do think though that we're about out of time." John's face was redder than normal and he perspired from the sincere effort he used in presenting the story.

Ed was slow to reply. Anger, which he seldom felt or displayed, had risen in him and he did his best to suppress it. "John, we're old friends and I wouldn't want to do or say anything that might hurt your feelings or hurt our relationship. I'm sure you believe everything you've told me but, John, I can't believe any part of it. You, of all people, crying doom? Unbelievable!" We've had quite a few political and philosophical discourses in the past and we're not that far apart in our beliefs. You'll have to admit this is quite a departure from all our past discussions."

John's face flushed scarlet at the rebuff. He wanted to leave immediately and fought an inner struggle before he could speak again. "Ed, isn't there anything else I can say to convince you?" He pleaded in a voice mingling sorrow and reproof.

Ed hesitated, searched for tactful words and finally answered, "I'll keep an open mind on this and will be watching for any other signs. I appreciate what you're trying to do for me and know how hard this must be for you."

"Ed, I pretty well expected your answer," John answered in a resigned voice. "Keep a close watch on happenings throughout the world. If anything occurs that could help you believe, then get busy! I'm afraid when events begin taking place, there won't be much time."

Ed fidgeted and said defensively, "John, I promise you I will! On the other hand, you should go see a doctor. I'm afraid you've confused yourself with a lot of garbage and I'm concerned that you're moving in a direction that will alienate all your friends, cause you to lose your job, and destroy everything you have put together in a lifetime."

"Ed, I understand what you're saying. I've already seen a doctor and I am convinced I'm right or I would still be going." John rose from his seat. "There's one more thing and then I'll leave. If you decide to build a shelter, let us know and we'll do what we can to help."

"Thanks John. I'll keep that in mind,"

With a heavy heart, John returned home. He stopped at the end of their lane, retrieved the Breton Daily News and glanced at the front page. Sure enough, he had made the news. The headlines stated: "LOCAL PROPHET PREDICTS DEATH, DOOM AND DAMNATION!"

John laid the paper on the car seat and with anger welling, drove on up the lane to the house. Once inside, he took time out and read the complete article. "John Bailey, a self-proclaimed prophet who lives here in this area, delivered a letter to the congregation of his church Sunday predicting that the end time is here. Not near, but here. The letter stated that within a short period of time, a nuclear war will devastate the United States."

"Although obviously there's nothing to it, his letter caused quite a sensation among their congregation and large numbers of disturbed people have called in to the paper and local radio stations asking if we have any details or news that would confirm his claim. Again, obviously, we have none."

"I personally interviewed Mister Bailey yesterday and he couldn't offer any tangible reason for his thinking other than a series of disturbing dreams he experienced which led him to his conclusions. His stated purpose in publishing the letter is to warn his fellow citizens of the impending disaster so they would have time to construct bomb shelters and prepare for the Holocaust."

"Folks, you can do what you like. However, I haven't seen anything or heard anything that makes me believe I should rush out and spend my life savings on a shelter. Mister Bailey certainly couldn't give any concrete facts, just innuendoes and charges claiming all the signs point that way. If we do hear anything, you can be sure you will be the first to know."

John flashed hot and cold, angry and then calm, as he read the article. "Out of fairness to them, I don't guess they did any different from what I expected," he muttered.

After reading the paper, John went back outside and discovered intense activity around the pit. They were digging the dirt, filling buckets and lifting it out. Bob and Mark, both stripped to the waist, perspired profusely. Mark's glistening muscles rippled each time he lifted a full bucket above his head. Bob, less muscular but wiry and strong, took the buckets effortlessly and dumped them. Tim, bogged down in toil unfamiliar to him, blistered his hands quickly but continued to labor, although in pain.

"It's time to take a break, boys," John instructed after watching them for a few moments. "Tomorrow, Bob and I will build two trolleys above the pit. We'll install an electrical hoist with a large bucket on each trolley. When the hoist brings the bucket to the top, it'll roll on the trolley off to one side where you can dump the bucket."

"Won't that be expensive, father?" Mark asked.

"Yes it will, but expense is immaterial. As long as my credit holds out, we'll get whatever materials we need."

Mark thought, if we don't use the shelter, father will have wasted an awful lot of money. "Dad, what will we do about

Trixie, and my pigs, and chickens?" Tim asked, carefully hiding his hands and masking his pain.

"Tim, the chickens and pigs will have to stay outside. We will bring Trixie inside although it will be inconvenient. Trixie will be your project."

"Won't the pigs and chickens starve?"

"We'll leave the animals a good supply of food and water and open the gate so they can go in and out."

They worked until 11:00 p.m. that night and John closed down the operation. They were all dirty, sweaty and bone tired when they went in to bathe and prepare for bed.

John told Mark and Tim, "Since you've been expelled from school, as far as I'm concerned, school's out. Stay here tomorrow and help us."

The following morning, John and Bob returned the backhoe and dump truck, and then rented another truck for hauling materials.

They spent all morning locating the parts for the lifts and trolleys. They found the last piece and hurried home. John started making the trolleys and Bob returned to Breton and dropped off the rented truck.

Later in the afternoon, Mark approached his father. "Dad, could I go over and talk to Kathy?"

John thought a few moments. His strong feelings of urgency made him want to say no, but he finally decided to let him go.

"Mark, be careful what you say to Kathy about all this. I had a long talk with Ed and he's in complete opposition. If you get Kathy all worked up about it, Ed may stop you from seeing her at all."

"I'll be careful, dad."

John, Tim and Bob resumed work. Soon, dirt flowed steadily from the hole. John and Tim operated one trolley while Bob worked on the other. They shoveled feverishly, the sense of urgency now shared by the entire family. Tim, with every muscle in his body protesting the unfamiliar physical labor and with his hands raw, endured quietly.

By dark, both trolleys operated. The lights dimmed each time they used the lifts at the same time. "We'd better work the lifts alternately before we burn something up," Bob advised.

They kept at it until 11:00 p.m. and finally, worn out, they went in, bathed, and went to bed.

Mark didn't come home until after 1:00 a.m. He went to bed but couldn't sleep. Thoughts of his visit with Kathy kept racing through his mind. His whirling brain grasped at the significance of all that took place. Mark had bicycled to Kathy's house as usual and then they rode side by side the mile to their favorite spot on the creek. After parking their bicycles, they instinctively faced each other. Kathy, slightly out of breath and face flushed, with her hair hanging over her right ear in a pony tail, drew Mark like a magnet.

Mark took both of Kathy's hands and held them. "Kathy, I've missed you," he said shyly, looking deep into her eyes.

"I've missed you too Mark," Kathy replied softly, and trembling, returned the pressure applied to her hands. Mark pulled her to him, placed his arms about her tenderly and sought her lips. Kathy closed her eyes, surrendered to the embrace and they were electrified by the thrill as their lips met for the first time. Kathy sagged in his embrace. Mark held her tighter.

After several seconds, their lips parted and they

separated. Mark was smiling. Knees weak, Kathy returned the smile uncertainly.

Mark took her hand again. "Kathy, I love you."

Kathy stood quietly for a few moments and then replied in a barely audible voice, "I love you, too, Mark."

They embraced and kissed again.

Mark and Kathy remained at their sanctuary on the creek until after nine p.m., expressing their blossoming love.

"We'd better get on back to your house before we get in trouble," Mark exclaimed when he became aware of the time.

They got back on their bikes and returned to Kathy's house. She went on inside, informed her parents they were home and then joined Mark in the swing on the front porch.

They talked on into the night discussing their admitted love and, finally, Mark broached the subject of the shelter. "Kathy, have your parents said anything to you about the shelter we're building?"

"No. I don't know what you're talking about. I've noticed mom and dad holding some private conversations lately. They stop talking when I come around."

"I may get in trouble for telling you but I think you have a right to know what's going on," Mark stated grimly.

Mark spent the next thirty minutes recounting the story and then concluded: "Kathy, this isn't something you can discuss with your parents, for if they find out I told you, they may not let me come over any more. I'm sure they would get mad at dad, also."

Kathy was pale and shaken from the second bombshell in one day Mark had exploded in her otherwise ordered life. "Oh Mark, I'm scared. I don't know what to think."

"Don't worry too much about it," Mark reassured. "All

this may blow over and if it doesn't, I'm sure everything will turn out OK."

They held hands and talked until after midnight and then reluctantly, Mark took his leave. "I'm not sure when I'll see you next since we're going to be pretty busy the next several days. I'll call you and talk to you for a while each day but if you need me, let me know."

After a lingering good night kiss, Kathy went in the house and Mark went home.

The following morning after breakfast, John told Bob, "You stay here and work on the plan and I'll pick up another load of supplies. Make a list of the lumber we'll need and I'll have it delivered tomorrow."

John took a different road to town. He loved the beautiful trees and shrubbery lining the country roads and frequently traveled different routes. Man worked hard and long for years destroying the natural beauties of the world. In spite of this, reclamation and beautification projects restored many areas. Flowers bloomed, trees spread luxuriant leafed branches skyward and grass covered the hillsides and fields with a green down. Cattle grazed near the crest of the hill; birds flitted from tree to tree.

The sun shone nice and warm until the clouds, approaching and building from the west, obscured it. Darkness settled over the area. John unconsciously slowed the car, his eyes drinking in the peaceful landscape.

He passed a farmhouse with chickens in the yard. I should have been a farmer. Farmers are close to nature. John continued his reverie.

The planting of crops, first buds peeping above the row, plowed earth, dependence upon the God-given rains, farm animals giving birth to their young, bountiful years and lean years, all have special meaning to the farmer.

Wind accompanied the clouds and began lashing the trees and grass; clouds scudded across the sky; thunder rolled and reverberated between the low lying hills; lightning licked playfully at the earth. A large droplet splattered the windshield; another quickly followed.

Moments later, John turned the windshield wipers on. They thrust busily from side to side; rivulets of water ran toward the windshield corners. He loved nature's elemental displays and always felt closer to God during the storms. However, John suddenly experienced a chill and deep dread as if a black shadow had passed between his soul and his Maker. He shuddered. Thankfully, the feeling quickly passed.

John continued toward Breton and the spring thunderstorm rumbled on toward the west. The rain pattering on the windshield stopped abruptly and he turned the wipers off.

I hope this didn't make too much of a mess of the pit.

When John returned from town with the load of supplies they picked their way through the sticky mud and surveyed the results of the thundershower.

"Mark, you and Tim may have to work in the mud until you get the top part dug off."

"That's OK dad," Tim shrugged, then said with a grin, "it'll all come off in the wash."

Mark and Tim worked in the pit while John and Bob went back in the study where they pored over their drawings.

"Have you completed the plans for a water supply?"

"Yes, here's the layout." Bob selected a drawing from the sheaf of papers. "I based the capacity on sixty days."

John looked them over. The water reservoir consisted of three forty-gallon pressure tanks removed from hot water heaters. The piping arrangement made water flow through all three vessels in series and then on into the house. This insured that they would always be full of fresh water.

"That is very ingenious Bob. With the pump in the shelter, we can continue having fresh water even after the attack. In addition, we will store dozens of gallons of water in plastic jugs inside and use them first to free up space."

"What do you have planned for the electric Bob?" John asked.

Bob replied. "We'll need power for a lot of our equipment although we can survive without it if the worst happens. With electricity, life will be more pleasant. I'm planning on a two-thousand watt gasoline powered generator and a hundred gallon fuel supply which we will bury in the hole we have dug for it. We'll use remote controls for starting and turning power on and off. By keeping it separate from our shelter, we won't chance contaminating our breathing air with carbon monoxide. We can use a small hot plate and have some cooked meals for we must rule out cooking with an open flame due to the oxygen consumption."

John reviewed the rest of the plans. "This all looks good Bob. Our project is beginning to take shape. We can pick up some of this other equipment tomorrow."

He arose from his chair and stretched. "It's past mail time so I'll go down and check. I'm hoping to hear from Jesse. I'm writing him tonight and telling him of our progress and encouraging him to bring Karen and come on."

John got the newspaper and scanned the front page. He had been searching carefully since his dreams looking for anything in world news that would confirm his beliefs and to date, there was nothing.

As he spread the paper, headlines greeted his eyes. STOCK MARKET TAKES A PLUNGE. Under the caption, the reporter went into detail on the factors affecting the market. Consumer buying had been down on a wide variety of products now for several months. Manufacturers who continued building their inventories expecting an upturn finally reached their limits and the mandatory production cutbacks were having their inevitable effects.

"Nothing to worry about," said the paper. It cited similar slumps, or market adjustments.

Nothing there, John thought and glanced through the rest of the paper. The only hint of trouble was the clanking tools and humming motors from the back yard. I'll look and feel like a complete idiot if nothing comes of this, John reflected, serious doubts hitting him for the first time.

They completed the hole on Thursday night and, Friday morning, focused full efforts on building forms in the bottom of the pit. John made arrangements in Breton for a concrete truck and decided to do his own hauling for he didn't want too many people having their curiosity aroused. He also got a slightly cheaper rate by making his own delivery which provided him with an excuse for doing it himself.

Mark and Tim helped Bob build forms. John went after the cement and by the time he returned, they were ready. John positioned the truck, shifted a lever, and cement poured down the trough and into the forms at the bottom of the pit. Tim and Mark climbed down inside with rakes and hoes and leveled the bottom. An hour later, they finished the floor and the concrete began setting up.

John drove the truck down his drive and entered the lane. After driving a short distance, he spotted two men partially concealed in a clump of trees, clearly keeping the Bailey home under surveillance. John stopped the truck, dismounted and strode across the field toward the clump of trees and accosted them. "Men, I'm John Bailey. Could you tell me what there is about my home that is so interesting and can you tell me who you are?"

"Mister Bailey, this isn't your property and we don't answer to you for being here. However, for your information, we're from the sheriff's department and have orders to keep an eye on you."

"Can you tell me why?" John asked, incredulous.

"If you need more information, I suggest you check with the sheriff," one of them replied.

"I'll do just that. And I'm advising you, don't do any prowling on my property unless you have a warrant."

Steaming, John climbed back in the truck and went on to Breton.

His visit with the sheriff left him chilled. The sheriff pointedly questioned John's motive for obtaining the dynamite, cited questions raised in his mind related to the possible dangers to other citizens and gave John a stern warning that if there was any indication of arms or militancy from the Bailey place, the Sheriff's Department would have no choice but to conduct a raid and take them all into custody. He also confirmed that Mark and Tim had won the battle at school when the sheriff mentioned some parents were considering filing assault charges.

John said little and left the Sheriff's office thoroughly chastised and glad to be free. That's one angle I hadn't even thought about. We're going to have to be extremely cautious from here on out.

When John returned home he collected the family and apprised them of the new turn of events. "Keep your eyes open and see if you can spot any other visitors. I don't like the implications a bit. The more people that learn what we're doing the more chance we'll have for visitors after we go underground. Whatever you do though, don't show any weapons or make any threatening moves that could bring the law down on us. One thing we must do is cut down a couple trees out back and blow out the stumps. Whatever we do, we can't afford to lose the dynamite."

Changing the subject, he asked Bob, "When do you think we can move into the shelter?"

Bob scratched his head, "We could have it suitable for survival in a week. Making it livable will take longer.

"There's nothing indicating we won't have a week but I'll breathe easier when it's ready." John stated.

John and Bob worked late Friday night finishing plans and making a list of equipment Breton Electronics couldn't supply. They still lacked a few parts for the ventilation system, which they had ordered from Louisville and was due in on Monday.

The Baileys, hard at work again on Saturday morning, removed the forms from the foundation.

"The floor looks good, doesn't it, Bob asked, critically examining their handiwork.

"I hope we haven't forgotten any of the plumbing or wiring," John added.

Shall we start the forms for the sides? Mark, will you and Tim begin passing the two-by-fours down?" John initiated the next phase of their construction without delay.

Mark and Tim shuttled materials over the side while John and Bob received them and stacked them.

"That's enough for now boys; hand down the tools."

They laid out hammers, nails, power saw, level, square, and other carpentering tools on the new concrete floor. Sawing and hammering continued until noon.

They completed the four outer wall forms and left three openings. One provided an outlet for plumbing and wiring midway down one side, a second hole accessed the well casing, and the other aperture at the end of the pit farthest from the house opened into the entrance shaft.

They bored holes in the forms around the door facing and imbedded three and a half inch studs every twelve inches which would secure a large steel plate over the entrance.

Saturday afternoon, John got a visitor, dapper and well dressed in an expensive suit, along with a gray fedora. He identified himself as Delbert Conrad, Secret Service. "Could we go inside and talk privately?" he asked.

"Certainly," John agreed, leading the way. What is this all about, he wondered. "Have a seat, Mr. Conrad," John beckoned.

They sat and Conrad, without preamble, began asking questions and taking notes.

After John confirmed his full name, address and age, he interrupted. "Mister Conrad, could you please tell me what this is all about?"

"Your occupation?" Conrad asked.

John remained silent.

"Your occupation?" Conrad repeated impatiently.

"Mister Conrad, I'll answer your questions when you tell me what this is all about." John retorted.

"I can arrest you and take you in if you don't cooperate." Conrad responded imperiously.

John remained silent.

Conrad, who actually was a fairly decent sort thought for a full minute before breaking the silence. "Mister Bailey, this is your last chance. You can make it easy or hard on yourself. I'll get the information in time, either here or with you in custody. You will fare better by cooperating."

John seethed, sorely tempted to let the man take him in, but after considering the consequences, he swallowed his pride, cooled off, and answered the questions; he couldn't build shelters in jail. John gave his occupation.

Conrad continued interrogating John for an hour, finally ran out of questions, and then reviewed his notes, from beginning to end, twice.

John, impatient and angry, masked his feelings the best he could. A thousand things needed doing.

Conrad appeared satisfied with his answers. "All right Mister Bailey, I'll explain. The letter you wrote to the president triggered this investigation."

John's face took on an incredulous look.

Conrad continued: "Following psychiatric analysis of your letter, you were classified as a potential threat to the president and I came here to check you out. After our conversation this past hour, I'm convinced you're not. If you had been, you would be on your way to jail. I'm not sure though that you don't have a screw loose."

John stated, "I guess I should be more careful about what I say and write from now on."

"You're right," Conrad agreed. "It could get you in bad trouble."

"Thank you for the advice Mister Conrad," John managed.

Conrad gathered up his papers, stuffed them all in his briefcase and got up.

"Good luck John," he offered.

"Good luck to you, too." I'm afraid you are the one who will need it, John thought.

"What was that all about dad?" Bob asked,

"I got a response to my letter to the president," John answered ruefully. "I'm lucky they didn't lock me up."

When John returned, they had completed the forms. They worked on until 10:00 p.m. and shut the job down.

"Let's all get some sleep since there isn't much we can do before Monday morning. We'll all go to church tomorrow."

Several expressed relief when John's words ended their arduous day's work.

John arose early Sunday morning, poured a cup of coffee, went to his study and closed the door. He needed time alone. Were there any loose ends that needed nailing down?

His letter to the governor wasn't answered or acknowledged. The lack of positive response was really no different from what he expected.

John's brother Charles, his only close kin, lived in Cincinnati. He and his brother never were close but John still felt a deep concern. Charles totally rejected the idea a war could be imminent. John, almost certain of the response, had felt compelled to try.

Ellen and John's parents were dead but she had two sisters. She called and wrote them but so far hadn't heard.

Both of Ruth's divorced parents had remarried. Her two younger brothers lived with their mother. Ruth called her mother and father but they both expressed disbelief. They finally promised they would watch the news and if conditions warranted it, they would build a shelter.

I can't think of another thing that might convince people, John thought. If I become more insistent, somebody may have me locked up. To date, I don't know of one person, except maybe Dean and Hazel, who has accepted my theories. Apparently, except for the one article, even the papers decided I'm not newsworthy and won't even do a story on me as a nut. They may be afraid of starting a panic. When things get worse, I hope people will wake up and get busy.

The time finally came and they went to the church on Miller Street in Breton. They arrived in time for Sunday school. After they got out of the van, people studiously avoided meeting them but nodded and smiled from a distance. John caught the innuendo when a small girl pointed at him and said something to her mother who quickly shushed her.

Each of them went to their departments. Greetings from John's fellow members were civil but restrained. They filled the time before class with weather talk, job talk, and a profusion of small talk. John couldn't have edged in a word if he had wanted to. He sensed the strain and knew that every mind in the room dwelled on his letter of last Sunday. Evidently, they didn't wish to discuss it.

Fifteen minutes into the bible study, John, feeling compelled, interrupted the class and said, "Men, I realize the importance of this lesson but I need to speak."

The teacher stopped talking and John spoke hurriedly, keeping the teacher from regaining control.

"The things I told you in the letter are true. I'm convinced a nuclear attack is coming soon and there's not much time for getting ready. Please listen."

George Crawford, operator of the Crawford Mortuary interrupted and spoke bluntly, "You're wasting your breath on us. Everybody has his own opinion, I say. I would appreciate it though if you would keep these wild ideas to yourself. Your letter terribly disturbed my wife and your suggestions gave her nightmares. She went to the doctor three times this past week." George was definitely upset.

Bill Clayton spoke up. "You're not the only one having problems. My wife wants me to build a shelter. Women are much more susceptible to suggestions and I'm not happy at all having her disturbed like this." Bill looked directly at John, "Please keep your unbalanced thinking to yourself in the future."

Realizing they were all good, well-meaning, ordinary men, unable to remotely visualize what he was saying, John made one final plea. "Men, can't you see? Are you totally blind? Look at the world about you! Look at history! Don't you realize the potential for destruction in existence today?"

Don Adams, the Sunday school teacher, looked at first one and then the other, helplessly.

John saw the futility of trying, knowing he couldn't reach them with his reasoning. Other class members showed by their nods of approval at the speeches of George, Bill and Edmund that they were in complete disfavor with John's cause.

Don Adams regained control and haltingly continued

the lesson. His heart wasn't in it, their minds weren't on it, and everybody felt relief when the bell rang.

John left the classroom area, saw Ellen and Ruth standing off to one side, and sensed a problem. Ellen cried and Ruth comforted her.

"What is it Ellen?"

Ruth answered instead. "Oh, John, one of the women said rude and hateful things. She said you were crazy and should be locked up. Every time mother tried to answer or explain, she interrupted. She wasn't very nice."

Ellen spoke up. "Don't get the wrong impression though. Most of the people were sympathetic and kind even if they did express disbelief."

Bob, Mark and Tim joined the group. They related stories of snide comments and rejection of John's warning. Their peers hadn't been tactful at all. Their criticisms related by Mark and Tim mirrored conversations between their parents at home, heard and parroted by their children.

John, tempted to leave and not attend church said, "No, they won't run us off. We'll go inside and see this through."

"Let's go," John took Ellen's arm and they walked resolutely into the church auditorium and took seats in the middle section half way down toward the front. Other members of the congregation gave them a wide berth. Small children turned in their seats and stared curiously.

A person's past deeds don't count for much if he upsets the status quo. John's thoughts were tinged with bitterness, anger and indignation. I wouldn't have believed that people would turn against us so completely.

Actually, most of the congregation felt sympathy toward the Baileys but didn't speak out in support. The Bailey's position called for a firm commitment and the people just didn't believe.

Reverend Burger preached an interesting sermon. He mentioned people who were easily swayed and allowed anything that happened to divert them from their path. Another thrust of the message included the trying of the spirits, whether they are of God or the devil. John got the point. Obviously, Reverend Burger didn't think John received his revelation from God. Many of the church group apparently harbored the same opinion. However, John got calls from a few people later whom were in sympathy with him and nearly believed.

John thought, with rare exceptions, prophets of old were ignored, disbelieved, persecuted and even killed, especially in times of high prosperity when low morality, decadence and frivolity typified a way of life and people became enraged at anyone who hinted change.

The trouble was, John didn't feel like a prophet and didn't believe he was one. He didn't believe he should launch a crusade warning people. What kind of a fluke of fate brought me the message and not to other people? He pondered. The more John considered it, the more convinced he became that this was not a universal message. The insight brought another wave of serious doubts.

John could understand the rejection of his tidings. In this time of unequaled prosperity, people's minds wouldn't accept anything that could upset it. By rejecting the possibility, this present life of luxury and plenty would continue forever. What I suggest could destroy this, therefore they must disbelieve.

The sermon ended and the Bailey family made their

exit. John felt sad and sorry for the people but he knew they wouldn't change their minds.

The family got in the van. John turned the radio on and dialed KBRT. They always enjoyed the beautiful choir music presented on Sunday afternoons by the Breton Congregational Choir.

# CHAPTER IV
# THE SECOND SEAL IS OPEN

Matthew 24:7, 8: "For nation shall rise against nation, and kingdom against kingdom: and there shall be famines, and pestilences, and earthquakes, in divers places. All these are the beginning of sorrows."

Revelation 6:3, 4: "And when he had opened the second seal, I heard the second beast say, Come and see. And there went out another horse that was red: and power was given to him that sat thereon to take peace from the earth, and that they should kill one another: and there was given unto him a great sword."

The Baileys closely monitored the television all afternoon but news remained sketchy.

At 6:00 p.m. disturbing news flashed across their television screen. "Good afternoon ladies and gentlemen, Billy Darrell, with the news of fighting in the Middle East. Word just arrived that fierce fighting erupted about two hours ago between the Arabs and Israelis. This breaks a long period of peace and shocks the entire world. Early reports state the fighting erupted on several fronts but we don't know the cause. Stay tuned for developments." The TV station switched back to regular programming.

Ellen placed her hand on her husband's arm and looked at him. "John?"

"It could be, Ellen. I've been looking for an event like this now for several days."

The other Baileys' expressions became serious upon hearing the ill-boding announcement. They watched news broadcasts the remainder of the day and although the information stayed sketchy, it sounded ominous.

Early Monday morning, Ellen and Ruth took Sabrina and went to Breton for a load of food and other supplies while Bob, John, Mark, and Tim resumed work on the shelter. Bob and Mark worked on conduit, wiring, and their sound and radiation monitoring devices while John and Tim put the finishing touches on the cement forms and then studied their plans for the entrance.

At noon time Ellen announced, "Time to eat."

"Whew," Bob explained, wiping sweat from his neck and face. "Much more of this would develop into hard work."

"I'll leave after lunch and get a load of cement," John stated.

Ellen and Ruth had food on the table when the men entered the house. The Baileys gathered around the table and John said grace. Besides thanking God for all their blessings, he prayed for Karen and Jesse's deliverance. John felt a deep concern for them but didn't know how he could change their minds. He trusted that God would work a miracle and bring them home.

Mark turned the volume back up on the radio. They heard a discouraging news update on the Middle East conflict. Conditions were deteriorating rapidly and signs pointed to information censoring. This could only mean bad news.

Following the Middle East news, the commentator talked about the economic instability. The Baileys listened somberly without comment.

When the meal ended, John left for Breton. Bob, Mark and Tim resumed work and by the time John returned with the cement, the forms were ready. He drove the truck into position and worked the controls following Bob's shouted instructions. Cement flowed out of the spout and filled the voids within the forms. They poured the entrance portions and Bob positioned the bolts until they lay straight with the wall while Mark and Tim smoothed the wall tops.

John drove the cement truck back to Breton and when he returned, stopped at the mail box. He looked through the usual assortment of bills and advertisements, threw the irrelevant mail on the ground, including bills, and looked for some word from Jesse but found none. He took the Breton Daily News from the newspaper tube and the double headlines confirmed the recent newscasts.

Everybody suspected that the Russian advisers who were in the Middle East keeping the peace were now coordinating the efforts of the Arab nations' fight against Israel.

Under the headlines, the Middle East War story evolved. The Iranian Military forces, along with Syria, Iraq, Palestine and Hezbollah launched a coordinated land, sea and air attack against Israel. These armies contained contingents from several smaller Arab countries such as Libya, Morocco, Algeria, and others. Russian advisers possibly directed and coordinated the assaults at all levels of command. Large numbers of Cuban troops and contingents from Nicaragua,

Panama, Mexico and Venezuela, who seemingly materialized out of nowhere, advanced with the Arabs on the Hezbollah front in South Lebanon. It was unclear which foreign forces were sent by their governments, were mercenaries, volunteers or all of the above.

The Israelis responded bravely but were losing ground; their numbers dwindling through attrition.

The United Nations Security Council held multiple meetings. Russia used their veto power to forestall any resolutions or actions by that body.

The United States government showed deadly indecision and failed to use any proactive measures to aid or rescue Israel. Although the president threatened to act on his own, there was enough resistance from Congress and political parties to delay critical response.

Unless something changed, and soon, it seemed that those nations who chanted "death to Israel" might finally get their way. The only thing now that would save Israel it appeared would have to be an act of God Almighty!

In other headlines, the stock market continued sliding sharply for the fourth day. The plunge hadn't yet reached panic proportions but approached rapidly. Large and small factories announced the production curtailment and layoffs. Many industries shut down and wouldn't reopen until after depleting their bloated inventories. Hysteria crept into the economic and world reports.

John hurried up the drive in the dark. Time was running out. He gathered the family in the den and briefed them. "The latest events indicate the war is close and we still don't have a shelter. We'll work each night now until midnight. We would be foolish taking any chances."

"Dad, I'd like to go see Jesse," Bob ventured. "I know we can't spare the time but seeing him and talking to him would make me feel better."

"OK Bob, fly up there and back, but hurry. We still lack quite a bit and you must do the electronic part of it. Radiation monitoring is crucial."

"I'll leave first thing in the morning and should be back tomorrow night."

John called the Klines and Kathy answered. "Could I speak to Ed?"

"Just a minute, Mister Bailey," Kathy replied.

"Hello John."

"Ed, how are you doing?"

"Just fine. What's on your mind?"

"Have you been watching the news?"

"Yes I have. Doesn't look too good, does it?"

"No it doesn't. Have you seen enough?"

"No, not yet, John. I admit this looks bad but I doubt if it signals the end of the world."

"Ed, if you change your mind, let me know."

They said goodbye and frustrated, John sadly replaced the phone. He went on out to the kitchen where his and Bob's wives were busy sorting out foodstuffs. "Ellen, how are you and Ruth doing."

Ellen replied, "We have most of our supplies here already. We're going back over the lists making sure we aren't overlooking anything."

"Are you getting a good variety?"

"I think so. Mostly, we have been buying foods that doesn't require cooking. There is a lot of emergency food supplies on the market and we have been getting a lot of these. A lot of it is pre prepared meals. We are also getting a lot of canned goods that will store for a few years if needed. We aren't getting any of the 20 or 25 year storage stuff for we don't think we'll need it. We did get some soups and a few things we can heat on the hot plate. I know we can't afford much electric for cooking but a hot meal now and then will be a big help. In addition to the basic foods, we have included jelly, cereals, powdered milk, candy, crackers, and several other odds and ends. Jesse will be having a birthday and we even got a cake for him." Tears came to her eyes when she mentioned his name.

"Ruth and I prepared daily menus for two months and bought the food accordingly. We have actually figured in a ten percent excess and hope we can stretch it out even longer. We have a complete list of everything so you can go over it and see if there's anything else we may need. I have doubts though that the shelter will hold it all."

"What about the other household items?"

"We have been working on those also. I'll let Ruth tell you about them."

"We have first aid supplies, utensils, plastic and paper bags, stacks of newspapers, disinfectant, baby supplies, sewing kit, candles, matches and other things we might need. Bedding, clothing, towels, wash cloths and so forth can be moved from the house when necessary."

John was pleased with their progress. "We have what we need and now it's just a matter of completing the shelter. We are going to build us a storage pit where we can store about a six month supply of food and other household items. I suspect when we come out of the shelter, everything is going to be scarce or non-existent. Go ahead and get a good supply of the long term storage foods as well. We just can't know the future."

"Let's all turn in and get an early start in the morning."

The alarm went off at 4:00 a.m. and rang until John reluctantly got out of bed.

By daybreak, John, Mark, and Tim were out at the shelter and busy removing the forms from the massive two-foot thick cement walls.

"Mark, you and Tim roll the three forty-gallon tanks over to the shelter," John instructed.

Soon the first tank rested on the floor of the shelter and a half hour later, all three were in place.

"Let's get our bathroom tank in next," John directed.

The square tank, made of steel, measured five by five by three feet tall. It took some rigging with the ropes and a good bit of heaving and tugging to get it lowered into the shelter.

"Let the sandbags and lime down next."

Mark looked puzzled. "What are they for?"

"The sandbags will fill the area between the entrance plates after we have gone inside and the lime, we hope, will keep the restroom from stinking."

Soon, twelve sandbags and eight bags of lime were stacked in the corner of the shelter by the door. Pipes, fittings, tools and other plumbing equipment followed.

"We won't move anything else into the shelter until we do the plumbing," John told Mark and Tim.

By working diligently the rest of the day, John and the two young men installed the water tanks and piping and finished the bathroom. They installed a fifteen inch high platform on top of the tank equipped with a commode seat and lid. It opened directly into the tank, outhouse style, since they wouldn't use water for flushing. On the back of the tank, they welded a vent pipe and extended it above ground. Hopefully, this would take all the odors outside. They enclosed the toilet with walls, installed a door, and hung a light fixture. They all laughed when Tim picked up a piece of chalk and labeled the door "Throne Room" in large letters.

Bob returned at 11:30 p.m. on Tuesday night and found them still at work, lowering the table into the shelter. Bob looked tired and John knew without asking that his trip was fruitless.

"Let's knock off for today boys," John decreed, wanting to hear Bob's report. He crawled through the shelter entrance and climbed wearily up the ladder.

"You've made a lot of progress today," Bob noted.

"We should be pouring the top by late tomorrow." John remarked, leading the group toward the house.

The Baileys assembled in the study where Ellen and Ruth waited to hear the news about Jesse and Karen.

Bob didn't mince words. "Jesse says he doesn't believe anything will happen and he can't give up a good job just because you had some bad dreams. He did seem uneasy when I pointed out the latest happenings in the economy and world military activity. The only promise I could get out of him that if things get bad, they would come."

John replied, "I'm afraid he will see the truth too late. If they were close by, it wouldn't matter but a three hundred and fifty mile drive takes a long time. They could make it in a short time flying but there won't be any flights if an emergency develops. We can only hope they come in time."

"Dad, have you been keeping up with all the latest news?" Bob asked.

"Yes, we have. We heard about the partial military alert on the ten o' clock news."

The Bailey family went to bed on a sad note.

4:00 a.m. came quickly and they arose wearily and after a speedy breakfast, launched an all-out effort.

"Beds go in first thing this morning," John dictated. "After they are in place we can build the forms for the roof. We'll leave some of the bedding in the house and sleep on it and the couches."

"Can we move the food or other household goods in before the roof goes on?" Ellen inquired.

"Yes, John agreed. "It doesn't look like rain and since everything is in boxes it should be all right."

"Tim and I will start carrying it out," Mark volunteered.

He and Tim walked over, each picked up a large box, and went out the door. Ruth held it open for them.

"Hold off on carrying any more boxes, boys," John advised after they set down their first load. "Go ahead and tear down the beds and carry them out here first."

Bob and John began installing the beds. They built a sturdy frame five feet high and fifty-four inches wide down the east wall the entire length of the shelter. With this completed, Mark and Tim lowered the box springs. They placed the three double bed box springs at the end. The two young men passed the mattresses down and thus completed the sleeping accommodations for eight people, all but the baby.

"OK boys, hand the boxes and other stuff down," John instructed.

After most of the supplies were stowed under the beds, Mark and Tim made another trip and brought a four by six foot table which they maneuvered into the shelter. They left again and came back with eight folding chairs. The third trip, they brought a small desk which would be their operations center.

"All we lack now is building the shelves from floor to ceiling down the remainder of the west wall," Bob said.

"I hope we can get the forms built and this roof poured today. Any time now something could happen keeping us from getting the cement. That would be disastrous." John's voice revealed anxiety when he spoke.

They finished the shelves by 2:00 p.m., began working on the forms for the roof and suddenly John stopped working and said, "I'm leaving right now for the cement truck. We may have to let it sit for a few hours but at least it will be here."

The forms should be ready by about 10:00 tonight," Bob stated. "Father, pick up two fifty-five gallon drums and have them filled with gasoline while you're in town. We only have four five-gallon cans full which wouldn't last long."

As each hour passed, John felt the tension building and a greater sense of urgency. An inner voice seemed to be saying to him, "Hurry! Hurry! Hurry!"

John returned with the cement. He also brought the daily paper and the news sounded anything but encouraging. The war in the Middle East went against the Israelis. They held their lines tenaciously and when orders for retreat came, few were able. Superior arms and overwhelming numbers were grinding them into oblivion.

Arab bloc and Latin American communist bloc forces, relatively unopposed, bludgeoned their way across the Sinai toward Israel's heartland. Russia supplied most of the air support and co-ordination. The Israelis worked desperately, bolstering their second line of defense with women, children and old men who shouldered arms and manned the trenches.

The United States issued serious warnings ordering the Arabs and Russians to stop their aggression. Russia denied complicity and reminded the United States that interference from the U. S. could result in a military response. Meanwhile, the fierceness of the attacks against Israel intensified.

On the home front, woes increased. The economy shrank in spite of all the government sponsored injections which should have cured any slumps. The stock market hadn't made any drastic changes in direction but persisted in a steady downward plummet.

Factories continued cutbacks and layoffs. In some areas such as the auto industry, layoffs had reached alarming proportions. A growing unrest in these cities created tensions that could erupt in violence at any time. A few sporadic incidents were already occurring.

John discussed the day's news with the family. "We really have no idea what can happen, even in the next twenty-four hours. We'll install one radio at the work site and another in the kitchen, turned up loud."

John thought a moment and then continued, "For the next few days, Ellen and Ruth can take care of monitoring from midnight to four a.m. Once the shelter is complete, we can all take turns."

Mark approached John. "Father, could I talk to you for just a minute?

"Sure Mark."

John and Mark remained in the study. Bob and Tim left.

"Father, I'm going over and visit Kathy one more time. I'm getting scared and I'm very concerned about her."

"You like her a lot, don't you?" John asked gently.

"Yes I do. We have become much closer the last few months. I'm afraid they will wait too long and get caught."

"Mark, I'll tell you what. You go see Kathy. Invite her over here if anything happens. I'll discuss this with Ed and make the same offer to him and Marge. This could throw us in a bad position for we haven't prepared for that many people, especially if Jesse and Karen come."

John, Bob and Tim resumed work on the shelter. Ellen and Ruth continued working in the house. In spite of the bright sunlight and the warm seventy-five degrees, a sense of foreboding and chill permeated the Bailey home.

Bob worked at installing a radio by the shelter while John and Tim hammered away on the forms. Music soon accompanied their hammering and sawing. Bob picked a station where national and world news aired frequently. On the hour and half hour they broadcast the latest events.

Mark returned in two hours from his visit with Kathy. He whistled cheerfully and appeared in high spirits. John could tell Mark exacted a favorable promise.

They completed the forms at 9:30 p.m. John placed the truck into position and dumped the cement until the truck was empty. They lacked six inches filling the forms, which left them with a three and a half foot thick roof.

"This should be enough," John decided. "With the dirt filled in on top, we can take anything but a direct hit."

"Nobody would waste an A bomb on one shelter so we shouldn't have to worry," Mark commented.

"All bombs aren't going to hit their targets," Bob noted.

At a little after 11:00 p.m., John felt he could take the time to call Ed. John was tired and Ed had been asleep so their conversation started on a strained note.

"Can I come over and talk to you, Ed?"

"If you feel that you must," Ed answered grumpily.

John hung up, slipped out to the garage and straddled Mark's bicycle. The air and the light refreshing breeze felt good as John made his way through the star-lit night to Ed's house. The trip actually revived his body and cleared his mind.

Ed waited for him on the front porch. "Come on in John," Ed led him into the living room where two cups of hot, fresh coffee awaited them.

John sugared and stirred his coffee and then began. "Ed, I'm extending an invitation from my family for you and your family to share our shelter with us if war comes. I'm also offering my help and that of our entire family if you build your own shelter."

The unselfish offer momentarily overwhelmed Ed. He brushed tears from his eyes and waited several moments before he could trust his voice.

"John, I really appreciate what you and your family are offering us and, believe you me, I'm watching world events closely. I'm sure though if any real danger develops, our government will warn us in plenty of time."

"Ed, Ed," John chided, "you know better than that. By the time they give the word, it'll be too late."

"John, I know it's late but could you go over all this with me again in depth?" I'm listening but so far I just can't accept any of it."

"Sure Ed, I'll be glad to if you think there's a need. Can you give me some idea of what you're thinking?"

"I don't want to hurt your feelings John but I'm going to level with you. First, I'm thinking that maybe you've turned into some kind of a religious nut or fanatic. Since you've been seeing visions, then you must believe you are getting the messages from God - or the devil."

John replied dryly. "Ed, I'll have to admit that I don't know why I dreamed what I did. Since the devil never authored any good thing, and if the dreams had to come from one or the other, then I feel safe in assuming the dreams were from God. However, the psychiatrist I talked to has a theory that I may have dreamed because of an accumulation of information in my sub- conscious about world conditions and current happenings."

"Another thing John, could this whole thing have come to your mind because of the world population situation? For much of our lives we've been warned of overpopulation calamity and maybe this is your sub conscious mind's way of solving the problem. You will have to admit, it would solve that problem."

John shrugged, ""What can I say? I've questioned these same things in my own mind and I've even considered the theories that some have expounded on mankind's self-destruct inclinations. I keep drawing blanks and eventually revert to my original decision: build a shelter."

"Ed, back to some of my original lines of reasoning, you know how I distrust the Russians, all communists for that matter, and their philosophy of Dialectic Materialism. Since the hardliners are sure to take over in Russia, what do you think you can expect? Who do you think is behind the war in the Middle East?"

Ed got up from his chair. "John, I understand what you're saying and I can see some of where you're coming from. I'm almost convinced but I need just a little more time. I'm truly grateful for all you've done for us and I'll let you know if I change my mind."

"It's late." John stood, stretched, shook Ed's hand and, without further words, left. When he arrived home he went to the study and slumped down in his chair.

"I've talked to every friend, acquaintance and relative until they have all essentially said bug off. I don't know of another thing I can do." John muttered.

Thursday morning dawned bright and sunny and with the shelter built, John felt more at ease. Today they could concentrate on and finish the vital systems. He and Tim would work on the ventilation equipment, while Bob and Mark completed the more technical parts of their audio, radio and radiation monitoring. They hoped that by nightfall they would have everything finished.

At the breakfast table, Ellen reported on the newscasts she monitored overnight.

Rioting erupted in several cities nationwide at 2:00 a.m. central time. Preliminary reports indicated the disturbances were widespread but due to disrupted communications, the news remained sketchy.

However, the ominous Middle East news reported Arab and Latin American troops advancing on Tel Aviv. The Israeli's fanatical resistance exacted a terrible toll on their enemies but the overwhelming odds slowly pushed them back. The Israeli foreign minister continued making direct appeals for help to England and the United States but, so far, neither country would honor their requests for direct military intervention. The feared Israeli genocide became a distinct possibility unless a miracle happened.

Israel vehemently claimed Russian involvement but the CIA, whose delicate network of intricate tentacles, stripped away callously by liberal administrations, lacked the ability to confirm or deny the reports.

The United States, fatally inflexible from years of isolationism and the downsizing of the military through sequestration, plus severe downsizing through the Obama administration, hesitated to intervene militarily. Regardless of the tremendous power and influence of the American Jews to exert pressure on the administration, liberals in Congress, both Democrat and Republican, maintained enough clout to keep our forces out.

Diplomatic efforts continued unabated in the U. N. and through all other available channels. The Russians remained polite but evasive and denied involvement. They pointedly insisted that the United States should not interfere. Third world nations took the floor, delivered lengthy vituperative attacks on the "American Imperialist" and blocked diplomatic maneuvers to stop the war.

The Bailey family ate breakfast hurriedly and went to work. Mark and Tim started removing the roof forms while John and Bob tackled the ventilation and monitoring systems. The ducting, piping and other materials, pre-cut from drawings Bob worked up, went together quickly.

John installed a filter holder above ground, allowing the vent pipe to end in the center of a twelve cubic foot filter. They were installing the filter under a picnic table in such a way that it would disguise it and also shield the filter from direct fallout. The other end of the pipe extended into the shelter and the threads would take any one of three blowers. The 115 volt D.C. blower got power from the battery bank when the gasoline generator wasn't running. The 115 volt generator supplied the A.C. blower. The hand operated air mover provided air if they couldn't use the others.

Once John knew they were prepared, he felt infinite relief. There's nothing more to do here until we fill the hole and we can fill it by hand if we have to, he thought.

"Come here father, we're getting more news," Bob said.

The announcer sounded upset. "According to our latest news bulletin, the United States landed troops in Israel this morning. Russia is furious and warns she will commit her forces with the Arabs unless the United States pulls out immediately. The White House Press Secretary informs us the President of the United States is confident that a show of force will convince the Latin Americans and Arabs they should stop their aggression. The White House also announced the President will deliver a major `State of the World' speech tonight at eight p.m. and also give details on the nation's internal disturbances."

Following a pause, the commentator continued: "The stock market, fluctuating wildly in the face of the unrest throughout the country, rallied for a short time this morning but later in the day took another plunge. Computer trading stopped at mid morning and the market closed temporarily at noon today. Experts expressed confidence the unstable conditions are due entirely to the national unrest and are sure that when order is restored, the market will correct itself."

"World conditions aren't looking too good, are they

father?" Bob questioned, following the newscast. "Sending help to Israel now is "a day late and a dollar short" I'm afraid. This so-called national unrest is also scary."

"No, world conditions aren't looking good. The lid could blow off at any time. Let's get busy."

John and Tim dismantled the piping from the water well and pump, removed the upper joint of the well casing, re-routed it to the inside of the shelter, and installed the pump. It fitted nicely alongside the forty-gallon tanks. Tim helped John assemble the pre-cut piping. It was hot and stuffy working inside the shelter.

Ruth came out and reminded them, "Aren't you men going to eat today? Dinner's ready."

"We'll be right there Ruth," John assured. "Let's hurry boys. We can't spare much time." There were still so many things that needed doing and no way of knowing how much time remained.

When darkness came, water flowed through the plumbing, flushing it. Bob continued working on the wiring inside the shelter. A cord from the house supplied power for the water pump, lights, and ventilation blower.

Bob's control panel bristled with loose wires, many of them exiting the hole in the side of the shelter. The other ends of the wires were wrapped around a tree above-ground for use later.

"We can fill the hole any time dad," Bob reported.

"We could be wasting our time working on that tonight, Bob. I'll try to get a dozer out here tomorrow and scoop it back in. Let's go in and listen to the president's speech and then we'll concentrate on finishing the generator system."

As they entered the room, the president began speaking.

"Fellow citizens, I don't wish to cause panic but I'm highly concerned about the worsening world conditions, especially in Israel and here in the United States. We don't have proof but we're positive the Russians are behind the trouble in the Middle East and much of this here in this country. However, to the contrary, they claim they're doing their best to restrain the Arab countries who are attacking Israel. In view of the worsening world conditions, I advise you now, begin making shelter space arrangements as a prudent measure. I assure you, there's no reason for panic and the shelters are precautionary."

"Concerning the sabotage, rioting and unrest within the country: The scope indicates this is highly organized and here again, although we haven't proved it, we're positive the Russians are behind much of it. We believe the ten thousand or so Russians who entered the country in economic and trade groups are in reality highly trained Speznez teams placed by the KGB and have joined up with "sleepers" to cause maximum sabotage damage and confusion."

"In addition to the attacks we believe may be from the Russians sleeper cells, we are seeing dozens of additional and seemingly unrelated acts of violence and terror, from multiple sources. Radical Islamic terrorists, some home grown and some coordinated by ISIS or al qaeda remnants are one category. Left wing and right wing radicals are involved. Apparently we have a mish mash of sedition traitors, and who knows what else, getting involved. All the enemies of our American society are taking advantage and coming out of the woodwork."

"We are reaping the results of years of slack immigration policies and downright outlawry of Democrat and Republican administrations in essentially throwing the borders open to anybody who wanted to come in. It has been especially bad in the last few years.

"Rioting erupted in medium and large cities nationwide at 2:00 a.m. Eastern time. The coordinated disturbances drew our police forces, fire fighters and public attention to the riot zones where hundreds of fires are being started and scores of people are dying from indiscriminate gunfire."

"Once the officials became preoccupied with the diversionary riots, the saboteurs attacked their primary targets - communications centers, nuclear and conventional power generation, substations, water supplies and mains, police headquarters and disaster control centers -which they destroyed or disabled. Their destruction of communications lines was so effective, it was several hours before we realized the extent and seriousness of the attacks.

I'm instructing cities and outlying areas to form their own militia and protect their territories. We can no longer tie up federal troops in their defense."

"I have declared martial law throughout the United States and all its territories."

"Bob, what's a sleeper?" Tim asked curiously, following the president's speech.

"Sleepers are people sympathetic to the Russians or other anti-American groups. They have laid low in this country, maybe thirty or forty years, waiting until the opportunity came for them to do dirty work."

John told the family, "From now on, each of us will go armed. Keep some kind of gun close by at all times. We are also going to keep a lookout posted. We'll let the women do that for us until we get the heavy work done."

"Let's go back to work men," John led the way outside after Bob finished his explanation.

"Who is the president trying to snow with this shelter bit," Bob growled. "He knows there isn't adequate shelter for one percent of this nation's population."

They worked on into the night, completed a wooden housing for the generator and batteries and lowered them into the pit. John, pleased with the day's progress, felt immense relief. Given another twenty-four hours, they would have everything ready.

They kept silent as the four made their exhausted trek to the house and to their beds.

Four a.m. Friday seemingly arrived immediately after closing their eyes. They forced themselves stiffly from their beds, ate a quick breakfast, and went to the shelter.

"Mark and Tim, work on the entrance. Bob, finish the electrical system and bury it. I'm on my way to Breton to try to get a bulldozer."

John went back to the house and located Ellen and Ruth. "Well girls, you can move everything to the shelter today except the bedding. When the time comes to go, we don't want to spend a lot of time fumbling around." John left his family making last minute preparations and went to Breton. On his way, he tuned in to the local radio station and at six-thirty, heard the news.

The Israelis continued their embattled retreat on all fronts. Accurate Surface to Air Missiles (SAMs) had annihilated practically all of their air force and their ammunition and supplies were dangerously low. American marines and aircraft were already in battle, hoping they could help stem the tide.

Israel sent out identical cryptic messages to all the forces fighting against her, including Russia.

"This is a grave warning! Stop your aggression!"

"Remember Hitler! We shall not die without fighting!"

"Remember Masada! We shall not take our own lives!"

"Remember Sampson! Our enemies shall die with us!"

"Remember Gideon! God is on our side!"

Rioting, burning and killing in the US assumed major proportions. Terrorists and radical groups, or guerilla groups, coming out of nowhere, continued to raid soft targets, block roadways and cause chaos across the country.

The most cynical morsel from their bag of dirty tricks involved the nation's prisons. Teams overpowered the prison guards, loaded inmates in buses, transported the rapists and murderers to the cities, armed them and turned them loose. Death row inmates, who should have died years before for their crimes, generated their share of terror against all they could of the society who had imprisoned them.

Defense forces hadn't yet regained control. Desperate efforts were underway to organize local civilian units to defend the urban areas. Conditions throughout the nation continued deteriorating. All major cities became armed camps under martial law, with roadblocks controlling all entrance and exit points. Ill equipped and poorly manned police patrols roamed the streets seeking to ferret out the guerillas; ambushes chopped the patrols to pieces.

Food would become a serious problem in a matter of days since the saboteurs destroyed or disabled distribution centers. Looters continued stripping stores and supermarkets while guerillas aided by holding the police and guardsmen at bay.

John went to Breton and made arrangements for a bulldozer. They promised delivery within an hour; Time was running out.

When John arrived back home, he parked his car halfway between his house and the road so the truck bringing the dozer would have to stop, then he went to the shelter area and stood studying the work needed on the entrance.

They had gotten a corrugated steel culvert four feet in diameter to use for the vertical passage. Before lowering it into the shaft, John used a cutting torch and burned an opening in one side that matched the shelter entrance. He then welded horizontal steel bars at twelve inch intervals from top to bottom in the pipe to serve as ladder rungs.

After making a quick survey of the shelter area, John glanced at his watch. If I hurry, I should have time to call Jesse before the dozer gets here. I can't give up hope that he will come.

John went to the phone, punched in Jesse's number in Detroit but, instead of making the connection, he heard the intermittent tone signifying a phone out of order. No doubt, phone service was cut off. John shivered; no more contact with Jesse. I'll fly out there tomorrow and try one more time.

Shortly after, John heard the truck with the bulldozer approaching. He walked down the drive and met it.

"Hello Tony," John greeted the bearded, unkempt man. "You'll have to unload here; there's no room there to turn."

"What are you doing with the dozer, Mister Bailey?"

"I need to level some piles of dirt out back."

"I'll stay and do it for you."

"That's OK Tony. There's a good bit of work and I

can't tie you up. The dozer comes much cheaper without an operator."

"What time should I return for it?"

"Four p.m. would be about right." John could finish the work in an hour but to have Tony return too soon could arouse his suspicions.

John waited until the man left, climbed aboard the dozer, and in slightly more than an hour, filled the hole, scraped the back yard off, leveled the back of the property and drove the dozer down the drive, ready for loading.

John returned to the shelter and paired off with Tim to complete the entrance. Tim held the steel plates in position and John built the short tunnel from the shelter to the vertical shaft. Four hours of work brought this phase to completion and they began building the barbecue pit to disguise the entrance. I hope this mortar has time to set before we have to use it, he thought.

Mark spotted a familiar car at the end of their drive. "Dad, that car down there belongs to one of the guys Tim and I fought with at school. I wonder what they're up to?"

"No good, I'm sure. Keep an eye on them until they leave. If they come up here, we'll try to get rid of them without trouble. If not, then we'll do what we have to."

The people stayed about five minutes and then left.

"Tim, when you finish bringing the brick, go ahead and install the table over the air vent," John instructed. "Be sure you have the filter tight."

"Alright, father. Does it matter which side goes up?"

"No, either way will be OK."

Bob worked in the garage, in the shelter, and on top for hours with Mark helping him. They did things with the dozens of wires, routed earlier to several vantage points. The wires extended from two runs of conduit which originated in the shelter. They poured seals in each conduit to prevent any dust or surface water from running down it to the inside.

Bob stepped into the generator pit and connected wires to the ten batteries. He then fastened a pair to the starter circuit of the gasoline engine and a third, heavier pair, to the output of the generator. He looked carefully at the fifty-five gallon gasoline drum and pipe connections for leaks and then placed the cover over the equipment. An air intake and exhaust vent stuck through the top of the cover.

"Mark, I'm going below and check out the generator. If everything works OK you can cover it with dirt." Bob said. Two minutes later, the gasoline engine throbbed to life and Bob let it run for five minutes while he tried out the equipment downstairs.

"Cover it over, Mark," Bob directed, climbing out of the shaft.

Mark shoveled vigorously and completed that part of the task while Bob went to the remainder of the wires. He hooked a shielded pair to a microphone and concealed it in the limbs of a tree and then connected another pair to a microphone at the opposite end of the shelter. He installed a third mike in the vertical shaft. Bob hooked a fourth shielded pair to a remote radiation monitor pickup at the north end of the shelter. This left only one other pair of shielded wires which he connected to a radiation monitor pickup located at the south end. It wouldn't pay to trust just one reading for something as important as this, he thought.

"Mark, help me string up this antenna wire," Bob requested." He boosted Mark up to the first limb of a pine tree and Mark climbed ten feet higher before securing the wire to a limb. The antenna, a must, established their sole link to the outside world since they would be underground with shelter walls and ceiling containing steel. There would be no reception without it. TV, internet, cell phones and all electrical and electronic technology would be the first to go.

John finished the shaft entrance, stepped off to one side to survey the area, and liked what he saw. He had dozed off the entire back yard and instead of disturbed earth just in the vicinity of the shelter, a large area was bare.

"Tim, make up two signs that say, `Keep Off! Seeded Grass'. Stick one at each end of the yard with the signs facing the house, John instructed. "While you're doing that, I'll plant small bushes by the intake and exhaust of the gasoline engine."

After they did that, John took another look. Unless someone suspected something, this should fool them.

Bob came out to the shelter. "We should be in pretty good shape, dad. I've checked out all the systems and everything works."

"Are you ready to connect the explosives?" John asked.

"As ready as I'll ever be."

"Tim, you and Mark go get the dynamite. Bob, go down in the shelter and double check all of the detonator wires to make sure they're shorted out. Bring the meter back up with you and we'll take another reading on this end before hooking them up. I'll get the caps."

All four again gathered at the top, just in time to hear a news bulletin. "Following a special session with congress, the president affirmed the state of national emergency and martial law. He extended enlistments for all the military for one year and ordered up Reservists and the National Guard."

The Baileys stood listening intently until the commentator concluded his broadcast and then resumed work.

"Mark, you and Tim go back inside the house while Bob and I plant the explosives," John directed. John removed four sticks of dynamite from the case, walked the fifty feet to the base of the tree where the caps were located, took one, and returned to the vicinity of the end of a wire pair. He took a pencil, punched a hole in the end of one of the sticks of dynamite, inserted the electrical blasting cap in the hole and gently pushed it farther in with the pencil eraser. He looped the cap wires over the end of the stick, pulled the loop tight and then taped the four sticks together firmly into a neat bundle. He placed the package in a hole in the earth under a pile of brick bats with the charge oriented under the bricks to propel them toward the shelter area.

*I sincerely hope we never have to use this.* When John considered the possibility, he shuddered.

"Bob, I don't believe we'll connect the wires just yet. Go ahead and check them out but I'll hook them up after everybody goes inside."

"Good idea dad."

John went back to the dynamite box, picked up four more sticks and then went over to get another blasting cap. He prepared the second bundle and laid these on top of the ground, concealed by a bush.

Altogether, they placed sixteen charges, some of them only one stick. Most of them lay concealed on top of the ground, covered by a thin layer of dirt, where they would make a big bang and heavy concussion to scare, rather than do physical damage. Only five of the charges were designed to harm. The last charge to go in consisted of two sticks sandwiched between two bricks, inside the vertical shaft. If anybody found the entrance, this shot would be a last resort.

A news bulletin interrupted the radio program. "White House Press Secretary, Bert Mosby, released the news that the President of the United States will speak at 8:00 p.m. this evening. The president requests that all citizens remain calm, stay at home unless absolutely required to travel, and pay no attention to rumors."

Bob came out of the shelter. "Everything is in pretty good shape. We're ready except for a few odds and ends."

"Tim, tell everybody to come on into the house. By the time we eat, it will be time for the president's speech," John directed.

After supper, the Baileys assembled around the television. The news analysts, looking subdued, discussed various aspects of the world and nation's conditions while waiting for the president's address. Finally, they concluded their talk and the channel switched to the White House. The president sat behind his desk in the oval office. He leaned forward in his seat, placed both hands on top of the desk, with fingers pressed together. His face was grim. He made an obvious effort to appear relaxed.

The president spoke. "Fellow Citizens of the United States of America, it is with a heavy heart I come before you tonight; the times are perilous indeed."

The president paused, shuffled his notes, then continued, "I went before the Congress of the United States today and with a bare margin in both the House and Senate, received their permission to engage our forces in the Middle East conflict on the side of the Israelis. Although we have already committed troops and air power under the War Powers Act, I now have congressional support. We have been landing troops and armament most of the day and shortly, our ground troops will engage hostile forces in battle with good chances we will soon be in direct combat with Russians, if not already. I can't predict what this means for the future.

"Fellow citizens, I don't wish to alarm you but I must speak candidly. We are receiving a constant flow of reports from the combat area. Aerial fighting throughout the Middle East is fierce, with our aircraft carriers in the Mediterranean supplying the bulk of our fighters. They are terribly outnumbered but are fighting valiantly. Due to the loss of all our bases in the area in years past, it will be several hours before we can offer them relief."

The president shuffled his notes again. "And now, I will report to you on the fighting within the territorial boundaries of the United States. "Beginning at 2:00 a.m. on May 26th, what appeared to be a riot broke out in Chicago. Shortly after, another erupted in New York and within minutes, Los Angeles, Houston, and New Orleans reported similar disturbances. Thirty minutes later, hundreds more had reported in. It wasn't a total surprise for the intelligence community advised us three days earlier that active sabotage and guerilla warfare would begin throughout the country. We placed internal security forces on alert at that time. "However, these hostile activities have been far more widespread and savage than anticipated."

"I declared martial law nationwide earlier today. I'm asking all able-bodied men in the country to voluntarily contact their local law enforcement agency and offer their services in militia units to cope with these traitorous groups. If the response is not enough, then we must draft."

"Effective this hour, a 10:00 p.m. curfew is in effect nationwide. I urge you to remain in your home for you could get shot. Also, I urge you to restrict your movements to emergency travel only."

"Moments before this appearance, I received a message from the CIA station chief in Berlin which states the Russians, who have been mobilizing rapidly the past seven days, are now rolling toward their release points. We believe a massive invasion of Europe is taking place."

The president's visage became even grimmer. "Fellow Citizens, we have not yet been able to determine the motives for the hostilities in the Middle East and here in our own country. However, we have issued grave warnings to the Russians."

The president paused, raised a glass of water to his lips, and sipped. He set the glass down, shuffled his notes again and continued: "Fellow Citizens, I have requested a meeting with the joint bodies of Congress in emergency session immediately following this speech. We will meet throughout the night if necessary and try to chart a course for this great nation through these perilous times."

"In conclusion, I request the prayers of all citizens that we will make the proper decisions." The president's image slowly faded from the screen.

The two network newsmen who had made the commentary before the president's speech came back on the air to make an analysis and do the wrap up. Their consensus was not surprising: The speech not only affirmed to the world that we would defend Israel but also warned Russia that she treaded on dangerously thin ice.

It became chillingly clear that the world teetered on the brink of a major war.

Local news reported sporadic rioting and lawlessness in Breton and Lexington. It also said several people were taking an interest in fallout shelters. John shook his head sadly; *I'm afraid they're too late.*

"Father, do you think we should start keeping watch? Do you think there's any chance of people bothering us out here?" Tim asked.

"Keeping watch may not be a bad idea Tim," John replied. "We'll at least start keeping our weapons close at hand. From this time on, just about anything can happen. We know we've had people from the Sheriff's Department out here watching us and there's no telling who else may have been out there spying. I hoped we could keep this operation secret but I should have known better."

"Dad, are we going to volunteer for the militia?" Mark asked.

"Not at present, Mark. Unless conditions improve, we can't afford to get very far away from the shelter."

The Baileys sat around a while longer discussing the president's speech and their plight and then went to bed to spend an uneasy night.

John, pleasantly surprised when Saturday morning arrived with the world still intact, called the Lexington airport for a flight to Detroit but found that all airlines had cancelled their services. He checked the possibilities of a chartered flight in a small plane but found nothing. John swallowed his disappointment.

John called Dean Davis. "Dean, thought I'd check in and see if you decided to build a shelter?"

"Yes I have John. We've started working on it but it's a long way from being done. I'm hoping we haven't waited too late."

"Dean, time is short; it may be too late now."

"I realize that John."

"I'll let you get back to work. I know you have a lot to do." John said goodbye and placed the phone on the cradle.

John decided to call Reverend Burger.

"Yes, John, what can I do for you this morning?" His pastor answered with a hearty voice.

"Reverend Burger, I wondered if you gave any more thought to what I said about shelters?"

"Yes I have, John. In fact, I've done quite a bit of review in the books of Daniel and Revelations, trying to equate the present with the end-time. I see several things happening in the world, and several nations in the right relationship that could fit the scheme of things. However, there's something that still eludes me."

"What's that?"

"The best I can tell, the United States is conspicuously missing from my interpretation of the prophecies, or if mentioned at all, falls into the category of obscure and insignificant."

"Hmmm, that's interesting. I would think that a great nation like the United States would play a significant role in the end-time events."

"John, if you look at the United States in history, we've only been around a little over two-hundred years. I realize God has blessed this nation tremendously; probably no other nation except Israel has ever been blessed more; this is why we enjoy the power and prosperity we have today. Who's to say though where we'll be two hundred years from now, if the Lord tarries. We are a unique people; we have control of our own government through the power of the vote. Along with that power, we as individuals are responsible for what we do as a nation. If ever a people were ripe for judgment, this nation is. We have allowed the separation of this nation from God by our illustrious Administrations, Congress and the Supreme Court. Separation of Church and State is one thing; separation of God from State is something else. Unless the people of the United States turn it around immediately, and it may already be too late, then judgment will surely fall."

"And another thing John, judgment can fall on this nation without it necessarily being the end time."

"Reverend Burger, I realize that we have some serious problems in this nation but there is a lot of good things about it too. There are millions and millions of good, solid people sincerely concerned about the way things are going. Why would God punish us all because of the actions of a few?"

"John, you make a good point. If you review the history of the United States, you see a big-hearted nation of people, caring for one another and caring for others. What we did for Germany, Japan, and other nations of the world following World War Two, was truly magnificent. Our efforts to spread Christianity around the world through missionaries, the way we help ourselves and each other through The United Way, Red Cross, Salvation Army, churches, civic organizations, volunteer workers, benefits, I could go on and on, are unsurpassed by any other nation in history."

"Let's stop right there, John. No generation can bask in

the favor earned by a previous generation. We must stand entirely on our own. Next point: In recent years, definite moves were made to separate this nation from God and His teachings. By failing to protest in the strongest way possible against these evils, and by not putting a stop to it, we the people, the government, are condoning it and will pay the price for allowing it to happen."

"The Bible teaches that Christians are to assemble themselves together and worship. Multitudes of Americans stay away from church. Some of them salve their consciences by watching TV evangelists - a good case of the blind leading the blind. There's no wonder we're way out in left field."

"Reverend Burger, what can we do?"

"As I said John, if you're right about all this, then it's probably too late to do anything. If you're wrong and there's time, then concerned people need to take the time, set up local action groups, develop into larger and larger action groups and either develop another political party and wrest control away from the existing parties, or bring so much pressure to bear on the elected officials, the people can regain control of their nation and their destiny. However, if the majority of Americans like it the way it is, I suggest that everybody just sit back, relax and wait for God's judgment."

John laughed. "Thanks a lot Reverend Burger. I've sincerely enjoyed my discussion with you and believe I have a better feel about what's happening. I'll see you Sunday, if we're all still here."

After hanging up the telephone, John related his conversations to the group, and then the Baileys spent Saturday monitoring the news on radio and television, working at odds and ends about the shelter, and resting.

After their furious pace of the past several days they felt ill at ease, not having anything to do.

Ellen went to her work room, strolled from painting to painting, selected one of her favorites, took it down, wrapped it in brown paper and tied it with a string. She went about the room tidying up, putting away paints and brushes and, after a long look about the room, picked up the wrapped painting and left.

Ellen met her youngest son. "Tim, will you take this to the shelter and leave it on the bed?"

Bob and Tim made a patrol of the area and reported. "Father, we didn't see any people out there but we did see signs. I believe we have had quite a few people prowling around the past several days."

"That could be bad news. We're pretty well at the mercy of the Sheriff's Department if they decide to do something."

Gravely concerned about Kathy, Mark mounted his bicycle shortly after 9:00 a.m. and rode off toward the Klines. Ellen's heart went out to him when she saw him leave.

Ed Kline called John shortly after noon and stated his intentions to build a shelter. Monday, he would launch out in an all-out effort. John cautioned him that it could be too late and again welcomed the Klines to their shelter.

Tim, out back visiting with his animals, fed the pigs and chickens and romped and wrestled with Trixie.

Television programs brought frequent news flashes throughout the day giving updates on the Middle East fighting and guerilla activities in the United States and Europe. Major network broadcasting became sporadic after sabotage interrupted many of the communications paths. Civil defense officials stepped up recommendations for the populace to prepare shelters but in a degree calculated to prevent panic. John detected officialdom's quandary in trying to cope with the rapidly worsening grave conditions. The commentator admitted that even with U. S. forces fighting alongside, the Israelis were still being overwhelmed.

The southern invasion of Israel had stalled, at least temporarily, ten miles south of Tel Aviv with the battle line running southwest from the Mediterranean coast, through Bethlehem, to the Dead Sea. The Israelis were still holding along the Jordan River but were being pushed back slowly on the northern front. Pressure in that area had slackened and the stabilized line formed a crescent from Caesura on the Mediterranean, through Megiddo in the center, to Beit Shean on the eastern flank. The enemy seemed content to hold in place on the southern line, and were massing all the incoming forces on the plains north of Megiddo where a major battle would probably be fought within a few days. Megiddo and the surrounding area had seen its share of battles in centuries past.

Gigantic transport aircraft, taking off every few minutes, formed a tremendous airlift pipeline to Israel; seaports loaded ships for immediate dispatch. However, there were not nearly enough American forces on the scene in the Middle East to make a difference. Intelligence sources detected furious activity among Russian sea forces, whose warships, armed with Cruise missiles, were deploying to intercept stations on the traditional shipping lanes. Our skimpy merchant fleet wouldn't stand a chance.

The president came back on the air at 7:00 p.m. Saturday evening and made an unprecedented announcement. "At 3:00 this afternoon, our nation received an ultimatum from

Russia demanding that we not interfere and defend Israel or Europe. Russia threatens us with nuclear annihilation if we fail to comply. I have just come from a meeting with the Congress of the United States where they took a vote deciding whether we should declare war on Russia. Both House and Senate voted nay. However, they passed a stern resolution condemning Russia and stating that we have left all options open for our defense and the defense of free world nations. Our strategy stresses negotiations through diplomatic channels on the issues which face us. Both houses of Congress will remain in session throughout the night, debating on actions we should use to combat the threat."

"There's no doubt we were tricked by the Russians. They duped us badly and we don't have the same retaliation readiness held in past years. We have told the Russians, we will continue mobilizing and transporting troops and equipment to Europe and Africa. However, we have assured them that, at least for the time being, we won't commit any additional forces to battle, although the ones presently fighting in Israel will remain."

Following the president's announcement, the usual network rehash of the speech was curiously absent.

The Baileys remained huddled around the television, talked in hushed voices and tried to absorb the meaning of all they heard. They heard a shocker that none of them had ever dreamed possible - Russia issued the ultimate threat; the United States backed down.

Following the 10:00 p.m. newscast, the Baileys retired to their makeshift bedding to spend a restless night.

The president's telephone rang at 1:32 on Sunday morning. The CIA chief spoke urgently. "This is Mark

Taylor, Mister President. I'm sorry to disturb you but Israel dropped a H bomb on Moscow at 1:30 a.m."

"Oh, no," groaned the president. "Do we know yet what response Russia may be making?"

"It's too early to tell sir. However, we're adding this information to the situation computers and will have an answer shortly, therefore, it's imperative that you proceed to the emergency command center at once."

"I'll leave here immediately," the president responded. He experienced a moment of total despair and frustration and, without prompting, his mind flashed back to the late sixties when the United States enjoyed overwhelming superiority in nuclear and conventional military power.

The president rushed to the waiting `copter. His mind rapidly reviewed events of the past few days. The military might of the United States had been on alert status now for several days. When the fighting escalated in the Middle East, more and more of the American strategic and tactical combat forces deployed closer to the Middle East and Russia. As the American and European forces reached higher degrees of readiness, so did the communists. Both sides, tense and poised, waited for the slightest provocation; therefore, conditions couldn't have been more volatile for the spark which Israel's H bomb provided.

By the time the president arrived, his key advisors, top brains in his administration, waited, assembled around the conference table.

"Have we raised the Russians on the `hot line'?"

"No, Mister President. Apparently the H bomb on Moscow knocked out all communications with the Russians. We've tried every way we know how, military and civilian, to link up with them but without success," the Secretary of Defense explained.

The president turned to the CIA chief. "Do you have the situation estimate?"

"Yes we have sir."

"And?" The president queried impatiently.

"We should launch an immediate attack," the CIA chief stated flatly.

"You mean 'we' should attack the Russians immediately?" The president asked incredulously.

"Yes sir. The Russians. The Chinese. All Communist forces worldwide. You are well aware sir, this has always been one of our contingency plans for such emergencies. We have been feeding massive quantities of information to the "sit" computer for several days and it predicted a possible nuclear war two days ago."

"Yes, I know all that. For that reason our forces went on full alert at that time. Please continue," the president spoke sharply.

The CIA chief resumed. "The computer went to condition red twenty-four hours ago. We have interrogated it every five minutes since and it issued predictions each time, possible attack within twenty-four hours. This estimate hadn't altered until we fed in the data about the H bomb on Moscow and then it immediately replied, 'attack is imminent!'"

"What about the option of 'surrender'?" The president asked. "I fully understand our nuclear deterrent capability compared to theirs and in comparison, we're sitting here helpless and hopeless. We gave up on M A D several years ago."

"Mister President," the CIA chief sneered, "If you and the Congress considered surrender, you missed your chance. You no longer have that option. We can assume Russia is launching her weapons now."

The President turned to the Secretary of Defense and spoke crisply. "What is your estimate David?"

The grim faced secretary replied, "We should attack immediately or lose all the first strike advantages."

"What is your opinion, George?" The president looked directly at the Chairman of the Joint Chiefs of Staff.

"The same," He replied firmly.

The president appeared harried. His feelings switched quickly from arrogance to chagrin, facing the realities of the moment and the decisions being forced upon him. He knew there were no alternatives but searched his mind desperately for any other action which would stay the inevitable and awful consequences sure to follow.

The president studied this eventuality many times in the past at leisure and understood full well the conditions of the moment. So did every other man sitting around the table. It was simple.

A snake, before striking, must coil. Russia had been "coiling" now for several days. Her Bear, Bison, and Backfire bombers, ICBM's, SLBM's, sea power and cruise missiles, were all at full alert, ready to pounce. A poised snake constantly surveys the point of danger.

Russian intelligence knew of our intercontinental bombers orbiting close to her borders, atomic submarines with exotic, nuclear tipped missiles prowling within striking distance, and the multitudes of cocked missiles in their hardened silos standing, waiting.

A snake, if attacked, strikes instinctively at the suspected point of danger. The assaulted Russia's response would be swift.

The president mentally reviewed the meaning of the contingency plan. If intelligence positively establishes that an attack is underway, the threat constitutes an attack and permits retaliation.

"Gentlemen, I think we all realize that we can't win. This nuclear attack on Russia and the communists is nothing more than an exercise in futility. You all realize what a sorry state our strategic forces are in. However, we'll take as many of them down with us as we can."

The president took a deep breath and raised the receiver to his ear.

"General Whorton, Omaha War Room," a detached voice spoke.

"General Whorton, this is the president."

"Yes, Mister President?"

The president took another deep breath and spoke. "Initiate 'Recompense'!"

General Whorton reached forward to the center of the control console and flipped a switch. "I'm ready to receive your voice code, Mister President," he intoned clearly and impersonally.

The president spoke a series of unrelated words into the telephone. A computer in the Omaha War Room digested the information, read out, and then printed out.

"I have received a green light, Mister President," General Whorton informed.

"Launch the attack," the president said in an

emotion-filled voice and, with a sinking feeling, replaced the telephone on the cradle.

He felt a terrible sense of guilt and remorse, thinking of the circumstances. The defenseless American people bothered him most. As president, he saw volumes of information and facts that the ordinary citizen knew nothing about.

During the cold war years, the Russians had quietly spent more than two hundred billion dollars on civil defense. Access roads radiated from all the cities like tentacles and evacuation routes were wide and plentiful. Russia could empty all her cities, even the largest, within thirty minutes.

The American people were vaguely aware of the city evacuation plans and fallout shelters of the Russians but the U. S. government and news media downplayed and ignored it. Following the end of the cold war, the evacuation and shelter capacity of the Russians was essentially forgotten.

The president could rationalize the suppression of this information but the factor that really tore at his heart was the lack of shelters for the American people.

The basic pattern for each Russian city was pretty much the same. Dozens of evacuation routes radiated out from the cities like spokes on a wheel. Fifteen miles out from the heavily populated hub, roads began branching off each spoke, first on one side and then on the other, a mile apart. Each of these branch roads terminated at a shelter, an elaborate, underground structure containing all the facilities required for five-hundred people to survive for thirty days.

A high-speed teleprinter chattered. An aide tore off the message and handed it to the president. "Reports swarming in from cities all over country; key overpasses, underpasses, bridges, tunnels and railroads being destroyed or blocked," the cryptic message stated.

"Evacuation routes! They are trapping our people inside the cities!" The president ejaculated.

General Whorton received the green light at 1:40 a.m. and in less than ten-seconds, high-speed teleprinters in all major military command headquarters angrily chattered the fateful message. Tense command personnel burst into feverish activity the moment the message came.

In Strategic Air Command headquarters, the alert officer, Major Strom, a highly skilled and dedicated professional, read the message and immediately pressed a button activating klaxon horns and flashing red lights in SAC communications centers throughout the world.

On a large console to his right, close to two hundred red lights came on illuminating the names of all SAC bases, missile sites and support groups. Major Randall, at another console, called up a computer display and filled in the blanks on a pre - programmed message. He pressed a button on the computer entry device and the prepared message printed out on a teleprinter. At this time, Colonel Bolton made his appearance and took charge. It took him ten seconds to assess their current status and proof read the emergency message.

Colonel Bolton nodded curtly to Major Strom who picked up a mike, delivered a short voice broadcast to the entire command, a prelude to the alert message. Major Randall and Colonel Bolton then completed the activation of the system.

The message was on its way!

Within five seconds more, the red lights on the console began turning green and at the end of twenty seconds all lights were green, confirming receipt of the message at the two hundred locations. Fifty-five seconds from the time the president gave the word, the entire Strategic Air Command reached active combat status and the colossal war machine went in motion.

Similar messages went out also to Navy, Marine and Army forces throughout the world.

The first ICBM lifted off at 1:42 a.m. plus two seconds.

The United States of America launched in anger their first nuclear bomb since Nagasaki and thereby entered World War Three.

Intercontinental strategic bombers wheeled from their holding patterns and immediately penetrated Russian air space. The few B-1 and Stealth bombers sped on to their targets; ancient B-52's lumbered in their wake. ECM aircraft accompanied them to perplex enemy defenses with their electronic madness. Payloads of individual bombers ranged from five megaton H bombs down to two dozen nuclear tipped cruise missiles.

Aircraft commanders opened top secret sealed orders, studied their flight instructions and designated targets; then, like Lemmings on their march to the sea, they winged their way to their destiny. The first strike was on its way!

Over a thousand gigantic arrows bearing the Titan and Minuteman ICBMs dancing on shafts of brilliant fire, rose from the Continental United States and arched lazily toward the north. MX ICBMs emerged from their tunnels, assumed their firing angle and followed only seconds later, their four-hundred kiloton payloads programmed for ground bursts to maximize fallout in the heavily populated target areas.

Dozens of atomic submarines, on station at strategic

locations throughout the world, ended short countdowns and began launching their MIRV tipped Trident and Poseidon missiles toward preselected targets. Each Trident submarine launched its twenty-four missiles with monotonous regularity. The eight MIRV's riding each nose cone broke away and transported its one hundred KT payload to key areas of the enemy heartland.

Klaxon horns sounded at hundreds of alert pads around the world. Frantic ground crews prepared hundreds more aircraft for flight. The plane crews finished briefings and rushed to their waiting planes.

Evidence of damage abounded where saboteurs, partially effective, attempted to destroy aircraft and strategic installations. Their efforts to hamper the arrival of key personnel from their off base homes were equally damaging. Nevertheless, a second wave of strategic and tactical bombers became airborne in three minutes.

A few anti-missile weapon crews rushed to their posts and readied their hardware for action. However, the ABM treaty and other strategic defense agreements, which the Russians ignored and we obeyed, restricted us to the few weapons built in the twentieth century. Reagan's SDI or "Star Wars," a brilliant idea whose time had come, one that worked, had gone the way of the shelters.

Powerful radars scanned near space for the entry of hostile vehicles. Air defense aircraft with pilots strapped in their seats awaited instructions.

The Russians launched their first missiles at 1:48 a.m. and, at the time, were unaware that death was already winging their way.

China, not to be denied, unleashed her forces at 2:00

a.m. Naturally, when major conflict came, the International Brotherhood of Communism united her with Russia. However, ironically, Russia and China used the opportunity to obliterate certain pet targets within each other's boundaries; they would never have a better opportunity.

Nuclear age time, which had been running since 1945, was fast running out. Time previously measured in years now measured in minutes and seconds.

Raw force, second only to that generated by the sun, streaked its way to earthly targets as mankind, infinitely skilled in the art of killing, in their hour of darkness, slipped over the nuclear edge.

All nations around the world with nuclear weapons in their possession responded as if a diabolical, invisible hand controlled their actions.

In many cases, devices were programmed for ground level bursts. The driving urge in the hearts and minds of men - destroy and kill each other to the utmost.

John woke at one-thirty-five on Sunday morning to Ellen's insistent shaking of his shoulder. "John, John, wake up. Some bad news just came over the radio."

John became instantly wide awake and sat bolt upright in bed. "What is it?"

"Israel dropped a H bomb on Moscow at 1:30 a.m., just about five minutes ago." Ellen shivered.

"Oh, oh, this is it. Go wake the others and we will move to the shelter. Have everyone assemble in the den." John leaped out of bed and dressed hurriedly.

Ellen ran from the room and down the hall to the other bedroom doors. Five minutes after she woke John, all the Baileys assembled in the den.

"Ellen, you and Ruth take the radio and all the bedding you can to the shelter. Once you get inside, stay there. Mark, you and Tim take the remainder of the bedding and then come to the garage and help us. Move quickly!" John talked fast and urgently.

After John finished speaking, the Baileys exploded in every direction. A scene of feverish activity followed.

John went to the phone. He punched in the number for Ed Kline and the phone rang seven times before Ed answered.

"Ed, this is John. Israel just dropped a H bomb on Moscow and I believe that in a matter of minutes Russia will retaliate against us with all-out war. Get Marge and Kathy and come on over--quickly!"

"Thanks John." Ed replied. "We'll turn on our radio and if things look bad enough we'll come."

"Don't wait! John exploded. "You may be too late if you do! Think about your family!"

John slammed the phone down and strode swiftly for the shelter entrance.

Mark met him at the top and asked, "Dad, what about the Klines?"

"I called Ed, Mark. He said they would come when they felt the conditions warranted it. That's all I can do."

"Father, I'm going after Kathy!"

John's first instinct was to forbid Mark to go. He considered his reply for a few moments and then replied, "Son, I'm terribly afraid for you to leave but I won't try to stop you. There's no way of knowing the dangers the next hour will bring. What will you do if Marge and Ed won't come and Kathy refuses to leave them?"

"I'll cross that bridge when I get to it," Mark replied grimly.

"Mark, go, but hurry. If the Klines won't come, leave them. Don't allow Ed to destroy you because he's stupid."

Mark ran to the car, and then sped down the drive.

When Tim finished with the bedding he ran down to the pig pen and opened the gate. He had installed an automatic feeder and it was full. He opened the chicken house and one or two of them squawked but all stayed on their roosts.

John waited at the shelter and shouted, "Hurry Tim!"

Near the shelter entrance, Tim met Trixie. Tim spoke softly in his dog's ear, hugged it and tickled it's ears. He called and Trixie followed Tim into the shelter.

"Where's Mark?" Ellen asked when John entered the shelter and it became obvious no one else was following.

"He went after Kathy."

"No! How could you John?" Ellen screamed and started for the entrance. "You can't leave another one of my babies out there!"

John stood blocking the tunnel.

Bob and Ruth moved quickly to her side and Bob spoke reassuringly, "Mom, Mark will be back. I know he will. Don't worry."

Ruth offered encouragement and comfort and Ellen calmed down somewhat but remained agitated and near hysteria. Her crying upset Sabrina who began whimpering.

"Dad, the newscaster said they were implementing the Emergency Broadcast System and to tune in on the EBS frequency. I turned the dial to 560 but so far there hasn't been anything new," Bob reported.

The time was 1:45 a.m. Hydrogen warheads riding

intercontinental ballistic missiles continued lifting above the sands of Arizona and Midwest plains. Strategic Air Command bombers already flew in Soviet air space.

John and Bob crawled back through the tunnel, up the shaft and into the open. Stars were shining brightly and a half moon added its light to the scene. The warm and balmy night, noisy with the croak of frogs, appeared calm with only wispy breezes stirring the leaves in the trees.

An eerie feeling of eternity in suspension passed over John and he made a conscious effort to get back in motion. "Bob, this is like being in the eye of a hurricane."

"You're right dad, in more ways than one."

Bob and John went hurriedly from charge to charge connecting the wires and in less than five minutes, completed the task.

Bob re-entered the shaft and descended. John hesitated and looked about him, running details through his mind to make sure nothing had been overlooked.

John took one last long look at the moonlit area. The view looked infinitely peaceful bathed in the soft light and the freshly scarred earth surrounding the picnic table and barbecue pit gave the only sign of anything amiss.

John entered the shelter holding mixed emotions. How I wish Mark and Jesse were here, he agonized.

Ruth raised her voice to be heard above the noise in the shelter, "A special news bulletin just came on."

All activity stopped and a hush settled over the shelter. Everybody listened tensely.

The commentator spoke excitedly. "We have just received word from the Omaha Air Defense Center that the BMEWS early warning radar spotted objects rising from

Russia. Trajectory information indicates they are ballistic missiles. However, the number of missiles and prospective targets are unknown. All persons are advised to take shelter immediately; I repeat, take shelter immediately. Stay tuned to the Emergency Broadcast System for further bulletins."

"Bob, turn on the outside radiation monitor. Go ahead and buck out the background noise and establish your reference zero. This may be your last chance. Select an outside microphone also. We may be able to hear something."

The waiting became slow motion. Ellen cried as if her heart would break; hope for her sons diminished rapidly. Tim looked scared and excited.

Ruth went to Bob where he sat at the small table, now the operations center of their small world. "Bob, I'm scared. Where will it all end?"

Bob took her hands in his. "I don't know Ruth, we can only wait and see. Our lives are in the hands of fate, and God."

The sensitive outside microphone brought them the voices of the croaking frogs and singing insects. The radiation monitor picked up normal background noise. It was impossible to believe that anything could be wrong.

John thought, surely this is just another bad dream and will soon go away. It can't possibly be happening. John felt distressed and began trembling. Reality came crashing down. We're actually under attack! Atomic bombs are coming! His knees felt weak; black spots began dancing before his eyes. I must be blacking out. He sat down suddenly and placed his head between his knees.

Bob spoke anxiously, "what's wrong father?"

John answered in a muffled voice. "I'm OK. I'll be alright in a minute."

The radio broke silence and issued a news bulletin. "Official news media reports that hostile warheads detonated over Washington, DC at 2:22 a.m. Eastern Standard Time. The extent of casualties or damage are unknown. However, reports indicate the full Congress may have been in session at the time. Stay tuned for later news."

Five minutes later, the commentator returned. "A late bulletin reports that several other cities are being attacked. New York, Newark, and the outlying areas have sustained multiple hits. Some of these appear to have been one-hundred megaton warheads. Observers outside the industrialized areas of Chicago, Detroit and Cleveland report numerous fireballs and mushroom clouds. Only God in Heaven knows the damage done and the lives lost," he concluded solemnly in an awe-filled voice.

Ellen's sobbing became more pronounced when she heard Detroit mentioned. Hope for Jesse, Mark and Karen waned.

John tried consoling Ellen. "There, there Ellen, we've done all we can. If it's God's will they'll make it safely."

Ellen drew little comfort from the words but stifled her sobs.

Tim stood just behind Bob at the console. He thought of his brothers, pigs and chickens and brushed an occasional tear from his eyes.

Ruth, crying quietly, tears trickling down her cheeks, went over and placed her arms around Ellen, trying to offer some comfort.

Sabrina slept peacefully in her bed, totally oblivious to the fact her world was being destroyed.

Morale ebbed low.

When Mark arrived at the Kline's house, he got out of the car, ran to the door and banged on it until Ed answered.

"You don't need to knock it down Mark," Ed greeted gruffly.

"Mister Kline, we're worried about you and want you to come on to our shelter," Mark replied anxiously.

"Come on in Mark," Ed invited.

In the living room, clothing and foodstuffs set next to the door gave evidence the Klines finally believed. Kathy and Marge came in from the kitchen, each carrying a sack.

Ed came to an instant decision. "Mark, take Kathy on with you. Marge and I will gather up a few more things and come right over."

"Should I take some of the stuff you have laid out?" Mark offered.

"No, Ed responded. "We'll bring it with us. Go ahead and leave, now." Ed realized that time had run out, the situation no longer urgent, but desperate.

Mark took Kathy's arm and started for the door.

She stopped. "I won't leave without mother and father."

Mark looked at Ed, appealingly.

Ed urged, "Kathy, go on. Your mother and I will come along as soon as we can get the car loaded."

Kathy reluctantly started again for the door; Mark took her arm and persuaded her to move quickly. Shortly, they were back at the Baileys and Trixie whined when Mark and Kathy came inside the shelter. Ellen and Ruth greeted them tearfully.

The shelter trembled; tremors continued for several seconds then subsided. "That one must have been fairly close," John speculated. "Anything yet on the radiation monitor?"

"Not yet," Bob answered. "I thought the needle made a slight upward swing when the earth shook but this may have been due to vibration."

The earth trembled again for several seconds and the microphone picked up a faint muttering like distant thunder.

At 2:45, Bob spoke. "Father, look at this." He indicated the radiation counter. The needle had lifted off the peg and climbed slowly. Bob stated: "We're reading on the most sensitive scale. It isn't high yet but it's moving rapidly; it will soon become dangerous outside."

"What levels of radiation do you consider dangerous, Bob?" John asked.

Bob explained. "Radiation dosage is measured by an amount called a rad. Rad stands for Radiation Accumulated Dosage. A person accumulates one rad if exposed to one roentgen of radiation for one hour. A five roentgen rate for one hour produces five rads. "Few people get sick or suffer any ill effects if exposed to 100 rads or less. Above 100, a person may have different degrees of illness. There are a few deaths at 300 to 400. 600 is almost sure death and 1,000 is certain."

"This means then, a low radiation level could prove deadly over a long period or, on the other hand, a person could survive a high level over a short period?"

"That's right."

They stared in fascinated horror at the rising needle.

At 3:00, Bob switched to a higher scale; the reading now exceeded ten roentgens per hour.

Occasionally, the earth trembled and distant muttering sounded over the speaker.

At 3:15, their shelter shook and they heard a crashing

noise on the speaker, followed immediately by a booming explosion. They could hear crackling and hissing noises, then a series of staccato bursts of smaller explosions. It gave them all a scary feeling, not knowing what was happening on the outside.

At 3:20 a.m. the radiation count reached thirty-five roentgens per hour. "It wouldn't take a person long to get sick if he were outside in this," Bob remarked.

The civil defense broadcasts gave a long additional list of bombed cities. There were numerous other localities mentioned, indicating misses of aiming points. From these reports, the countryside wasn't much safer than the cities.

John felt tormented. "If I only had the power to know about Jesse and Karen; not knowing is maddening."

At 3:30 a.m., the roentgen count reached sixty. 3:45 came and the needle climbed past seventy-five. Nobody could live long in this, John thought.

By this time, Kathy had become frantic. "Where is mother and father! Why aren't they here?" She sobbed hysterically. "I want to go back and get them! Let me go!"

Mark implored his father. "Dad, can I go see about them? It won't take long."

"No Mark, don't go. It would be suicide to go back outside. They should be along any minute unless something happened to them."

The failure of Marge and Ed to appear at the shelter caused complications. Kathy, hysterical, made the shelter sound like a madhouse. This woke the baby who added her screams to the medley. Mark tried desperately to console and quiet Kathy, with little success.

After Mark and Kathy left, Ed and Marge completed filling the sacks and carried them to the car.

"Are we ready to leave?" Marge asked.

"Marge, let's listen to the radio and if conditions worsen, we'll go on over." Ed stated.

Ed went to the living room and turned on the radio. Marge went out to the kitchen, put on a pot of coffee and then joined Ed in the living room. He finally located a broadcast at 560. The news at 2:25 of the first bombs detonating over Washington frightened them.

"Ed, let's go on over," Marge urged.

"We'll wait awhile Marge. I don't see how we could be in much danger. Fort Knox is the closest place they would hit and a bomb there shouldn't harm us here."

Marge and Ed drank coffee and monitored the news until 3:15 a.m. They felt the trembling of the earth at 2:30 and again at 2:45.

Marge started to speak several times and urge Ed but each time she held back. She decided to trust Ed's judgment, but Marge didn't realize that Ed, like her, was also ignorant of fallout and radiation hazards. Unknown to them, tiny grayish flakes already drifted in the atmosphere above them. At present, they were sparse but becoming more numerous with each passing minute. An occasional flake drifted down and settled on the rooftop, in the drive, and on the window sill.

At 3:15, they heard a terrific crash and a booming explosion. Their house shook when the concussion reached them. Ed and Marge ran outside to see what happened. About two or three miles away, they could see flames leaping hundreds of feet in the air and while they watched, the staccato burst of exploding shells reached their ears. They watched in horror for a full ten minutes before returning to their house. Upon approaching the lighted doorway, Marge asked curiously, "What is this Ed? It looks like snow." They could plainly see the small gray flakes drifting downward like tiny random snowflakes and settle on their lawn, sidewalk and door stoop.

Ed galvanized into instant action. "Marge! That stuff is fallout! Let's get out of here!"

At 3:45, they were in their car driving down the lane toward the road at eighty miles per hour. Ed was looking directly into the fireball of the ten megaton bomb when it exploded over Lexington. The flash blinded him. The shock from the searing pain in his eyes froze his hands on the wheel and his foot on the accelerator. They were still doing eighty when their car bulleted across the roadway at the end of their lane, leaped a ditch and smashed head-on into the trunk of a large tree. Both died instantly.

Friday, May 27$^{th}$, Jesse arrived home from work, discouraged. He was laid off, along with 250 other Lawton Motors employees.

"Karen, I'm home."

"In here Jesse, I'm making a cake."

Karen's lively voice buoyed Jesse instantly.

"Karen, I'm afraid I have bad news."

"What is it Jesse?" Karen looked at him apprehensively.

His dry voice registered disgust. "Lawton motors laid me off today; I no longer have a job." Jesse turned a chair backwards and sat down on it.

"What will we do now?" Her calm voice held a trace of disappointment.

"We can draw unemployment and try to exist or we can accept father's invitation and go home. The way these riots are spreading it might not be a bad idea if we got out of here for a few days."

"Your father seemed to really want us," Karen recalled. "We can come back when your company calls you back to work."

"Pack a few things and we'll leave first thing in the morning. We can get there tomorrow afternoon. Karen, a lot of the things have taken place that father said would happen right before World War Three. You don't suppose he's right, do you?"

Karen's face turned pale. "I hope not. I can't bear to think of such terrible destruction."

"How long is it before supper?" Jesse changed the subject.

"Another hour, at least," Karen replied.

"I'll take the car down and get it serviced." Jesse dismounted from the chair and left.

Karen shuttled between preparing supper in the kitchen and trying to pack their suitcases in the bedroom. She had supper ready and warming on the stove when Jesse returned.

They ate and then resumed their packing.

"I know I'm forgetting half of what we need but maybe I'll remember it in the morning," Karen commented, closing the lid on the last suitcase.

The alarm went off at six-thirty. Jesse woke first and lay there a few moments savoring the softness and comfort of his bed. He reached over and touched Karen, already awake.

"Time to get up Karen," Jesse said as he gently shook her.

Karen sat up slowly, yawned and stretched. "I'm still so

sleepy." She slipped one dainty leg and then the other over the side of the bed.

Jesse marveled, viewing Karen in her negligee. She appears so frail, and yet, what strength! I still can hardly believe I could have such a beautiful, lovely, and nice person for a wife, he reveled.

Jesse's mind snapped back to the present realities; he got up and dressed.

"Let's hurry, Karen, we have a long drive ahead."

"What time do you think we'll get there Jesse?"

"We should be there easily by three this afternoon."

Karen fixed breakfast while Jesse filled a thermos.

"Do you want two eggs or three, Jesse?" Karen asked as she cracked two eggs and placed them in the skillet; she held a third one poised.

"Two will be enough this morning," he replied, pouring two cups of coffee.

Karen placed their eggs and bacon on plates and removed four pieces of toast from the toaster.

They ate their breakfast quickly and in silence. Now that they had decided to make the trip, they both felt an urgent need to be on their way.

Jesse carried luggage to the car while Karen cleaned the kitchen. She finished about the time he came through from the bedroom with the final load. They went outside and Karen locked the door.

Jesse opened the car door on the passenger side and closed it behind her. He stopped at the trunk, tossed in the luggage, and quickly got their car underway. At seven-forty-five they were on the road headed south, and home.

They travelled two hundred miles by noon and were

over halfway home when Jesse pulled into a service station. "Get out and stretch your legs. Sitting in one spot so long is tiring," Jesse suggested.

Karen got out on the driver's side and walked to the rest room.

Jesse waited while the attendant serviced the car and then went over to pay. "How much do I owe?"

"You got twelve gallons of gas and one quart of oil. That will be twenty-seven dollars and twenty cents please."

Jesse paid the attendant, wiped off the windshield and, after visiting the rest room, they continued their journey.

At 1:15 p.m., a police officer dressed in combat attire and holding an assault rifle flagged them down at a roadblock and approached their car. "What is your destination?" He asked in a brusque voice.

"Just this side of Lexington, a city called Breton."

"I'm afraid you can't make it there using this route. There's rioting in Cincinnati and the expressway is unsafe for travel. Sniper fire killed two motorists this morning and wounded several more. Where are you coming from?"

"Detroit."

"It probably isn't much of a choice but I recommend that you go back and stay off the roads."

"We're heading on south," Jesse stated firmly.

"Then you'll either have to wait, or detour by Ripley."

"But Ripley will make it fifty miles out of our way," Jesse protested. "How long do you think it will be before this highway is open?"

"We may have it cleared by five or six but there's no way of knowing for sure."

"Then we will detour," Jesse decided. He placed the car in gear, turned down the ramp and off the expressway.

They were soon driving along a two lane secondary road in a direction that wasn't taking them any nearer home.

They arrived in Ripley at 3:30 p.m. As they drove through the town, they saw groups of people milling around. When near the center of the business district, they approached an intersection almost totally blocked by people. The mob had stopped other cars and loudly harangued the drivers. Several of the crowd stepped into the middle of the street to block their passage. The implications were frightening.

Jesse made an instant decision. "Duck down and stay down Karen!" Jesse bore down on the horn, stepped hard on the accelerator and began weaving the car wildly toward the mob blocking the street. The throng involuntarily parted and allowed them to pass. One person stuck his arm out and the hurtling car struck it. He cursed wildly, gripping his stricken elbow.

Jesse could see other groups on down the street moving out from the curbs. He maintained the initiative and kept gaining speed. Some hesitated but all gave the hurtling car room as they went by. A volley of shots rang out and he and Karen heard bullets thudding against their car.

Jesse didn't slow down until outside the town and on open road. It was 3:45 p.m. and they were still sixty-five miles from home.

Fifteen minutes later when Jesse glanced down, the gas gauge registered considerably less than a quarter of a tank.

Almost empty! Jesse looked again at the instrument. It can't be!

"Karen! Look at the gas gauge! We should have well over a quarter of a tank left!"

Realization dawned on him and he began braking. He shouted, "Those shots! I'll bet they hit our gas tank when they hit the car."

When the car stopped, Jesse and Karen got out and Jesse slid under. The gasoline, already drained down past the hole, had quit running. He reached his hand up the tank and felt the hole, fairly close to the bottom. Undulating waves of fear swept through him as he realized the implications. Jesse crawled out from under and brushed himself off. "We're almost empty. All we can do is get back in and drive until we either run out of gas or find a service station."

At 4:15, they hadn't found a place to refuel and the car quit. They coasted to a stop with thirty-five miles to go.

"Maybe we can get a ride," Karen said hopefully.

"Maybe so," Jesse's voice reflected his doubts. "This doesn't look like a much traveled road."

Jesse opened the car trunk. "Karen, take one small suitcase and pick out what you think we must have. We'll lock the rest in the car and come back for it tomorrow."

Karen opened all three bags and spent ten minutes sorting the contents. "I have everything we need. You can put the rest back." Karen sat on the one small suitcase, trying to fasten the catches.

Jesse laughed. "Just a minute and I'll help you." He finished latching the suitcase and then locked the trunk.

"Let's go," Jesse picked up the valise and, hand in hand, they walked briskly down the road toward home.

A dozen vehicles passed them before it got dark. At first, Jesse and Karen tried sticking out their thumbs and then, when that failed, Jesse tried flagging them down. Jesse became more insistent for them to stop and one of the cars darted toward them. Afterward, he thumbed cautiously.

After dark, they saw less traffic and their chances became more and more remote. With all the rioting and unsettled conditions, Jesse couldn't blame them for not stopping.

At midnight, they turned off the Breton road onto a narrow, black topped road and continued walking. It was a warm, balmy night. Even though a slight breeze blew, Jesse perspired heavily. He cast occasional worried glances at Karen for theirs was a brutal, killing pace for her. Although he wanted very much to stop and give her rest, he didn't dare, for the feeling of urgency continued building in him, to a high pitch.

1:00 a.m. found them nine miles from home.

"Oh, Jesse, can't we stop and rest for awhile. I'm so tired," Karen implored in a weak, trembling voice.

Jesse stopped and set the suitcase down next to a tree. "Sit on this, Karen."

Karen sat and slowly pulled off both shoes. Jesse expressed dismay at the sight of her raw and bleeding heels. "Karen! Why didn't you say something sooner? How can you walk with those blisters?"

Karen smiled painfully. "They aren't hurting much now; they feel numb. This road is pretty smooth so I'll go barefoot for awhile."

"Here, put on my socks." Jesse removed his shoes and handed her his socks.

At 1:10 a.m., they resumed their journey. Karen and Jesse trudged wearily on. Their forward progress became slower and slower. At 2:00, they were still six miles from home and Karen walked unsteadily, extremely exhausted.

"I don't believe I can make it any farther," she gasped in a quivering voice and plopped down on the ground. Can't we spend the night here and continue in the morning?"

"It isn't very cold so I'm sure we can. I'll look around and see if there's a good place to lie down."

Jesse walked down the road a hundred feet and then back. "I didn't see a good spot so we'll rest here for a few minutes and then look for a place a little farther on." Jesse caressed Karen's hair tenderly.

A glowing light appeared in the east and remained.

"Hmmm, that must be lightning but it sure looks odd," Jesse thought.

The glow remained in the sky for a full minute and then began to fade. Another light appeared in the northeast, this time much brighter. This puzzled him even more when he saw yet another bright light glowing in the east. Some minutes after the first light appeared, they heard a muttering like thunder, yet not quite like thunder.

"Karen, I don't think we should stay here tonight. It looks like it will rain," Jesse said, still puzzled.

He thought, I don't believe this is lightning; it may be the Aurora Borealis. It's unusual for them to be so far south though.

They got up stiffly and set out on down the road. The short rest revived Karen somewhat and they made good time. The glowing lights kept appearing, first one place and then another, in the night sky.

A brilliant flash lit up the southern sky. It resembled a

huge, glowing, orange ball, hanging above the horizon. They stumbled to a stop, momentarily blinded.

"Karen! Those lights we've been seeing the past half hour are nuclear explosions! Let's hurry!" Jesse grabbed her hand, and after their vision returned, they half ran on down the road.

The orange fireball began to fade until only a faint glow remained. They had no way of knowing, but the origin of the flash was three hundred miles distant.

At 3:00 a.m., they were only three miles from home with Karen exhausted to the point of collapse. She fell. Jesse stopped and tried to help her up.

"Go on without me," Karen gasped. "Save yourself. I can't go another step."

"Get on my back and I'll carry you," Jesse ordered, kneeling down next to her. Though slight of build, five foot, eight inches and weighing one hundred and forty pounds, Jesse was wiry and strong.

Karen, hiking her skirt well above her knees, used all her remaining strength to sprawl across his back.

"Hold tight around my shoulders," Jesse instructed, standing up. "Put your legs around my hips."

When she brought her legs up, he hooked both arms under them, locking them in place. He partially knelt, trying to retrieve the valise, and then decided to abandon it.

Jesse walked stubbornly and unevenly down the road, blood vessels standing out on his handsome face, indicating the strain. Was it his imagination or could he detect a faint trace of dust in the air?

Fallout! We're too late! He staggered, appalled by the possibility.

Jesse trudged doggedly on. His pace slowed; he stumbled and nearly fell. We're too late. We'll never make it in time, he thought. Jesse took a few more stumbling steps and then pitched headlong.

They were only a half mile from home but Jesse had exceeded all bounds of his endurance; it was 3:30 a.m. Jesse saw a haystack about forty feet away, picked up Karen's soft, limp body and staggered on until he reached it. He fell to his knees and laid her gently on the ground. In a few moments he burrowed out a space large enough for them both. Jesse placed his helpless wife in a more comfortable position, overlapping her hands tenderly just below her breasts. Her eyelids fluttered and closed, her wan face framed by the tangled, wild mass of unruly red hair. Nature demanded they stop and rest.

We'll stop five minutes and then go on, he decided, as he lay down and snuggled against Karen.

Jesse again seemed to smell the dust in the air as he drifted off into an exhausted stupor.

At 3:45, a ten megaton bomb made a direct hit on Lexington. It exploded at two thousand feet and in a fraction of a second, the down-town section became engulfed in a two-hundred-million-degree fireball.

Sixteen city blocks surrounding ground zero instantly converted to a white hot, gaseous incandescence in the fervent heat. All matter, including steel and concrete, all became a part of the fireball and billowed upward into a gigantic mushroom which towered fifty thousand feet into the sky. The explosion flattened another nine hundred blocks and ignited everything flammable. Within minutes, all life ceased to exist in the three mile radius as the fireball sucked out their oxygen and devoured it.

Gregory Beall lived five miles from ground zero. Sirens signaling attack sounded almost two hours earlier. Civil Defense workers went from door to door urging people to take shelter.

Gregory chose to stay in his apartment. He watched out a window facing away from the center of town when the bomb hit. The black of night transformed to a ghastly brilliance; the utility pole across the street smoked and burst into flames.

Gregory saw curtains and shades ignite in neighboring apartments; wooden exteriors and roofs flamed from the intense heat. Seconds after the flash, the shock wave hit. A near solid wall of air pressure rushed away from the fireball at two thousand miles per hour. It slowed to a thousand, generating a thirty pound per square inch over pressure by the time it reached Gregory's apartment house.

The wall of air pushed steel reinforced buildings awry and flattened all the others. Fires, started seconds before by the flash, burned at furnace-like intensity. Apartments collapsed and gas pipes ruptured, adding fuel to the flames. Gregory's window imploded, the ceiling descended and he raised his arms protectively.

The blast wave fanned fires kindled by the flash ten miles from ground zero and knocked houses flat.

The blast wave expended its force and fires began to lose their intensity. Air, forced away from the center and oxygen consumed by the flames, left a partial vacuum over several square miles.

The brilliant fireball changed from white to red and after three minutes, faded into the sky.

The partial vacuum sucked fresh air back in toward Lexington's center and converted the entire city into a raging inferno. Smoke and ashes zoomed skyward becoming a part of the gigantic, expanding mushroom.

The rising columns of hot gasses continued sucking in the oxygen-laden fresh air and generated hurricane-force firestorms which raged throughout the city.

All humanity up to three miles from ground zero perished quickly from blast debris, flash incineration and suffocation.

John's employer, Mister Blanton, heeded John's advice after he finally realized that trouble was imminent. Having all the materials, equipment and manpower available, he swiftly built and stocked a shelter at his house, ten miles north of Lexington.

When the bomb came down, he and his wife were in their shelter. The incandescent flash ignited their house; the shock wave jostled them crazily inside their shelter; the tornado like winds howled overhead, fanning their torched house. After the winds receded, rushing air from the opposite direction whistled overhead and then died down. It got quiet except for the crackling fires.

Battered, bruised and terrified, they held each other in a dazed embrace, not knowing what would happen next. They had survived the flash, the blast, and the intense radiation burst, leaving them with a glimmer of hope.

Unfortunately, their ordeal wasn't over. Super lethal clouds of swirling radioactive dust and smoke filled their shelter and particles settled on all flat surfaces and in every nook and cranny. They died quickly from the intense radiation poisoning, never knowing why.

No doubt, properly built shelters and "Star Wars" would have saved many lives. However, the American Congress, Government and News Media emulated the ostrich, and on the day the bombs came down, Americans found themselves nude in the firestorms that laid their homeland waste.

The "Designated Fallout Shelter", inadequate for the fifties, was totally ineffective for the present. However, they did offer some protection from the initial blast.

The people in Lexington who died unprotected in the fireball were lucky. Most of the blast victims died within the first hour from mutilation, burning, radiation, and suffocation. The remaining survivors, doused with a vast shower of radioactive fallout which resembled fine, grayish flakes and sand raining from the sky, wouldn't survive.

Stunned men, women and children ran and staggered, crying and screaming, through the streets. All about them the inferno raged and ravaged their city. Many of them fell dying on the pavement; while some of them staggered, bumped into buildings, cars, fences, or any other object getting in their way, their irrational behavior triggered by irradiating rays bombarding their brains with thousands of roentgens. Some fell to the ground in convulsions.

Thirty minutes after the blast, swirling clouds of radioactive dust raised the roentgen per hour count past ten thousand and shelter occupants couldn't avoid inhaling the deadly particles.

Reverend Burger awakened at 2:00 a.m., an hour and forty-five minutes before the blast, when the air raid sirens sounded. He reached over to the night stand and turned on his radio.

"What's wrong, Arthur?" His wife asked anxiously.

"I'm trying to find out right now."

The broadcast stations were off the air so he tuned in to 560 and soon discovered the reason for the warning. John Bailey was right after all, he realized.

He answered a knock on the door. George Labry, a deacon, stood outside. Terribly disturbed, he came to his pastor for advice and comfort in this fearful hour. "Do you think we should gather at the church for prayer?" George asked.

Reverend Burger replied kindly. "We can if you like, George. Those who have shelters should go to them but I'll be here at the church if anyone wishes to come."

Several of the congregation and many who were not members of the church gathered in the auditorium.

Some of the more devout Christians came, realizing their nakedness to the coming wrath, to be in the sanctuary where, many times in the past, they felt the close presence of God. In their maturity, they were calm and resigned.

All who came sought God in their own way for their own reasons. The pastor ministered to members and non-members alike.

"Reverend Burger, don't you think we should pray for this war to stop and especially that no bombs hit Breton?" Bill Davidson wanted to know.

Their pastor answered kindly, "Bill, we can pray but I think it's really too late for that now. The Bible teaches that once God allowed judgment to fall on a nation, He never stayed his hand until He finished it."

"Do you believe this is God's judgment?" Martin Devers asked, amazed.

"Martin, we can't say whether it is or it isn't; it could very well be," Reverend Burger answered. "We, as a nation, along with all the other free world nations, neglected multitudes of opportunities to make this a better world. We enjoyed the unique position of being the most enlightened nation on earth, and with that enlightenment, we bore a responsibility. We could be reaping the results of our failure to respond. This could be God's recompense. We can pray for mercy; we can pray for God's will to be done."

A hundred and forty-four people were on their knees in the sanctuary moments before the bomb hit Lexington, fifteen miles to the south. The flash ignited the church, the parsonage, and many other buildings up and down the street. The brilliant light blinded the remaining occupants.

Several seconds later, the shock wave hit. The building shuddered violently and the rear section collapsed. Flames erupted spontaneously throughout the wreckage; the few stunned people who remained tried to free themselves and flee. Those who were able to reach the outside found no haven for their entire world was aflame.

Although Breton stood fifteen miles from the bomb that hit Lexington, she still received a devastating blow and when the fire went out days later, most of her was gone.

A city Breton's size doesn't die easy. Humanity survived for several hours in agony and suffering.

Large mobs of people materialized on Breton's streets shortly after the blast, many severely injured, some screaming and cursing, others praying.

Although the electric went off, there was no absence of

light. Flames billowing high into the night sky lighted the city in lurid and ghastly detail.

George Donner led a band of looters down Bowling Street. Bowling received light blast damage but several fires burned. George lowered the eight-foot length of two-by-four from his shoulder and rammed it through a liquor store window. More blows cleared the glass in an area large enough to enter. Larry Bates stepped inside and began passing bottles out to the other men and minutes later, they rambled on down the street, tilting bottles to their lips as they went. They left the liquor store in flames. "Come on, let's go," and led the band on down the street.

Farther out in the suburbs, the damage lessened. Here and there entire families worked feverishly trying to complete shelters they started at two a.m. when the warning sounded. They worked on, unaware that their bodies were already riddled by fatal doses of lethal alpha and beta rays from the grayish ashes drifting gently from the sky and settling around them.

Martha Eastman, an attractive young mother of twenty-two, worked in an all night diner on the east side of Lexington when the air raid warnings sounded. Her first thoughts concerned the safety of her children; she dialed her mother's number but the exchange was dead.

"Mister Jenkins, I must go home," she said anxiously.

"Go ahead Martha; I doubt if we'll have much more business tonight anyway."

Martha picked up her jacket and purse, left the diner, looked up and down both sides of the street for a taxi but didn't see one. She began walking swiftly toward home.

Martha's route led through cheap tenements and

unkempt neighborhoods. She felt uneasy and kept glancing behind her frequently. During one of these backward glances, an arm shot out from a narrow alley between buildings and grasped her. The death row inmate, freed earlier by a Speznez team, hurled Martha to the ground and pounced on her before she had a chance to scream. A heavy fist slammed into her face.

Martha died before the bomb came down.

At 3:45 a.m., the shelter shook violently. Dishes rattled; pots and pans clattered; stacks of boxes tumbled, and in several seconds, sound from the outside microphone howled and roared when the blast wave passed. The lights flickered and went out. The radio, loudspeaker and radiation monitors all went dead.

In the unnatural quiet which followed, John spoke. "Turn on emergency power Bob; it doesn't appear that the electric will come back on."

Bob switched over to "battery" and a light came on. He turned the radio, radiation monitor and amplifier system over to battery power. The needle on the radiation monitor hovered on 100 per hour, and then slowly and inexorably crept upward.

John tried to get reception on the radio but all he could hear was heavy static and a rushing noise. Radiation totally blanketed the radio waves.

The earth's trembling subsided.

"Tim, you and Mark pick up the boxes that fell to the floor. Bob, see if you can get the gasoline generator started. We can save the batteries and won't have to switch blowers," John advised.

Bob turned on the ignition switch and manipulated

controls until the generator lined out. He positioned more switches until all the equipment ran on generator power.

The civil defense broadcaster in Breton came back on the air. Static and interference made it almost impossible to understand him. "This is to advise you that a bomb exploded somewhere to the south of Breton and the best we can tell, it probably hit Lexington. Although we didn't take a direct hit, Breton suffered severe damage. Everywhere I look, I can see fires. One of our ground observers reported in person moments ago that the entire downtown area is a mass of flames. The burst flattened quite a bit of the city, especially on the south side. The outside radiation monitor here at the station is climbing rapidly. The winds are out of the south and we're already receiving fallout from the blast. We have a roentgen count of 1500 and it's rising rapidly. We just had another . . . "The civil defense broadcast faded out, the radiation interference completely blocking it.

Kathy screamed hysterically. "Mark! Mister Bailey! Go help my mom and dad!

Something has happened to them!"

Mark tried desperately to console the distraught girl and looked imploringly at his father. "Dad, please let me go see about them."

"Mark, Kathy, I'm terribly sorry but it's impossible. The radiation would kill us in just a few minutes," John replied, making another unpopular and hard decision.

Mark tried to console Kathy but she wouldn't be.

At 4:00 a.m. the roentgen count outside their shelter reached 600. Less than one hour's exposure at this rate would be fatal, John thought. He picked up a portable radiation counter and carried it over to the entrance, checked carefully, and detected only the barest movement on the instrument. John felt relief.

At 4:05, they heard a voice call out over the loudspeaker. "Father! Father!"

They couldn't believe their ears. Ellen screamed. "It's Jesse!"

Bob activated the microphone. "Jesse, do you see the barbecue pit?"

"Yes I do."

"That's the entrance to the shelter. Just inside is a vertical shaft with a ladder. Come down it and wait until we get the door open."

John rushed over to the entrance. Mark and Tim worked frantically removing the cover. Minutes later they grabbed and tugged the sandbags out that filled the short connecting tunnel. With the sandbags removed, John crawled inside the tunnel and removed the outer panel.

"Father, are we ever glad to see you!"

"Thank God you made it."

"Jesse, before you come in, we need to decontaminate you and Karen. You may have enough radioactive material on your clothing to kill you. Both of you strip; I'll bring water, soap and towels, also blankets, to wrap you in after you've washed."

John went back into the shelter and issued rapid-fire instructions. "Mark! Pour a pan of water. Tim! Get two towels. Ruth! Find blankets. Ellen! Get soap."

"How are they John? Ellen asked, tears streaming down her face and overcome with joy at having Jesse returned to her so miraculously.

"They look well Ellen. I hope and pray they didn't get too much radiation."

John crawled back through the tunnel, handed Jesse and Karen the pan of water, soap, and wash rags and cautioned, "Be sure you wash all hairy areas and all cracks where particles could lodge." He turned his back and waited until they finished washing and handed them the towels. "Drop the wash rags and towels on the floor when you finish."

After a time, Jesse reported, "We're ready to come in."

John handed them the blankets, then backed through the tunnel and into the shelter with Jesse and Karen following.

"Stop just inside the shelter and let Bob check you with the counter. If you have any more contamination, we need to find it now."

Karen stood just inside the shelter, grimacing and swaying. Jesse placed his arm around her slim waist and steadied her.

Kathy made her way past all obstructions and grasped Jesse's arm. "Jesse! Did you see my mom and dad?" She sobbed loudly.

Jesse hung his head. "No we didn't, Kathy."

"Where are they?" She screamed.

Ellen and Ruth made it to her side and placed their arms about her.

"Kathy, I don't know of any good way to tell you but they must have had an accident on their way over. It would be suicide for any of us to go back outside," John told her.

"No! No! She screamed. "We can't just leave them!"

Mark made his way to her side, took her in his arms in a protective embrace and tried again to console her.

John paused a moment to reflect on Marge and Ed. He

felt sincere regret at the loss of such nice people and good friends. Poor trusting, procrastinating Ed, trusting society to a fault and believing to the end his government would protect him. Marge, that good soul, followed Ed loyally to the end.

Bob crossed the shelter, ran the detector up and down Jesse and Karen's bodies and spent several seconds checking their hair. "Both of their heads still have several radioactive particles."

"Tim, get another pan of water. Ellen, since you are dying to get close to them, you can wash their hair."

John turned to Bob. "Check the radiation level in the vertical shaft and tunnel. We left their clothing back there and also, we may be getting some dust."

Bob took the portable counter, carefully surveyed the vertical shaft and the clothing Jesse and Karen discarded; the pile read twenty roentgens per hour.

Suddenly, the shaft lit up well enough to see the ladder rungs. Bob looked up and saw a steady light at the top. He watched it for a minute and it began fading. He backed into the tunnel, took another reading and, next to the shaft, it indicated five roentgens. Where the tunnel entered the shelter, he changed to a lower scale on the Geiger counter, read twenty milliroentgens, and then reported the findings to his father.

"OK Bob, you and Tim can close off the entrance. Be sure you get the bolts tight."

Kathy overheard John give the order to close and accused him bitterly: "You had plenty of time to look for my mom and dad. You're just letting them die! I hate you! I hate you!" The last rose to a scream and then she broke down and cried noisily and bitterly. Helplessly, Mark looked on and gave up trying to console her. At this stage of grief, Kathy wouldn't accept comfort from anybody and wouldn't let Mark touch her.

John searched his conscience wondering, should we have taken the chance? He got some small comfort knowing he did the right thing.

The shock from another bomb reached them and the shelter trembled faintly.

"What is our count inside the shelter now, Bob?"

"The last time I checked, about two minutes ago, the needle barely came off the peg; it's about five milliroentgens per hour."

The report helped relieve John's fears. "We're still within a safe range. If it doesn't get too much worse inside, we'll do just fine."

Ruth finished drying Karen's head and she and Ellen helped her, pale and trembling, onto the bed. Ellen ordered, "Tim, get me the first aid kit. We need to get Karen's blisters cleaned up before they get infected. Ruth, your clothes will come closer to fitting Karen than mine will. She's going to need everything. Bob, you'll have to give Jesse something to wear."

By the time Ellen completed dressing her injured feet, Karen had drifted into an exhausted sleep.

"Jesse, we're all beside ourselves with joy that you and Karen are here. If you feel up to it, we'd like to hear about your trip," Bob suggested.

Jesse quietly recounted the events of their journey and harrowing ordeal while his mother washed his head. He paused at the point where he and Karen lay down in the haystack, long enough to get a drink of water.

Jesse continued, "At 3:30, we both lay down and went to sleep. We were so tired our bodies refused to function any longer and we would probably still be sleeping if it hadn't been for the bomb at 3:45. The light glared so brightly I thought my eyes were open. Luckily, we were lying in the haystack on the side away from the blast. I kept my eyes shut tight until the light began to fade and then I woke Karen. The flash torched the haystack and flames shot up thirty or forty feet above us. Fence posts, trees, weeds, and everything else smoked and smoldered. We could see around us in pretty good detail from the light of Breton burning; the fires reflected off a huge cloud above Breton and it looked almost like day. I thought we were goners when the high winds hit us and blew us down. All we got was a few scratches."

"Surprisingly, the fifteen minutes sleep left us somewhat rested and we ran most of the way home. We took a shortcut across the fields. I could see our house burning for the last mile.

"A large airplane of some type crashed about a half mile from here and is still burning. Our garage is on fire also."

Jesse paused and looked at their intent faces. He continued, "Karen was terrific throughout the entire trip. She's a brave and fantastic girl and I love her very much."

After the family group broke up, Jesse got his father off to one side and spoke to him in low tones. "Father, Karen and I will probably die from radiation. We stayed exposed for a long time."

"Surely not, Jesse. I don't believe God would bring you to us and then take you again," John reassured gently. "Go on to bed and sleep for a few hours. I know you're ready to drop."

The total situation remained quite grim but John and the

rest of the family felt in much better spirits following Jesse and Karen's arrival.

Thirty minutes after Karen and Jesse entered the shelter, Bob exclaimed excitedly. "Father! Look here!"

John crossed the room and peered over Bob's shoulders. Bob had switched to the 5000 roentgen per hour scale which was the highest range on the monitor. The reading, already past the 4500 roentgen mark, increased visibly. Even while they watched, the pointer reached 5000, moved past, and then stopped and trembled when the needle arrived at the limit of its travel.

"Since the wind is out of the south, we must be getting the full effects of the fallout from the bomb that hit Lexington," John noted.

"I hope this shelter is good enough to protect us," Bob spoke ardently in a low tone.

Shortly after 6:00 a.m. they heard a scuffling noise over the loudspeaker.

John whispered a warning. "Quiet."

Bob dashed over to the operating console and turned off the generator. It shut down and the lights dimmed and went out and the blower coasted to a stop. They lost the audio until Bob switched them to battery power. The light came back on and they again heard the outside noises.

Everybody in the shelter became still and quiet except Sabrina who was in the process of waking. "Get that baby quiet!"" John admonished in a loud whisper.

Chubby Sabrina, with folds of fat under her chin and dimpled arms flying akimbo, looked at Ellen with her bright-blue eyes from a small cherub face highlighted by fat cheeks and an uplifted nose.

Ruth grabbed Sabrina and urgently placed a nipple in her mouth, instantly restoring the blessed quiet.

They all listened carefully. The scuffling noise came again and this time, much closer.

Bob switched microphones from north to south, listened a few moments and then switched back to the north.

"They're on the side of the shelter next to the house." More scuffling noises came over the speaker and they heard a voice. "The shelter should be somewhere in this general area. See if you can find where it goes underground."

A second man answered, "I don't see anything yet."

"Keep hunting for it. The entrance should be close."

"What will we do with the people in the shelter?"

"Kill the men and keep the women." The first man answered coldly.

John glanced at Ellen and Ruth and caught their terrified expressions responding to the shocking, brutal statement from aboveground.

John reassured them. "We took this danger into account when we built the shelter. There are ways to prevent their molesting us."

The optimistic words relieved Ellen and Ruth somewhat.

Bob flipped switches and adjusted the volume to a high level. Voices and shuffling noises came clearly over the speakers. The talking stopped and they heard retching.

When those noises stopped, they heard a string of abusive profanity. "It must be that _______ _______ _______ radiation sickness we heard about on the radio."

John spoke. "Bob, switch to 'mike' position and we'll speak to them."

Bob positioned the switches and handed the microphone to his father.

John spoke clearly with an authoritative voice. "Men, this is John Bailey, the owner of this property. I'm asking you to leave the area immediately." He paused, allowing them to overcome their surprise.

Whispers came over the speaker. One of the men answered. "We're only trying to get away from the radiation. All we ask is that you let us in to share the shelter with you."

"How many of you are there?" John asked.

"Four," the man replied in a slurred and halting voice. "Four. Ah, two are still in the car. One is unconscious and the other one's out of his head. We're all real sick."

John thought for some time before he replied. "Men, if there were any hope for you I would consider it. However, your exposure outside this morning was more than enough to kill you and, even if you came in here you would still die. Shelter now couldn't prolong your life even for a few minutes. Therefore, I beg you, leave, and find yourself a comfortable place to spend the next few hours."

A stunned silence, except rasping breaths, was the only response. Obviously, the men weren't aware they were dying.

Finally, with trembling voice, the man replied. "We don't believe you. Open the shelter and let us in."

John answered, "Impossible. It would kill us all and it wouldn't help you one bit."

"If you don't open up, we'll force our way in," one of the outsiders blustered.

"Men, I warn you that we can defend ourselves and we'll kill you if you don't leave," John advised grimly.

The voices outside held an unintelligible whispered conversation.

Ellen blurted suddenly and anxiously, "John, maybe we should let them in. Surely they wouldn't harm us if we helped them."

"Ellen, we're talking about survival and I don't have time to argue the point. You'll have to trust me to do what I believe is right."

Ellen stared at John in horrified disbelief, burst into tears, covered her face with her hands, turned away and blubbered, "Things aren't bad enough so now you're going to start killing people."

John ignored the remark and ordered: "Bob, select a small charge on the south side, farthest from them. We'll try to scare them away. When I give the word, set it off and then select a four-stick shot on the west side."

By using the different microphones, they could tell the men were getting closer to the shelter entrance.

John switched on the microphone and his voice lashed out cuttingly. "Men, this is a warning. In thirty seconds, I'm setting off dynamite which will injure or possibly kill you if you are still in the area."

The breathing outside quickened and the man hesitantly shuffled back a few paces and stopped.

"Set off the first shot," John snapped.

Bob pushed the button; the shelter shuddered and they heard a muffled roar. He immediately toggled another switch forward, selecting another charge. Scuffling and coughing noises receded.

"Turn on a microphone," John directed crisply.

Bob selected an external mike and they could hear the men returning.

"Fire the next shot," John ordered.

Bob pressed the button; the shelter shuddered and they heard a loud roar.

"I hope this discourages them from trying anything else," John remarked grimly.

"What will we do if they keep coming?" Bob questioned.

"We still have the other charges, the ones with the brick bats. I hope we don't have to use them though."

They could hear a voice from aboveground shouting bitterly. We're going to town for dynamite and we'll be back! We'll dig you out of there and kill you like rats!"

The angry voices faded away and the men seemingly made their departure.

"The air in here is getting pretty stale. Do you think it would be safe to start the blower?" Bob asked.

"No Bob, I believe we should wait and make sure they left. If they find the vents we're in serious trouble."

Only breathing sounded inside the shelter. They all sat and listened intently.

Bob continued switching from mike to mike. Ten minutes later, a barely perceptible noise came over the mike in the entrance tunnel.

"Father, those men are still out there and they're moving quietly. I believe they've found the entrance," Bob said.

John ordered: "Ready on the blasting panel. Those men are desperate and won't stop at anything to get in."

A voice declared excitedly, "Jack! I've found the entrance and also the ventilation duct. We'll block off their air first and then they'll be glad to let us in." The voice stopped, replaced by horrible retching and gulping noises. The man cursed weakly and continued, "Hurry, Jack, we need to get inside fast. I don't believe I can hold out much longer."

"Bob, select a loaded charge. We can't afford to wait until they wreck our ventilation. They could kill us all."

The sound of excited voices came to their ears. Evident from the commotion, the men stood just above the shelter.

"Fire!" John commanded.

Bob pressed the button and twelve sticks of dynamite shattered a pile of brick bats, converting them into shards and splinters of deadly shrapnel. They heard pitiful screaming and crying after the deadly missiles found their mark. At least one of the men could still move for they heard a dragging noise.

John, pale and shaking said, "I'm so sorry we did that but we didn't have any other choice."

Ellen sobbed even louder following John's statement.

"What now father?" Bob inquired in a whisper.

"We can only wait and see what develops. We don't know how badly those men are hurt, whether they will live or die. Select another brickbat charge in case we need it." Although badly shaken, John stood firm in his resolve.

Ruth and Kathy also cried and the men stood, unnerved and pale, reliving the horror of the past few minutes. Karen slept through it all.

"Mark, turn the speakers off and use the headsets."

"Tim, turn on the stereo and play some music."

Lying quietly and listening to the soothing music did little to dispel the horror. Injuring people or possibly taking lives deeply shocked them all. Even the knowledge that the men were already mortally wounded with radiation didn't relieve their guilt.

"Mark, let me know if you hear any noises at all."

"OK father."

The shelter became quiet and still except for the soft music. The occupants sat, looking bewildered, each wrapped in their own thoughts.

Around 9:00 a.m., Karen tossed restlessly in her sleep and at ten, awoke and lay quietly in the bed, her face pale and wan. With sensibilities returning, she suddenly began understanding the situation and that her parents and sisters were probably in mortal danger. Realizing they were probably beyond help, she turned her face to the wall and sobbed quietly.

Jesse woke at 11:00 and immediately got out of bed. He felt shaky in the pit of his stomach but otherwise OK.

Occasional tremors continued shaking the earth until late Sunday afternoon. They slowed in frequency, until at 5:00 p.m., they occurred only once every thirty or forty minutes. Two blasts that morning delivered sizeable jolts but all the other explosions were distant.

The needle on the radiation monitor stayed pegged out at the top of the 5,000 roentgen scale. They had no way of knowing the actual level outside.

Bob scanned the radio bands searching for news. All he got was static and interference. Since Breton went off the air early in the morning, they hadn't heard anything.

"Mark, read all our radiation check stations and see what we have. Be sure you log them in the record book."

"Right father," Mark turned to the radiation monitor and recorded the above-ground readings first; it still pegged out past 5000. He switched to the probe installed in the ventilation intake duct just outside the filter; it read five roentgens per hour. He next selected the point where the air entered the shelter; it read four millioentgens. Some contamination, but not a dangerous amount, he thought. He checked the probe in the water supply intake from the pump; it registered zero. The one attached to the ceiling of the shelter indicated one milliroentgen. The last probe, located in the shaft just outside the door, read sixty roentgens per hour.

"Here they are father." Mark handed him the clipboard.

John looked over the results and then wrote on the sheet. "We'll log the date and also the time. We'll keep an events record for any unusual happenings."

## CHAPTER V

# THE THIRD SEAL IS OPEN

Revelation 6:5, 6: "And when he had opened the third seal, I heard the third beast say, Come and see. And I beheld, and lo a black horse; and he that sat on him had a pair of balances in his hand. And I heard a voice in the midst of the four beast say, A measure of wheat for a penny, and three measures of barley for a penny; and see thou not hurt the oil and the wine."

John moved to a point where he could see all the shelter occupants. "All of you give me your attention."

He paused until all the others settled down and listened. "We're going to be living in this shelter for quite some time and we need some organization. First, it's absolutely necessary that we maintain a watch twenty-four hours each day. Here are the things to look for."

"The air blower must run constantly. If it doesn't, fumes can back up from the toilet and smell terrible. Also, the air will get stale. To conserve fuel, the gasoline engine will operate only during the day. We can't afford to waste the battery power so each night we'll use the hand operated blower. Everybody except one should be asleep and oxygen consumption will be at its lowest. Using the hand blower will also help the one on night duty stay awake. I'm sorry the shelter is hot and muggy but there's probably nothing we could've done about it even if we'd known."

"We'll have six four hour shifts. Bob is working the first shift which ends at midnight. I'll take over then and Jesse at four. Mark will take it from eight to twelve and Tim from twelve to four. The girls will take day about picking up the four to eight shift. Any questions?"

Mark asked, "Will we have this same shift every day?"

"Yes, unless something happens later to change it. That should make it easier for us to adjust."

"What else will we do besides operate the air blower?" Tim wanted to know.

"The next item is radiation monitoring. We need to make hourly checks for the next several days. We can't afford any surprises. They could kill us. We can't be sure that something won't change that will allow radiation inside the shelter and, if that happens, we need to know about it immediately. Bob has prepared a chart for recording all the different points and he's also writing an instruction sheet explaining which scale to use and how to read it for the different places we're checking."

Bob interrupted, "This also includes maximum allowable readings. If any of them go higher, wake me or dad."

John continued: "The third item is the outside microphones. We have one north of the shelter, one to the south and one in the shaft. There's a selector where we can choose each of these individually or all at the same time. For normal listening, monitor all the microphones. If you hear anything, pick first one microphone and then the other to localize the sound. If at any time, day or night, you hear noises, wake me immediately."

John paused, "Bob, do you have anything to add?"

"Yes, I would like to point out that they can choose either headphone or speaker. At night, we'll use the speaker. Wear the headphones during the day to cut out all the talking and other shelter noises."

Bob cautioned, "Be sure you always keep the volume turned up to ten. With that setting you should be able to hear even a dog walking."

The shelter got quiet and the silence continued for several moments, with the only sound a light popping noise from the speakers. Tim shifted his weight and his bed squeaked. Mark cleared his throat.

John broke the silence. "In addition to the monitoring schedule, we need to work out a daily routine. It's important to stay busy, confined as we are. The routine won't start though for a couple more days since everybody needs to learn their shift duties. It's imperative that you pay close attention to the microphones for the next several days. We must know immediately if we have any prowlers."

John changed the subject, "Ellen, since you decided on the bed arrangement, I'll let you tell everybody where to sleep. We're all exhausted from the day's activities and need to get some rest."

Ellen, red-eyed but over her crying spell, adjusting to reality, took over. "Bob and Ruth will take the bed in the corner, Jesse and Karen next, then you and me. Tim and Mark will sleep in the two single beds at the far end; we'll fix a bed by the entrance for Kathy. There's extra bedding to put down and we can take it up each day to give us more room."

"Use the mattress off my bed for her and give me the extra bedding," Mark insisted.

Kathy, still deep in grief from the apparent loss of her parents, didn't seem to notice the discussion.

Ellen looked fondly at the baby. "Sabrina seems well established in her sleeping quarters already."

Tim said, "I'm hungry."

"I am too," Mark chimed in.

"We probably all are," John added.

"I'll start the gasoline generator and we can make some soup," Bob advised.

"Good idea Bob, if we can talk our cooks into it," John said jokingly.

"The soup will be ready in ten minutes if you think you can stand the extra heat,"

Ellen replied.

Sidestepping and climbing around and over boxes and furniture occurred while the shelter occupants shifted positions to make room for supper preparation. Their quarters were even more crowded than expected; the air was hot and close.

The lights dimmed slightly when Ellen plugged in the single burner hot plate. The elements glowed a cherry red by the time Ruth emptied the first can of soup into the pot. She opened two more and dumped their contents in the pan, adding a corresponding amount of water. Ruth brought out the crackers, bowls and spoons while the soup simmered.

Karen whispered to Jesse, "I'm not sure I'll be able to eat anything. I feel nauseated."

She looked pale and when Jesse took her hand, it felt moist and cold. When he put his arms about his wife and pulled her close, he could feel her trembling. "Try to eat something and maybe you'll feel better. It's been a long time since we ate; you may just be weak from hunger."

Jesse was trembling somewhat himself but attributed it to lack of food.

Ruth and Ellen filled the bowls with steaming soup and all the Baileys waited expectantly. After they filled the last one, all of them bowed their heads.

John prayed, "Our Father and our God, we humbly thank you for saving our lives. 'Yea though we walk through the valley of the shadow of death, we will fear no evil for Thou art with us.' We thank you God, for this food and this shelter, Amen."

The Baileys remained subdued and thoughtful during supper. For the most part, their minds still rejected the terrifying reality outside the shelter. Thankfully, mankind possessed a safety outlet in his mind allowing him to cope with unlimited adversity.

Each of them topped off the soup and crackers with a glass of flat tasting milk reconstituted from powder. They drank it hurriedly.

Jesse tasted his soup, felt nauseated, and quietly emptied his and Karen's bowls.

They finally settled down for the night at 10:30. Although weary, several minutes passed before any of them could relax enough to even consider sleep. Eventually though, light snoring sounded throughout the shelter.

Bob sat at the monitor console; a faint light illuminated the dials and meters. He turned the gasoline generator off immediately after supper and switched to battery power. The only equipment operating was the audio system, radiation monitoring and the light. Bob had rigged a rheostat in series with an eight watt light bulb and could vary the intensity down to where the bulb filaments just barely glowed red in the dark. Even at maximum brilliance, the bulb wasn't much brighter than a candle. The light made a negligible drain on the storage batteries.

At 11:00, Bob made his routine radiation check and the outside level still read 5000 plus. The needle quivered as if it were about to move off the peg. Sure death in less than fifteen minutes' exposure, he thought. Bob took the last reading, made his final entry and flipped the range selector to the top scale and probe selector to aboveground.

Bob carried his chair and walked over to the air blower. He sat down and resumed turning the handle. I won't wake dad at 12:00; he needs the rest. I'll wait until 4:00 and wake Jesse. Gears whined faintly and air whispered from the blower while Bob turned the crank, on into the night.

Monday morning came and the Baileys awakened to a new day in the shelter, less than thirty hours since the first bomb fell. John slept soundly through his scheduled shift at the monitor and didn't wake up until almost 8:00 a.m. He felt wonderfully refreshed and wide awake.

John wrapped a quilt about his body and carrying his trousers, stepped into their wash room and dressed. He walked over to the monitor and peered over Jesse's shoulder. "What are the latest readings?"

"Here they are father," Jesse handed him the clipboard.

John scanned the readings closely. The outside level had dropped back on scale to the 4000 roentgen mark at three this morning and subsided to 1700 by seven. He noted that two readings went up slightly at 3:00 a.m. The air intake outside the filter read thirteen; the vertical shaft increased to eighty. All the other readings remained the same. That shaft area is really dangerous, he thought.

"Jesse, start the gasoline generator and hook up the electric blower." John instructed.

The noise and commotion woke everybody except Bob. Different ones got up and began dressing and within a few minutes, there was activity all over the shelter area.

"Ellen, what's for breakfast?" John asked.

"We'll have dry cereal, cookies, orange juice and coffee. I know it isn't much but maybe it will do until lunch." Activity was good therapy for Ellen, who was having a hard time adjusting to the new world.

Jesse switched on the ignition, pressed the starter button, and seconds later, the voltmeter needle flickered, climbed to 115 volts and steadied.

"OK mom, you can put the coffee on any time." Jesse felt even more nauseated this morning but hid it.

John removed the manually operated blower. "Jesse, hand me the AC rig and I'll install it."

Jesse took the blower from its storage and handed it to his father who slipped it over the four mounting bolts. He plugged it in and turned on the switch. Fresh and cooler air from above ground poured into the shelter.

Karen spoke weakly from the bed, "Jesse, come here."

Jesse hurried over to the bed and peered anxiously at Karen. "What is it?"

"Jesse, I'm sick; help me; I'm about to vomit."

Ellen hurriedly took a pan to the bed. "Use this."

Retching noises issued from the bed; Jesse held Karen's head and offered what comfort he could. A sour smell quickly spread through the shelter confines.

The thoughts of Karen suffering from radiation sickness left them all heartsick.

Karen finally finished vomiting and lay back weakly. Jesse stayed at her side and Ellen resumed breakfast.

"Mark, if you and Tim will put the table and chairs up, I'll place the food on it," Ruth suggested.

Mark spent all the time he could holding Kathy's hand and trying to comfort her. Although still deeply grieved, she finally began accepting the harsh reality.

Mark removed the card table from behind the bed and unfolded the legs while Tim got folding chairs from the same location. Ruth set the table with cereal bowls, sugar, milk container, and spoons.

The Bailey family gathered around and John said grace. The Baileys ate their breakfast, mostly in silence.

The second day in the shelter crept along at snail's pace. They were still apprehensive and listened carefully for outside noises. They did their routine duties and all the talk throughout the day remained subdued.

The clock on the shelter console finally showed that night time had come. The marauders didn't return and the Baileys began breathing easier. All except Karen, who appeared pale and wan. She hadn't said hardly anything all day and Ellen occasionally cast worried glances her way.

Finally, at 9:30 p. m., Bob picked up a civil defense station located in central Tennessee. The news sounded grim. As expected, Washington and New York got hit first. Washington absorbed three hydrogen warheads spaced at five minute intervals. The first two were air bursts centered in the north central and south central sectors of the city, but the third bomb detonated one hundred feet underground. The crater, three miles in diameter and six hundred feet deep, severed the Potomac River, which filled the hole immediately.

Fortunately, the president and other select members of the United States Government moved to the super-secret underground shelters north of Washington just before the attack and from there, coordinated the war effort.

New York and outlying cities took a cluster of twelve hydrogen bombs, two of them 100 megaton, early in the attack. Five more hits at planned intervals fanned the flaming cauldron. Casualty figures weren't available from any locale since all communications and most semblances of civilization ceased to exist following the attack.

The enemies saturated the entire eastern seaboard with dozens of five- to one-hundred megaton bombs which left several hundred square miles devoid of life. Even the vegetation perished. These expanses wouldn't be habitable again for hundreds of years.

The newscaster listed the larger cities destroyed, mostly by multiple warhead hits. Thousands of smaller cities became targets, also.

Quite a few of the warheads traveled by missile from Cuba, Nicaragua, and Panama. Our intelligence sources failed to uncover them, but they were there.

Preliminary information showed the death toll would rise much higher than the wildest previous estimates. The newscaster gave an analysis of the phenomenon. The15,000 megaton yield of all the atomic devices dropped on the

United States, fantastically higher than anybody could have dreamed, blanketed the entire country with super-lethal levels of radioactive fallout.

***The third seal is open and the rider of the black horse is riding, riding, riding.*** *Starvation and pestilence followed swiftly on the heels of the nuclear war.*

Hundreds of millions died within just a few days following the nuclear exchanges by all of the nuclear armed nations. Nations such as Pakistan took the opportunity to vent their spleen toward their enemy, India. India, of course, retaliated. Pakistan also attacked American interests in Afghanistan and the surrounding area. Israel took their opportunity to destroy most of the nuclear and missile facilities in Iran, as well as Tehran. Israel also hit Damascus and several more of their pre-selected targets.

North Korea, of course, took the opportunity to destroy Seoul and much of South Korea. American forces in South Korea were a primary target. China attacked Japan and the Philippines. They also targeted American interests in the Pacific as well as Alaska and the Aleutian islands.

Needless to say, Russia and the United States held back nothing in their exchanges. It was a world gone mad. God's spirit hovered over the world as satanic influences were allowed to lead nations of the world to their mutual destruction.

Tens of millions died quickly from the initial blast wounds. Tens of millions more died within the first week from lethal radiation. Tens of millions more would die within the next thirty days from radiation.

Following the deaths within the first thirty days, the world was now vulnerable to widespread starvation as food supplies diminished and distribution systems remained paralyzed.

Starvation set in almost immediately. Only those who prepared in advance, and especially the rich, still had food for the near future. Even before the nuclear war began, food supplies were already getting short because of the interrupted delivery caused by sabotage of roadways and distribution systems.

In picking the targets for the nukes, all sides were selective in their targets, insuring the generating of Electromagnetic Pulses (EMP) would have maximum effect in shutting down power grids, communications, and all systems electrical and electronic. Television, cell phones, tracking device, most radio, are all gone. Internet . . . gone. Communication satellites . . . gone. Microwave communication . . . gone. Power grids around the world . . . shut down . . . gone. Even electronic devices on automobiles which supplied their ignition . . . gone. The world went off, as if the MAKER had thrown a giant switch.

Word filtering through indicated that governments were attempting to function and regain control. This would be a nebulous and sketchy process for some period of time. For weeks and even months, people around the world, especially in the US, would be on their own.

After the CD broadcast, they searched the dial on the broadcast band but only heard static of varying intensity.

Bob, why don't you tune in the short wave receiver and see what you can pick up," Jesse suggested.

Bob turned it on and searched the twenty meter band first. Static and interference hindered badly but he found a few amateur stations still on the air. Some of these operated from the security of shelters and some didn't. Those without adequate protection cried pitifully for help. Bob tuned away after noticing the stricken faces. He jotted down the frequencies so he could check back later.

When bedtime finally arrived, all retired except Bob. He busily turned the crank on the manual air blower when he wasn't occupied taking radiation readings. The shelter became quiet and still except for the whirring blower and light snores from the direction of Mark's bunk.

Midnight came and Bob woke his father. John dressed, took his place at the monitor and scanned the latest reports. The outside radiation count continued dropping and now read 250 roentgens per hour.

John spent an uneventful four hours and woke Jesse who spent an uncomfortable morning, vomiting twice before the others woke.

Tuesday morning, Karen looked even more pale. Her forehead was moist with cold, clammy sweat. Her breath came in short, deep gasps and she suddenly reached for the pan on the corner of her bed. She retched violently for several seconds but nothing came up.

Ellen and Ruth went over and fluttered about like helpless hens. Ellen held Karen's head; Ruth took a wash cloth, soaked it in water and applied the cool compress to the back of Karen's neck.

Karen finally quit retching. She shook uncontrollably and her skin looked pasty white. Ellen and Ruth helped her lie back down and tried to make her comfortable. Jesse went to her side, took her hand, looked at his father helplessly, started to say something, then changed his mind. The same thought ran through all their minds. Radiation sickness!

That dreaded condition of massive cell destruction which could prove fatal. Karen seemed to be much worse than Jesse.

True, Jesse and Karen absorbed the deadly rays for the same period but several factors influence an accumulated dosage. First, a killing dose of radiation for one person could be much less than that required for another. Second, there was also the chance that Karen breathed more radioactive particles than Jesse during their ordeal. With no way to determine how much each absorbed, they could only hope it wasn't a fatal amount. The Baileys started their day deeply concerned about Karen's health.

Kathy migrated to Karen's bedside, hovered about her, and watched over her constantly. The apparent loss of Kathy's parents had been deeply shocking but she was beginning to bring her thoughts to bear on other matters. The Baileys noticed her interest in Karen and hoped this would be the therapy needed to ease her grief.

The family performed their routine tasks. Bob started the generator, hooked up the AC blower, and transferred all the equipment from battery to AC power. He checked the ammeter to make sure the batteries were recharging. Ruth plugged in the hot plate and started the coffee. Ellen, with Tim and Mark's aid, prepared the table and dishes. They ate breakfast without interruption.

Kathy prepared a bowl of cereal for Karen and carried it to her bed. "Karen, try to eat this and maybe you'll feel better."

I'll try Kathy, but I doubt if I'll be able to keep it down. I still feel sick."

Kathy placed pillows behind Karen who couldn't sit up alone. Karen carefully ate a spoonful of the cereal, waited long enough to be sure it would stay down, and then ate more. The food had a settling effect on her stomach so she hungrily ate the remainder.

This pleased Kathy. "Would you care for more, Karen?"

"No, that will be enough for now," she replied, smiling wanly.

Kathy helped her lie back down.

With breakfast out of the way, they placed the table, folding chairs and dishes in their respective storage areas. Movements almost equivalent to acrobatics took place when the underground tenants moved about the shelter in search of more comfortable positions.

Mark worked busily at the monitor panel. He read the radiation counts closely and kept the volume turned high, listening carefully for any possible outside noise that would detect prowlers. Through constant activity he forced Kathy's loss and their plight from his mind.

Eleven-thirty came and John checked the log for the latest readings. Most of them, except outside, were still much the same. The outside count, 100 roentgens per hour, had continued dropping rapidly over the past twenty-four hours. So far, nothing disturbed the exterior silence.

"Tim, I'll relieve you at the console," Bob moved to take his place at the eight p.m. shift change.

Midnight came and John relieved Bob. John listened carefully for an hour, hearing absolutely no sound from above. In fact, it was entirely too quiet.

I wonder why I can't hear the frogs croaking? Maybe I'd better wake Bob and have him check the amplifier. There may be something wrong with it, John speculated.

He got up from the console and walked over to where

Bob slept. "Bob, Bob, wake up!" He spoke softly and urgently, gently shaking his shoulder.

Bob woke with a start. "What is it dad?" He whispered.

"Bob, there may be something wrong with the amplifier. I haven't heard a sound of any kind for an hour. Usually, I can hear the frogs plainly."

Bob walked over to the console and began making checks. He determined that the system worked properly.

"Father, the amplifier system is OK. The reason you don't hear the frogs, they must be either dead or dying."

"I guess you're right Bob. I hadn't thought of that."

John installed the DC blower in place of the hand operated one. Soon, cool, refreshing night air came pouring in to relieve the stuffy atmosphere.

"Use the batteries tonight, Bob. After today, we need more air than I can supply with the hand blower."

"It won't hurt anything father. I'll recharge the batteries tomorrow. We could operate this way continually for forty-eight hours before running the batteries down. The only danger would come from getting the batteries too low to start the generator.

"Dad, I took a good nap and won't be able to go back to sleep. I'll take the rest of your shift."

John yawned. "OK, I'm pretty sleepy."

He got up from the console, stretched, looked about the room thoughtfully, and satisfied, went to bed.

6:30 Wednesday morning came and John, the first to wake, got dressed and walked over to the console where Jesse sat.

"What on earth is wrong?" John asked.

Jesse looked up, smiled wanly, pale and trembling, "Just a little upset stomach."

John clasped his arms around Jesse's shoulders. "Oh, son, why didn't you wake me. Go lie down. Ellen! Ruth! Wake up!" John felt deeply disturbed, seeing the radiation effects on his son. "Oh God, if you will only let him live," he prayed.

The Baileys rose from bed and soon a bustle of activity filled the shelter.

The commotion roused Karen and she saw that something was wrong with Jesse. Since she felt somewhat better she got out of bed and went to her husband.

"Oh Jesse, I'm so sorry," she wailed, clasping him in her arms.

"I'll be all right in a few minutes Karen."

John and Karen helped Jesse, definitely very ill, to bed. Karen appeared distressingly pale and shaking. Kathy and Ruth both went and propelled her back to bed.

Karen lay there for a few moments and then blurted. "I'm going to vomit," and started to get out of bed.

Stay there and I'll bring you a pan," Ruth ordered. She barely made it back in time.

The Baileys entered their fourth day in a depressed state. They had limited medical knowledge about radiation with no way to tell the severity of Jesse's and Karen's sickness. They harbored a dread that the sickness would be fatal, although both seemed much better yesterday.

Ellen and Ruth closely attended them most of the day and tried to make them more comfortable. They coaxed Jesse and Karen several times to eat but each time they did, it wasn't long until the food came back up. Everybody fostered a horrible, helpless feeling.

"Bob, could I see the 8:00 a.m. radiation reports?" John asked.

"Here they are, father," he complied.

John scanned the records closely. "Hmmm, the outside readings are still dropping but not fast like they were. Ninety roentgens per hour is still a deadly dose."

"The rate should fall off pretty fast for the next few days. Most of the fallout has a half life of only a few hours or days and as it decays, the intensity will fall off proportionally," Bob explained.

John scanned the rest of the readings. They were getting some radiation inside the shelter, but minimal. Every time he read the count at the air filter he was even more thankful for the foresight in installing them. Without the added protection, an intolerable amount of radioactive dust would probably have killed them all.

"Bob, start the AC generator. After they finish making the coffee, we'll pump some fresh water. What we have in the tanks may be good but it tastes terrible."

Ellen spoke up. "We can put the stale water to good use. I don't know how the rest of you feel about it but I think it's time some people in this shelter took a bath. Somebody's deodorant definitely isn't working."

"It's not mine for I'm not wearing any," Tim quipped.

"I wasn't going to say anything Tim, but since you let it out, I'll agree," Ruth joked.

The coffee finished making and the Baileys ate breakfast. Although confined only four days, most of them were already craving the bacon, eggs, toast and other tasty breakfast foods they always took for granted. Nobody commented. None of them wanted to be first to complain.

With breakfast over, each of them sought out their assigned duties and went to work.

John and Bob prepared the water pump for operation. John stood by the faucet with a bucket and Bob turned it on. John opened the faucet and fresh, clean, water flowed out.

"Turn it off Bob," he waved his hand when water approached the brim.

Bob turned the pump off and John carried the water over and set it down on the console. "Anybody that wants a fresh drink, come and get it."

"Wait just a minute dad. Let me check it with the Geiger counter," Bob got the instrument from the console drawer.

Bob turned the counter on, allowed it to warm up and adjusted out the background level. He placed the probe in the bucket and the needle came off the peg and moved up scale. He got a reading of three milliroentgens.

"The water is safe enough to drink."

John drank a glassful. "That's good stuff. I had just about forgotten what fresh water tasted like."

"I'll take some," Tim approached with a glass and John poured him a drink.

"Jesse, would you and Karen like to try some of this fresh water?" Ellen encouraged.

Both of them answered yes. They sipped cautiously and gratefully at a glass of the fresh liquid. Neither of them vomited and it left them feeling better.

The rest of the shelter occupants drank, leaving only a small amount. Quenching their thirst became a major event, breaking the monotony in their so far, uneventful day.

Obviously, the days would become more and more

boring. The cure for that, however, was a mental picture of the poor unfortunates outside the shelter.

"John, what's that awful scent?" Ellen, with her acute sense of smell, detected it first.

"It's probably just body odor, or the smell may be coming from the toilet. We may need to add more lime."

"We haven't eaten any hot food for a long time so tonight Ruth and I will cook. It won't be much but at least it will be a change." Ellen brought up the subject of supper, leading the conversation away from the odor.

They enjoyed supper. Fried spam became the main course, supplemented with peas, corn and green beans. Crackers substituted for bread and they topped off the meal with two large bowls of juicy, yellow, peach halves.

Kathy and Ruth prepared plates for Karen and Jesse who both nibbled at the food without appetite, and ate very little. The rest of the Bailey family tackled the meal with relish.

"What I need now is a hot cup of coffee," John hinted.

"We have some tea bags if anybody prefers hot tea," Ruth advised.

"I'll take some tea," Mark stated.

"Me too," Tim added.

With supper over, Ellen took charge of the bathing schedule. "You get two pans of water, one to wash and one to rinse. When you get done with it, dump it in the toilet. You may change your underclothes but everything else goes back on. Since washing clothes presents a problem, you can plan on wearing the same things for a long time."

Faces fell when Ellen broke the news.

She continued. "I know that's going to be tough but if

it's any comfort, you will get to change every now and then, especially shirts and blouses.

"Kathy, since you are our guest, you get to go first. You can change into some of my clothes and we'll wash yours."

"Mrs. Bailey, let somebody else go first. I'm too embarrassed."

"In that case, Ruth, you have the privilege."

They all shuffled and moved around, making way for Ruth. Bob drew water and placed it on the box. Ellen provided her with a towel and wash rag.

"This reminds me of my army days," John commented. "We referred to this operation as a spit bath. However, we didn't have quite this much water since we bathed in our helmet."

"I'm glad we had the foresight to bring deodorant and scented sprays. This place could get smelly in two months."

"I don't smell a thing," Tim commented.

"Don't raise your arms," Mark cautioned.

Following the bathing cycle, Ellen said, "We'll stagger the baths instead of taking them all on the same day. I didn't realize it would take so long. It's almost midnight."

"The place sure smells a lot better," Jesse remarked.

John spoke. "Bob, leave the gasoline engine running all night tonight, or at least while the air smells good. We may need all the fresh air possible tomorrow."

"Good idea father. I know it's late but I believe I'll tune in to the CD frequency and see if anybody's broadcasting. He turned knobs and twirled dials but all he picked up was a tone at 560.

"They should be on in about three minutes, dad."

"Go ahead and leave it on. We need to find out what we can about outside conditions."

Their local CD station never came back on the air and the broadcast at midnight radiated from the station in Tennessee. They could tell the announcer was ill from his quavering voice.

"Good evening ladies and gentlemen. This is Grant Morton, your Civil Defense Broadcaster from Sector Eight, Eastern United States. The following message includes updates and revisions on all previous broadcasts. Statistics are sketchy but represent the latest available information. Unfortunately, the news received today isn't encouraging."

"The nuclear attack destroyed most of our major cities. Surviving officials estimate that sixty million Americans died outright during, and immediately following the initial attacks and at least one hundred million others received fatal doses of radiation, meaning they will die within seven days. Thirty million more, exposed to undetermined amounts, may or may not live. The remaining twenty-five million are thought to be adequately sheltered and will survive. Keep in mind that these figures are only estimates based upon available information and subject to later revision."

"The President, Vice President, their families and some key government officials lived through the attack housed in the secret government headquarters north of Washington. However, I regret to report that the entire Congress died, except the truants, probably from the first bomb which detonated just above the Capitol building."

"Crews of technicians, with total disregard for their own safety, worked valiantly throughout the attack, and after, to establish a workable communications network. As a result, the underground White House is in touch with every state in the union, including Alaska and Hawaii."

Funny noises came over the radio and the voice broadcast ceased for a short time. The announcer came back on the air and spoke apologetically. "Excuse me please, ladies and gentlemen, I have been feeling ill today."

He resumed the news coverage. "Late this evening, we received a message over the EBS network from the President of the United States. Stand by please."

Following a short delay, the message started. "Good evening fellow citizens. It is with a sad and heavy heart I come before you. You have heard the Civil Defense broadcasts and are aware of the appalling destruction rained upon us by our enemies. I would say that I am sorry for what occurred but there are no words to express the grief and chagrin I bear over the calamity that befell us. I know it is no consolation to you but I will say that they forced the war upon us; it was not of our making. We retaliated with at least a two for one ratio on our enemies. Intelligence reports are incomplete but verify almost total annihilation of Russia, China, Cuba Iran, and many of our other enemies. Non-combatant nations throughout the world are reporting heavy casualties from fallout."

The president paused and then continued: "Fellow citizens, do not lose hope. The Government of the United States still functions with controls extending to every state in the union. We are neither defeated nor defenseless. Our military stands ready to guard us from attacks whether by land, sea or air. We still have atomic devices in our arsenals and shall retaliate against any enemy who may dare attack us."

Ellen laughed and cried hysterically. "We haven't learned a thing, have we?"

John, listening to the estimates of survivors and the defense capabilities, wondered at how much of this was fact and how much fancy. He hoped the president knew this for sure but seriously doubted it.

The president continued for ten minutes trying to reassure the survivors. His ringing oratory sounded hollow.

The announcer resumed his broadcast. "Ladies and gentlemen, this concludes our evening bulletin. The next scheduled broadcast comes at 9:00 a.m. tomorrow. Good Evening."

The tone came back on after he signed off.

"Oh Lord, please help us," Ellen moaned. "Won't we ever learn to live in peace?"

The news sounded awesome and sobering. It was impossible for the mind to grasp the reality of billions of people dying in just a matter of days. Destruction clearly exceeded the wildest estimates, beyond imagination. One tiny encouraging fact remained, who could conceive of an enemy attacking under present world conditions?

"Dad. Why? What happened? I believed in our political system and yet, obviously, it failed. Why?" Bob wanted to know.

"Bob, that's a question that will haunt survivors until the day we die. I'm convinced ours was the best political and economic system in the world. It's the best system that has existed in the history of the world and yet, although the best, it contained flaws. The wasteland about us bears testimony to that."

"Bob, tune in on the short wave and see what you can pick up," Mark suggested.

Bob turned the CD radio off and the short wave on. He scanned all bands, searching for available signals, rotated the dial and jotted down each carrier wave detected. Most of them appeared on the twenty meter band. I'll go back through them one by one and see what they are, he thought.

The next station was a voice broadcast but in a foreign language which Bob didn't recognize. He turned to another, weak and unreadable, an English language broadcast.

The fourth one, also in English, came through clear enough to understand and the man sounded as if he were out of his mind. Describing his surroundings, he painted a dreadful, ghastly picture. Thousands were in the last throes of dying, in the streets and in their houses. The operator described his family's plight, pleaded incoherently for help and cried hopelessly. Suddenly, his mind switched channels and he began describing his ham radio station. As quickly as he began the dialogue, he suddenly ceased talking altogether. The transmitter remained keyed and his gasping, rasping breathing permeated the airways. The man, obviously in the last stages of radiation sickness, was dying.

Bob switched to another frequency and then another. He finally located a signal from a fallout shelter in a cave in the Ozark Mountains. News from this source sounded more optimistic and occasionally took on a cheerful note. John wrote the frequency down in the log book. We'll monitor this one regularly, he thought.

The operator described his shelter which was isolated from the outside world like the Baileys. The only information he could relay came from the CD broadcasts and other amateurs. He described local conditions, current radiation readings, listed several helpful hints for shelter survival and then concluded his broadcast with a schedule for future transmissions.

When Thursday morning came Jesse seemed slightly improved; Karen still appeared deathly ill.

"Is it still too dangerous to go outside?" Mark asked.

"It's still dangerous out there but if a person doesn't stay out long, it isn't deadly," John replied. Every day it can be delayed the better off we'll be. The radiation level drops slowly now, but it's still falling, nevertheless. The outside reading this morning was eighty-five and now it's eighty-four."

Karen felt a little better in the afternoon, able to eat some food; Jesse felt much better. Ellen was in high spirits to see them showing such definite improvement.

John brooded. I don't have the heart to tell her not to get her hopes up too high for radiation victims sometimes show dramatic recovery followed by relapse, and in many cases, death.

Kathy and Ruth tackled the washing job and soon, underclothes, male and female, adorned the shelter area. They stretched temporary clotheslines from one end of the shelter to the other and soon, everything was hanging up to dry. The damp clothing raised the humidity inside the shelter but the blower kept the humid air moving and sped up the drying process. Kathy made sure her undies were in the least conspicuous place. She glanced at Mark occasionally, afraid he might see them.

At 2:00 a.m. Friday, John heard distant rumblings and mutterings. We aren't under attack again are we? He put on a pair of headsets and turned up the volume. John listened carefully. The mutterings and rumblings became louder and more frequent; he relaxed; he heard thunder. The air entering the shelter became cooler at three. At 3:05 a.m., the first rain drops pattered on the ground above them and grew into a downpour. He turned the volume down, hooked the speaker up and increased the volume until the sound of the rain became clearly audible.

It still rained hard when he took the 3:45 readings. The radiation count dropped several points with the coming of the rain. The outside reading came down to forty-eight and all the other monitor points decreased also. John felt as if a heavy weight lifted from his shoulders. This is our first real break, he reflected thankfully. I had begun to think we would have to stay in this shelter forever. Morning came and spirits rose when John told them about the rain and the decreased readings.

"Do you believe we will actually get to leave this shelter someday?" Ellen asked.

"It looks that way now," John replied, smiling. "It seemed for awhile that we would be here until Christmas."

"How soon do you think it will be safe enough for us to go out?" Tim wanted to know.

"At least another six or seven weeks. It may be even longer than that for we must be absolutely sure we're safe before leaving the shelter."

"How can that be?" Tim asked, raising his eyebrows. "Four days ago we read over 5000 and now it's down to forty-eight. I would think that in another day or two the readings would reach zero."

Bob answered. "Tim, it would be great if it worked that

way but because of the half life of radioactive materials, it doesn't."

"Half life? What do you mean by that?"

Bob explained. "When radioactive material loses half its strength, the time taken to lose it equals a half life. When the same length of time passes again, the material loses half the strength left after the first half life. Eventually, the material decays until only faint traces remain. There are certain elements, radium and uranium for example, with a half life of hundreds of years while others such as strontium, cesium and uranium, are much shorter, but still last for several years. Most of the isotopes generated in a bomb blast have a half life of seconds, minutes, hours, or days. A few of them will have a half life of weeks, months or years. This is why you saw such a fast drop the first few days. The elements with the short half lives have already lost their strength. As days pass though, you will see a smaller and smaller decrease, because the longer half life materials will hold the count up. I hope the radiation strength will drop low enough in a few weeks to where we can leave the shelter."

John added, "The sad part of it is, in a hundred years, we will still have significant levels of radiation on the earth. Some of the fallout residue consists of relatively long lived elements including Strontium-90, Cesium-137 and Carbon-14. If the scientific reports are accurate, this radiation will affect the health, genes, and reproduction capabilities of our future generations."

"Ellen, why are you crying?"

"Oh, John, all those poor people out there dead and dying, and our own son and daughter sick and maybe dying. I can't stand it," she wailed.

Ruth went to her side. "There, there Ellen. Don't even think about those things. Jesse seems much better and at least Karen isn't any worse. That should give you some hope. Try looking on the brighter side."

Ellen sobbed on for another hour and then finally went to sleep. All the others went about their tasks quietly.

"What do you think is wrong with mother?" Bob's voice registered his concern.

"It's probably a reaction from the strain of the past few days," John speculated. "I hope that's all anyway. This would be a bad time to need medical attention."

"Mark, you and Tim give me a hand. This is a good time to take a look outside." John walked over and started clearing the area next to the entrance. "Remove the panels and sandbags. Bob, stand by with the Geiger counter and see if we pick up any radiation inside when we clear the opening. I'm going topside and see what I can see."

John's four sons objected.

"No boys, I disagree. At the present levels outside there's no chance of my receiving a dangerous dose. It shouldn't even be enough to make me sick, no longer than I'll be out there. Remember our discussion about radiation affecting reproduction? Well, your mother and I have had our family while all of you are still young with your families yet to have. It's only common sense that I should go instead of you."

John didn't get any more arguments and they opened the tunnel.

Bob took measurements with the Geiger counter. Readings inside the tunnel were negligible but the meter showed twelve rads at the far end where the shaft went up.

"I'll be back shortly," John promised, ducking down and crawling into the passageway.

Minutes later, he stood on top under a heavily overcast sky. Their house was gone. It had burned to the ground. The prevailing light breeze from the south caused him to hold his breath as much as possible for he wasn't sure just how safe the outside air might be.

John took a quick look about him and strode rapidly back to the entrance. The charred remains of the house, garage, and Ellen's van testified to the devastation of the past few days. The flowers, vines and shrubbery which had grown profusely about their yard looked withered and scorched. He plucked a green leaf from a bush and it crackled, turning to dust when he rubbed it between his fingers. Although many of the leaves were still green, they were dead. He looked for the car that brought the marauders but couldn't see it. I guess they drove it away from here.

John didn't tarry but reentered the shaft, stripped off his outer garments and crawled, shivering, through the tunnel to the shelter. Bob checked him carefully with the Geiger counter and declared him clean, except the bottom of his feet. John took a wet rag, wiped them off and then threw the rag into the vertical shaft.

"Close it up boys," John ordered.

Bob informed his father, "You stayed exposed a total of twelve minutes. At the present rate of forty-eight, your dosage shouldn't have been over ten rads. I doubt if you'll feel any effects from it."

John sounded relieved. "I'm glad we know something of what we have outside. Incidentally, it's cool outside, probably in the fifties."

Ellen woke two hours later, and although calm and quiet, wasn't her usual self. She remained withdrawn and remote, slow to reply to comments and questions. The rest of the family became more concerned when Ellen didn't respond to any of the activities about her.

The first week of June drew to a close and the Bailey family experienced the oppressiveness and boredom associated with loss of freedom although they had been in the shelter for only ten days.

The radiation readings fell daily but were now falling stubbornly slow. John marked the date on his improvised calendar and noted under Tuesday, June 7, a reading of thirty-seven. Although it was a large drop compared to readings following the actual attack, they still had a long way to go before it would be safe enough to leave the shelter and spend time outside.

He also noted the improved air temperature inside the shelter. Whereas it was stifling hot in the beginning, it was now pleasantly cool.

"Does anyone have any idea why it's so much cooler?" John asked.

Bob replied, "Dad, the haze and particles in the air from the atomic blasts and the smoke from all the fires has probably caused it. Some scientists predicted a 'nuclear winter' following a nuclear war."

"Just what is a nuclear winter?" Ruth asked.

"The nuclear winter occurs when there's haze or overcast thick enough to block out the rays of the sun and cause a cooling effect. Predictions are that this can last for several months or years."

"How can this affect us?"

"I'm not sure, but it will make the winters colder and possibly retard vegetative growth."

"We're going to have quite a few problems when we get out of here," John added soberly.

Conversation lapsed and John looked around the shelter, assessing their current situation.

Karen and Jesse exhibited a general malaise, pallor, appetite loss and sore throats. Karen was becoming emaciated.

Jesse had lost some weight but so far, seemed to be holding up fairly well.

In spite of the daily duties, monotony and boredom began showing up in outbursts of temper in some and depression in others. Ellen, improved somewhat over the previous week, lacked a lot being her old self. The terror of the outside world bore heavily on her mind.

"Dad, why do you think all of this has happened," Bob asked.

"First, I don't think Russia intended for this to happen. I believe she miscalculated and the H bomb present from Israel triggered an event she really didn't want. The world finally experienced the big accident everybody worried about for years."

"I believe that Russia was pulling off a gigantic hoax which originated three or more decades ago. I doubt if very many Russians were in on it, probably not more than a dozen or so of the key leadership. Events that sent my sub-conscious into tail spins are obvious to me now; for example, the status of nuclear weapons. In the 1980's and 90's, Russia put on a tremendous show, destroying weapons and preparing to destroy weapons, but due to her supposed problems with logistics, personnel, communications, and so forth, she lagged way behind in the actual destruction. On the other hand, in anticipation, we got way ahead of the disarmament schedule. Many of ours, although not yet destroyed, were disassembled, warheads transported to one area and the missiles to another, or in other words, useless. Here, the old American trait of jumping in and getting things done worked against us."

"Our political system worked against us also since both our President and Congress were of the same political persuasion, highly cooperative and gleefully downsizing our military. I used to wonder why that party picked their particular political symbol but now I think I know."

Except miscalculating Israel, Russia already held a nuclear and conventional superiority which placed her in the position where she could ask for and get the unconditional surrender of all the world's free nations. Russia never got the opportunity to convey this information to our president for Israel's bomb pre-empted their message by probably seventy-two hours. I assume the electromagnetic interference and radiation from the H bomb kept them from issuing their ultimatum, although I'm sure they tried."

"Whew! Dad that sounds far-fetched even if it does make some sense. Don't you think we would have attacked Russia anyway if she issued the ultimatum? I can't imagine us just sitting back and allowing it to happen." Bob replied.

"Bob, I believe they could have offered proof forcing us to capitulate or commit suicide. Also, you'll find out sometime in the future that the Russians hurt us much worse than we hurt them in the nuclear exchange. The only reason we hurt them at all came about because we launched the first strike before they had a chance to vacate their cities and occupy shelters. Hundreds of thousands of them were probably en route when the bombs came down."

Bob, sitting at their operating console, started the AC generator and began tuning the radio to pick up the scheduled ten a.m. Civil Defense broadcast. The Sector Eight CD station had finally gone off the air. He suspected this was due to the demise of the operator rather than failure of equipment. By careful tuning, he located a faint, but clear, distant CD station.

The news reports were beginning to paint a faint, garbled picture of the state of the world.

The death toll in the United States exceeded by far pre-war estimates. Preliminary figures indicated survivors would number in hundreds of thousands rather than millions. It would take weeks or months to get close tallies, if ever.

From all accounts, fallout saturated the entire earth. News filtered in from foreign countries telling of the horror of quiet death drifting slowly and relentlessly from the skies.

Many countries besides the United States, Russia and China got bombed. Israel took hers in the destruction of Tel Aviv when Russia retaliated for the one hydrogen bomb Israel launched, triggering the holocaust.

Russia devastated England, along with the United States. European countries remained relatively untouched following the expedient accords agreed upon between them and Russia. In other words, they surrendered. Russia and China, although officially aligned, grabbed the opportunity and dropped unspecified numbers of nuclear bombs on each other's pet targets. As the bombs fell on major targets in the United States and Russia, each selected lesser targets for succeeding destructive waves. Occasional stray bombs fell on neutral countries.

The United States expended all tactical and strategic stockpiles but Russia and China held part of theirs in reserve.

And then the fallout came. It knew no national boundaries. The dark, grayish clouds of dust and smoke swirled from continent to continent, finally circled the globe at the equator, and then spread from pole to pole. Radioactive concentrations varied from place to place but in practically all cases, it was enough.

After a period of several days, the intensity of the interference began to decrease and a few AM civil defense channels came back intermittently and sporadically. A few amateur radio broadcasts were also trying to make contacts.

A very bleak picture began to appear. The world would never be the same in this age.

As Bob listened to the CD broadcast on the headsets, he jotted down notes on a pad so he could inform the others of his findings.

A tenuous administration in the United States claimed they had finally established communications with all fifty states. It was still a paper government since nobody could leave their shelters. However, plans existed for the day when it would be safe to emerge and orders given through the CD broadcasts.

Tentatively it appeared that the government would order all survivors to move to designated locations and concentrate the population for mutual safety. The White House leadership intended to dictate orders directing what was best for the survivors.

The Baileys listened but reserved judgment when they heard the plans expounded.

Several days passed and information received on short wave and CD broadcasts became more and more informative.

The report given by the president on how badly we beat Russia was erroneous. No. Not erroneous. A blatant lie! From all the information filtering in, the United States, for all practical purposes, was totally devastated. The thirty million American survivors was the figment of somebody's imagination. Russia, on the other hand, suffered much less damage by comparison and remained a powerful, functioning nation.

Europe suffered extensive casualties from fallout and would ultimately lose well over half of their people from starvation and pestilence. This became more or less true for the entire world. The earth remained obscured from the sun by particulate matter and smoke generated by nuclear explosions and firestorms. These particles would continue falling from the sky for the next three or four years and nobody knew what effect all that would have on people's health.

More interesting news came from Israel. Although Russia retaliated and totally obliterated Tel Aviv with a hundred megaton hydrogen warhead, Israel was pretty much ignored during the nuclear dual between Russia, the United States, and the rest of the world. All her leadership got wiped out and an obscure and relatively unknown Colonel Wolverstein conducted himself brilliantly in extricating their nation from the unholy mess with the Arabs, Russians, and all their helpers. He established his headquarters in Jerusalem.

An uncanny large number of motorized and armored

vehicles, along with crashed aircraft, littered the Israeli and mid-east countryside. It looked almost as if something or somebody had just pulled the plug on them!

At the moment, no fighting occurred anywhere in the world. All peoples used whatever protection they could find to ride out the nuclear storm which engulfed their world in an unseen lake of radioactive fire.

The information, passed from mouth to mouth by radio amateurs, newscasters and other sources, could have truth in it or it could all be fairy tales. The Baileys filed the bits of information away with a good deal of skepticism but could only wait and see.

Temperatures and radiation statistics from most states were being broadcast. Some areas had much lower levels of radiation than others. A strip just east of the Rockies and running the length of the mountain chain enjoyed the lowest readings and the people in that region would be leaving their shelters first if the radiation continued its decrease at the same rate.

Some portions of the United States were considerably more radioactive (hotter) than others, especially the eastern seaboard from New York state to North Carolina and then inland for one hundred and fifty miles. The west coast, especially in and around the larger cities, was also quite hot. Whether true or not, reports were that all that could be found of Hollywood was a big hole in the ground! Most of this territory would remain uninhabitable for many decades.

Former population centers, military complexes and industrialized areas bore the fiercest attacks and still showed the highest radiation levels. Temperatures dropped dramatically over all the country. Most places were in the fifties but some of the northern states had temperatures in the thirties. The nuclear winter was upon them.

After the CD broadcast, Bob tuned the short wave receiver and searched the different bands for new stations. He already had a list of frequencies and their times of broadcasting but was always looking for others. He could pick up a lot of useful information in these broadcasts, especially concerning Ohio and the few adjacent states.

Fifty miles east of their location, a short wave transmitter broadcast at regular intervals. Two families, with a total of eleven persons, lived in a shelter in a remote and little known cave in the hills that divided Powell and Montgomery counties.

Within a radius of one hundred miles, Bob knew of twenty-three survivors, including the Bailey family. Surely there were others such as they, with no way to communicate.

There undoubtedly were hundreds of millions of people killed in the war but the Baileys entertained hopes for large numbers of survivors. It would be a grim world indeed if only a few families escaped.

Karen lost most of her hair by the seventeenth of June. Kathy carefully collected the hair as it detached and soon had a long, round bundle which she carefully preserved inside a long piece of aluminum foil. Ruth had promised she would make a hair piece after it quit coming out.

Karen's appetite began improving. Thin and weak, Karen felt better now than any other time since arriving at the shelter. Although emaciated and almost hairless, she emanated an enchanting and ethereal beauty difficult to describe. Ruth fixed a head scarf about Karen's head which enhanced her appearance. Kathy applied make-up that somehow survived the war.

Ellen placed her arms about Karen and hugged her. "Karen, we all love you very much and we're so glad you're better."

"Thank you mother," Karen answered with tears in her eyes.

Ellen laughed, "I'll have to admit we worried until we got to knowing you better."

Karen smiled in return. "I'm glad you think better of me now. I was still pretty much of a brat when I married Jesse. Being an only child with a wealthy father, my chances of their spoiling me was pretty good. I can thank Jesse for helping me get my head on straight."

Jesse moved over and took Karen's hand. "I could see the pure gold under the brass exterior from the beginning," Jesse laughed. "I knew it would be impossible to explain so I decided to let time take care of the problem."

"Why were you staying with the old lady in that dilapidated, run down house?" Ellen asked curiously.

Karen explained. "That old lady was my favorite aunt on my mother's side. I ran away from home and knew that would be the last place my parents would look for me. That was so childish of me, running away." Tears came to Karen's eyes. "I was terribly selfish and self centered at that time. Thank you, Jesse, for saving me from that."

"Thank you for being the treasure you are!"

Jesse, much improved, suffered some hair loss but completely regained his appetite and, although still weak and somewhat thinner than before, had regained his color and much of his energy. The young couple's improved health helped the overall optimism considerably.

July the first arrived and shortly after breakfast, John called a meeting of the family.

"I believe it's time we looked at our supplies and see how they're holding out." He turned to Bob. "Do you have any idea how much gasoline we have left?"

"Dad, it's really hard to say exactly, but if my figures are correct, we should still have enough gasoline for three more weeks at the present rate."

"What about our food supply, Ruth?"

Ruth looked uncomfortable. "You know how carefully we've been controlling the food. It still seems to be dwindling too fast. At the present rate we'll run out in about two weeks.

John frowned. "I was afraid of that. We may have to go on more stringent rationing. At the present rate of decline in radiation intensity I wouldn't dream of going outside for another three weeks, and maybe not then. We also have no assurance we'll find any food once we get out."

The shrinking food supply crisis loomed before them demanding immediate attention.

Kathy burst into tears. "It's my fault. If you hadn't brought me here, you would all have enough food. I'm sorry I came!"

Ruth embraced her. "Kathy, we wouldn't have it any other way. We would gladly have taken more people in if given the chance."

John added his reassurance. "Looking at it from a starvation standpoint, we aren't that bad off, Kathy. Don't worry; we'll make it with plenty to spare." John was sorry he brought the subject up. It needed discussing but they could have waited until a time when Kathy slept. Oh well, he thought, may as well finish it.

"Ellen," John instructed, "You and Ruth sit down and make out menus for three weeks and proportion out the food accordingly. I would like to see a three or four day surplus on top of that if at all possible."

"We'll try." Ruth replied shakily. She left the meeting abruptly and vomited. Ruth's radiation sickness symptoms caused concern at first but, re-diagnosed, it appeared that in about seven and a half months she would have a baby.

Karen raised herself weakly on her elbow and remained silent, listening carefully to all they said. Karen had experienced a close brush with death but barring complications due to her weakened condition, her survival chances improved every day.

Bob briefed them on the latest readings, national and international news, and other items picked up over the short wave radio.

The Supreme Ruler of the world government and United States of Europe continued consolidating and strengthening their position in the world. Many volunteers, risking or giving their lives to the radiation, worked feverishly rebuilding communications lines throughout the country which allowed him to rule even during the time of fallout. This key factor allowed him to wrest the European nations away from Russia. Well before time to come out, he had a clear understanding with the Troika in Russia that they and the United States of Europe would leave each other alone. He planned on bringing Russia into the

World Government fold after he got the rest of the world absorbed.

He also established communications with Israel and set up an early meeting with the self-proclaimed Prime Minister Colonel Abe Wolverstein, when radiation levels would allow it. They made a tentative agreement that the United States of Europe would move in and fill the void left by the demise of Israel's friend, the United States of America. They set the date for the twentieth of July.

John concluded the meeting and announced, "Tim, it's game time."

July the fourth came and went without celebrating but with a good bit of reflection. Day followed day routinely and on the twenty-first of July, John called the family together.

"Well clan, it's time to make another survey of our predicament. We may be able to leave the shelter safely anytime now." he stated.

"I'm ready." Mark informed him.

"Me too," Tim agreed.

"Aren't we all?" Ruth added.

A surge of excitement ran through the room.

John explained the current radiation readings. They were still not down to zero, certainly not low enough, but bearable. The present reading was one hundred milliroentgens per hour and hopefully, would keep decreasing a little more each day.

John based his decision to leave the shelter at this time on their meager food stores. A three day supply remained and all of them were hungry from the lean meals they ate the past three weeks.

"We'll go outside tomorrow," John informed them. "If conditions don't appear conducive to remaining out, we can at least forage for food and then spend whatever time is necessary back here in the shelter." "Lord knows what we'll find out there," Jesse stated.

## CHAPTER VI
# THE FOURTH SEAL IS OPEN

Revelation 6:7, 8: "And when he had opened the fourth seal, I heard the voice of the fourth beast say, Come and see. And I looked, and behold a pale horse: and his name that sat on him was Death, and Hell followed with him. And power was given unto them over the fourth part of the earth, to kill with sword, and with hunger, and with death, and with the beasts of the earth."

The earth's ecosystems would be heavily impacted for years to come. Even though resilient nature would effect a quick recovery and hide much, the damage ran deep.

Civilization, as the world had known it, disappeared. It would never recover in the present age. The world population received blow after blow.

Initially, deaths from nuclear blasts and intense radiation dominated. Then deaths from injuries and lethal radiation followed. Many left protective cover too soon and were fatally sickened. Deaths from continuing intense radiation came next.

Death from pestilence, and disease spread like wildfire. Without any medical help, people were helpless and soon died. Only those who had foresight to store medicines and antibiotics could in any way cope. Within six months, the death toll would be in billions. ***The rider of the pale horse is riding, riding, riding!***

Very soon after the war, roving bands of scavengers and pillagers roamed the countryside seeking food primarily, but also gasoline and anything else they might need.

A government structure began to emerge that loosely encompassed much of the entire world. It would be centered in Rome. The continent of Europe was mostly spared. When Russian forces poised to invade Europe, they surrendered.

Two months following the end of the nuclear war, a fledgling government was in place. Pockets of fighting still occurred sporadically throughout the world but were negligible and immaterial insofar as the new world government was concerned.

Another nation that miraculously escaped destruction was Israel. Initially hard hit in places such as Tel Aviv, Israel had survived Jerusalem still its capital.

During the war, Israel had defended itself in such a way that an unprecedented accumulation of forces, ground and air, from Russia and the Middle East, ground themselves to pieces against the tiny nation.

It may have been the employment of Electromagnetic Pulses (EMP) or in other ways unknown to the outside world (or the hand of God) that literally caused aircraft to fall from the sky. In addition, mechanized and motorized vehicles just stopped in their tracks.

Leaders of the new world government, still puzzled and scratching their heads at their failure against Israel, forthwith practically begged Israel to enter into a seven year peace treaty with the new world government. Israel accepted, following the promise that they would supply material and other resources to expedite the rebuilding of the temple in Jerusalem and would not object to Jerusalem being the capital of Israel.

Part of the structure of the new world government included ten governmental areas throughout the world. This structure, loosely knit, excluded many pockets of humanity deemed immaterial to the overall scheme of things. That category would apply to large areas of the United States considered no longer material or just uninhabitable due to destruction and radiation.

In the next eighteen months, world commerce and internal commerce within some countries would begin to be established. Rome as the hub and Europe as the wheel was the center from which all activity radiated. Tentacles from there would go to the ten regional governments.

Regulations were quickly forthcoming as the new government began immediately establishing and tightening control over those governed. Rules detailed what was expected from those ruled and how all resources would be controlled and allocated.

One of the first edicts to come forth was to immediately brand all Christians as outlaws until each could be interrogated and given the opportunity to renounce God and Jesus Christ. A special identification and numbering system would be used. Any sign of opposition from members of their leadership was immediately eliminated.

John Bailey lay awake two hours, impatiently waiting for daylight on the momentous day of Friday, July 22. It seemed a lifetime since the first bomb fell but in reality, only fifty-six days had passed.

"Time to get up, folks," John said, going from bed to bed, shaking them. "Let's take a look at the outside and see what we have left." An immediate bustle followed as all the family moved with alacrity.

While Ellen and Ruth prepared breakfast, John and Bob began making plans for their egress.

The meal over, table, chairs, Kathy's bed, and many other articles got shoved out of the way and stacked to give access to the steel inner door. Tim and Mark joined in and helped Bob open it.

"Don't drop it," Bob cautioned, firmly grasping one side. When they lifted the plate clear of the studs one of the sandbags fell inside on the floor. The two young men removed the remainder and within minutes Tim busily removed the outer plate.

"Here it comes," he said, dragging the heavy plate back inside the shelter.

"Just a minute boys," John cautioned. "Let Bob take a reading and see if we have any hot material in the shaft and on top. It should be clear but we won't take any chances."

Bob retrieved the detector from the console and read safe levels in the shaft and at ground level. Tim, Mark, Jesse and John climbed the shaft and soon, all five of the Bailey men stood outside gazing about them in awe. Trixie stood looking up at Tim and wagging his tail.

The dark sky gave the appearance of twilight although it was 9:00 in the morning. The chill air, in the low fifties, caused them to shiver, standing there in their short-sleeved shirts.

"I can't believe it's just July. We'll need to put on more clothes if we stay out here long," Jesse remarked.

Their house and garage were large piles of ashes. The cars made two blackened lumps in the garage remains.

The dead leaves and grass as far as the eye could see was a stunning sight. Instead of midsummer, the landscape gave all the appearance of deep winter. The only signs of life were several flies buzzing around.

Bob checked the immediate area while John poked around through the ashes of their former home. Mark and Tim wandered around looking curiously at first one thing, then another. Tim searched for the animals but didn't find a trace.

"Dad, let's bring the rest of the family up and let them get some fresh air," Bob suggested.

"Good idea. However, from the looks of things we may have to spend another night in the shelter."

Soon, all ten of the group enjoyed the cool, fresh-smelling air. Even Sabrina, who appeared less fat and chubby, seemed glad to be back on the outside. She blinked in the light, revealing the bright blue in her eyes was taking on a hint of gray.

Ellen looked depressed and remained silent, viewing the remains that had been her home for twenty years. She sighed, conjuring up scenes from past enjoyable times she spent here.

John felt a deep sadness, noting Ellen's expression. I hope she can overcome her depression over this for the worst is yet to come, he thought.

John entered the ashes of their home and walked to the area where the study once was. He located their fireproof strong box, moved it around to where he could get to the door and cleaned it off.

Ellen walked over and watched him curiously. "What's in the box John?"

"Let's wait first and see if the contents survived," He answered and began opening it. John handed her their picture albums and Ellen's face lit up with joy. "Thank God those were saved," she said tearfully.

"Our marriage license and insurance policies are in here also," John stated inanely. Finding those items which would provide a link with the past injected a note of cheer to the otherwise grim scene.

"Bob, why is it so dark and cold?" Ruth asked.

"We are in a nuclear winter. All the bombs raised so much dust and started so many fires the smoke and ashes are hiding the sun. I would think that most of our forest land caught on fire from the atomic bomb flashes and burned completely up. In fact, some of them are probably still burning, even if it has been two months. You can imagine what we have between us and the sun. In fact, I think I can smell it."

"Won't this cause other problems?" Karen asked.

Bob responded. "This can cause problems we haven't even dreamed about yet. For example, crops can't grow without the sun. For another, plants can't make oxygen without the sun. I'm not sure what effect this may have on us. I hope there's already enough oxygen in the air to keep us going."

Jesse added, "From the looks of things, our troubles aren't over; they are just starting."

"Mark, go back inside and pass out the firearms," John instructed. "From now until further notice, we will all be fully armed when we leave the shelter. This includes rifles, pistols, knives and ammunition."

"What about jackets dad?"

"I think we'll be OK without the jackets once we start walking. We'll warm up pretty fast."

"Bob, I'll take Tim and Mark with me and we'll do some exploring in the immediate area. You stay and protect the family. We'll be back by dark," John concluded.

"Better take the Geiger counter with you and check for hot spots," Bob advised.

"Bob, keep one of these rifles handy while we're gone." John slung the counter strap over his shoulder and turned it on. Accompanied by Mark and Tim, he set off down the driveway toward the road.

"Father, can we go and see what happened to the Klines?" Mark asked.

"Yes Mark, we'll go there first," John answered kindly.

Silent and thoughtful, they walked down the road, lined with dead grass and brown-leafed trees. Most of the leaves were still clinging to the limbs but a few had begun to fall. A good rain will bring them down, John thought.

They approached the turn-off to the Kline's house and John spotted their car.

"Tim, you and Mark stay here." John could tell even at that distance their vehicle had undergone a terrific impact. He inspected the wreckage and then returned to his sons.

"Bob and I will come back over here later and bury them. They both died instantly."

Mark turned away quickly. John and Tim walked around and talked quietly until he regained his composure.

They walked five miles down the road toward Breton and everything they saw and felt reminded them of winter.

"What's that lump over there in the field, father?" Tim asked.

Probably a dead cow or horse," John guessed.

There hadn't been any signs of life anywhere in the countryside except insects. The quiet and stillness seemed uncanny with not a bird or any moving creature, except them and several insects, to break the silence.

Mark stooped over and carefully examined the grass. "Dad, look here. The grass may be alive. The burnt grass has green roots, although there are no shoots coming up."

John knelt down and looked. "This is good news. However, it will have to warm up considerably before anything can grow."

John shivered. "Boys we had better turn around and go back for today."

An hour and a half later, just at dusk, John and his sons arrived back at the shelter. Temperatures had dropped and it was even chillier than when they left. Bob, along with the women and baby, were back inside. Jesse, wearing a jacket, was still out on top serving as lookout.

"There's not a living creature in sight, father."

"I know, Jesse. We've been down the road five miles and haven't seen a sign of life of any sort, except insects."

"Let's all go back inside, eat supper and get a good night's sleep. Tomorrow, we'll start early, go into Breton and see what we can find," John recommended.

Ellen greeted him as he entered. "John, this place smells terrible. I don't know why we hadn't noticed it before."

John laughed, "The smell got worse gradually over a long time and we grew used to it. The clean air outside cleared our smellers."

John turned serious. "Kathy, your mother and father

died in a car wreck on their way here. I know it's not much comfort but they died instantly."

Kathy went to Karen for comfort and sobbed on her shoulder for a long time.

The Baileys dropped back into their shelter routine and settled down for another night underground.

Early the next morning, which was Sunday, they arose, ate a meager breakfast and then vacated their shelter.

"Mark and I will take a fast walk to town, survey the area, and see if we can pick up some kind of vehicle. Bob and Tim can go over and bury the Klines. We'll go over there later with Kathy and have a memorial service for them. Jesse, since you're still weak, stay here and remain on guard. If anybody or anything shows up, stay alert and don't take any chances. Shoot to kill if you have to. We shouldn't be gone for more than three or four hours."

John and Mark set off down the road at a fast pace, paused at Gary Burkhart's grocery, which miraculously hadn't burned, and then stared curiously at the remains of Earl Townsend's service station as they passed by. They didn't see the remains of either Gary or Earl. At 8:30, they entered Breton's northern outskirts. They were twenty-five miles from the detonation point of the hydrogen device that hit Lexington.

Radiation readings were somewhat erratic, bouncing between 100 and 200 milliroentgens. The readings were just high enough to make their safety marginal, which left John feeling uneasy. "Mark, keep a lookout and I'll keep a close eye on the Geiger counter."

"Right father." Mark intently studied their surroundings, keeping the rifle at the ready.

An occasional brick house still stood, where, by some miracle, the roof and trim hadn't been set afire by the flash. Although standing, these houses showed evidence of severe blast damage. On the right a collapsed supermarket hadn't burned. The metal trim, roof construction and other factors kept it from igniting.

They immediately discovered numerous decomposed bodies of humans, dogs, cats and birds in the streets and yards. Many of the bodies hosted hordes of insects and a faint, putrid smell was still evident because the cooler weather retarded the decomposition.

They continued their uneasy trek toward the center of town, eyes darting from side to side, in front, and occasionally to the rear.

"Dad, this is scary," Mark shivered, glancing again to his rear. He imagined myriads of ghosts were all about them, ghosts of the hosts of recently departed souls.

"I don't feel too comfortable about this myself."

Heavier damage appeared when they approached the downtown area where most buildings burned; the few that remained unburned had been knocked flat. They didn't see any signs of fire fighting.

Several abandoned cars and trucks cluttered the streets. Most of these had burned and only charred hulks remained. A few vehicles survived, sheltered from the incinerating flash by a building or other object. One car had crossed the sidewalk and buried itself halfway inside a burned out supermarket window. A dead man sat crumpled behind the steering wheel.

In the sturdier buildings still standing, plate glass windows were broken in all the store fronts and there were signs of looting everywhere. Broken bottles, cans of food, furniture, appliances, and many other articles cluttered the streets and sidewalks.

"What horrors these people must have endured during their last hour," John supposed, gazing about.

"Mark, let's find some wheels and whatever else we can and get out of here."

"I'm ready father. This place gives me the willies."

A thirty minute search produced a 2008 four door sedan. Keys were in the car and it had a full tank.

They stopped on the outskirts of town at the supermarket they had passed on the way in and began searching for food. John used the Geiger counter against the food stuffs but didn't detect any abnormal radiation. Unless the high levels spoiled the canned goods, they would have an abundant supply.

The produce, milk, and meat sections of the market, in advanced stages of decay, still smelled.

They dug through the wreckage, and although most of the canned goods had already been taken, they found some canned fruit, vegetables, and meat and carried them out to the car where John took a knife from his pocket, opened three cans and sampled them to determine if they were edible. When satisfied with the food supply, they got in the car.

"Mark, let's take a detour by the church before we go home. I've got to see if there's anything or anyone left."

They made several detours and stops to move debris before arriving at the former site of the church and parsonage. Nothing remained but ashes, steel girders, broken glass and brick. They left hurriedly. John didn't see any reason for lingering any longer.

After they returned home, the other family members gathered about them curiously when they got out of the car.

"What now, father?" Jesse asked.

It's time for a planning session. There are some things to decide. Should we stay in the shelter or move into one of the vacant houses in the area? Do we remain here or leave and try to join other people? Whatever we decide to do our safety and security will be our first concern. We need to stay well armed and vigilant. There's no telling if or when we may have visitors."

After a lively discussion with a free flow of comments and ideas, John held up his hand. "There seems to be a consensus we should find a home outside the shelter and for the time being, remain in the general area. However, the radiation readings are questionable. One-hundred milliroentgens is still too high to stay out all the time."

Bob asked, "what if we checked out a location and see what the readings are after we scrub the place and do everything possible to improve the radiation count?"

John responded, "Good idea, Bob. I saw a brick house about three miles from here. It's the Burton place. It is right next to the Breton Memorial Cemetery. We'll go over first, check it out and get some readings. If there's no problems or complications, and if the count is bearable, we'll start moving. The electric generator will need to go over though to operate the well pump. Water and a few lights should be all we'll need."

"Dad, don't you think it would be advisable to re-stock this shelter and keep it intact?" Bob suggested.

"Good idea, Bob. There may still be some periods of high radiation when we'll need to spend some time in it. I guess it's also possible there are still some kooks out there with some more bombs."

John paused a moment and then continued. "We don't have much left but time so let's not rush into anything. We can go back to town and shop for another generator. We will leave this one where it is. Also, we need to assure ourselves of an adequate food supply, water, and gasoline before doing anything else. Boys, let's all go over to the farmhouse, look it over, clean it up, take some readings, get a generator, and then come back for the others."

John led the way to the car and a few minutes later, drove into the farmhouse yard. They explored the house and found the dead bodies of a man and a woman in the master bedroom, He looked at the potential task of removing them and cleaning up adequately. I believe this can be done safely, he thought.

They wandered around the barn lot staring at bones of cows, horses and hogs. There were occasional feather bundles where the chickens had died. John kicked one of the piles and disturbed a horde of ants.

Four hours later the Baileys had the house ready for occupancy, including the electric generator. Their gasoline supply was dangerously low and replenishing that would be high on their list. Radiation readings were higher than desirable but marginally acceptable.

The Baileys spent the rest of the day moving radios, bedding and other equipment to the farmhouse.

They were well established by dark and the women prepared supper. They opened the canned goods found in Breton and poured it into bowls. The food tasted delicious and they ate heartily to make up for the lean meals eaten the past several days. With supper over and the table cleared, the Bailey family, along with Kathy, sat around the dining table and discussed their plans.

"Dad, I think Karen and I will move back into the shelter and stay for a few weeks."

"Why, Jesse? Don't you think this place would be more comfortable-and safer?"

"Yes, but since Karen and I have already absorbed massive doses of radiation, I don't want us to get any more."

"That sounds like a good idea. However, when we talk about separating, the safety factor concerns me."

"We'll keep the door bolted and make sure the monitor system and dynamite charges are functional. We should be safe enough by doing that."

"Another thing, you're going to have to seal that inside toilet and build yourself an outhouse outside. You still have the problem with air movement through the shelter."

"You're right. We'll have to stay here until we work out all those problems and then we'll move."

Mark walked over to Kathy, took her hand, led her in front of the group, and then spoke. "All of you listen. Kathy and I have something we would like to say."

Oh, Oh, here it comes, John thought to himself.

"Kathy and I would like to get married."

After a moment, Ellen spoke. "But you're both so young! Don't you think you should wait awhile? After all Mark, you're just barely seventeen and Kathy is sixteen."

"Mom, things aren't like they were. Our life is full of uncertainties. None of us have any idea how much time we have left and we've decided we're not going to waste any of it. We want to spend whatever time we have together."

John spoke. "I understand what you're saying Mark and I have no objections. What are your plans?"

"First, we'll get married. Since there are no churches, no preachers and no JP's, we've decided that you can officiate. We're not too concerned about how you conduct the ceremony or what you say. We just want to get married legally in everybody's eyes."

"When would you like to do it?" Ellen asked.

"Kathy, would this next Sunday afternoon be OK with you?" Mark asked.

"That will be fine with me," she responded softly, snuggling a little closer.

Ruth spoke up. "Looks as if we have a lot to do between now and then. There's the wedding dress, rehearsal dinner, and, well-all the other things."

"I guess we'd better get busy," Karen added.

Jesse spoke up. "Mark, have you and Kathy decided where you will live?"

"Not yet," Mark responded.

"Why don't you move into the shelter with Karen and me?"

"Thanks for the offer, Jesse. We'll think it over and let you know."

Bob spoke. "That sounds like an excellent idea to me. With the prospect of new babies, the less radiation exposure the both of you have, the better off you'll be."

The rest of the Baileys had a good laugh while both Mark and Kathy blushed scarlet and averted their gaze.

"Well, that's one bit of planning none of us expected. Now, we need to talk about our immediate future and decide what's best," John added.

Initially, Bob, Jesse and Mark would scour the area in and around Breton and within a fifty mile radius of their location. Their goal would be to contact survivors and at the same time, collect and stockpile food, clothing, gasoline and other supplies.

One immediate concern was the lack of any living domestic animals. Also, it was unlikely that crops would grow the following spring and bear their needed food but one bit of encouragement was the green just above the roots they had discovered in the dead grass.

John rode into Breton the next morning with his sons and they stayed long enough for him to locate another car and hot wire it. He then went by Karen's aunt's house and viewed the scorched fence and pile of ashes. He looked carefully but couldn't find any trace of her body.

John left there and went to Dean and Hazel Davis' house. He located their partially built shelter and not finding them, searched in the remains of the house and in the general area for their bodies. He never found a trace of them or their children but found the corpses of seven men inside the shelter.

After John left, his sons started their exploration and fifteen minutes later, they had gained only two miles in the direction of Lexington. Extreme blast damage blocked the roads and made a detour necessary. Bob watched the Geiger counter but so far, hadn't noted any increase.

The three men continued to circle Lexington but every time they turned to penetrate, more debris blocked roadways and stopped them. Finally, when they had circled to the west, they were able to move in farther toward the center.

With their arrival at the outer perimeter of the city

proper, Bob began to see an increase in the radiation levels. "Hold up Jesse. I believe we've gone far enough. We're beginning to get some pretty strong readings."

"Bob, there's a knoll ahead. If it's OK with you I'll ease up to the top of it and maybe we can see downtown Lexington."

"Go ahead. Take it slow though and I'll keep an eye on the meter. If I tell you to stop. Stop."

Jesse crept along the last several yards to the top. He stopped the car and they got out for a better view.

"I can't believe it!" Mark gasped.

A fifteen square mile egg-shaped depression occupied the heart of what once was Lexington. The bomb missed dead center by about three miles; in a five mile radius around the concavity, not a wall had been left standing.

"Lexington got hit by a H bomb by all appearances," Bob speculated. "I can't understand why they would use one that size since the city didn't have any strategic importance."

"Population and industry I suppose," Jesse theorized. "Probably, when they ran out of primary targets for their big bombs, they started singling out industrial and population centers."

"There's no need to go any deeper into Lexington. We could get into trouble with the radiation."

"Where to next?" Jesse asked.

"Since we're south of Lexington, let's head on down to Richmond and see what's down there," Bob directed.

Bob, Jesse and Mark continued combing the countryside and small towns until dark but didn't find any sign of life. They did, however, find adequate fuel stashes throughout the area. Unless evaporation and the age of the fuel became a problem, abandoned service stations assured their fuel needs for some time to come. A gasoline powered generator and a little hot wiring on the gas pumps would do the trick.

That evening when the boys returned, John called the family together. "It's time we tried to contact other people. Survival appears possible in this area but we might fare better among a group of others. We don't know yet what dangers there are out there and until we learn what they are, we need to remain cautious."

"Father, why don't we take a trip to the east and see if we can locate the family in the cave over in Montgomery County?" Mark suggested.

"Good idea Mark. You, Bob and Tim can make that trip tomorrow."

Bob spoke up. "According to the information we have been getting over the CD and short wave radios, there will be at least one assembly point in each state and in some cases, more. Columbus, Ohio and Cave City are the assigned locations closest to us."

"I believe I would prefer moving in a southerly direction, don't you?" John looked around the circle and got assenting nods from all of them. John continued: "Since we are all in agreement, we'll send a party to Cave City in about a week and scout out the conditions. After they return we'll decide whether to check out Columbus. On your trip tomorrow, carry rifles and ammunition and, whatever you do, be careful. All the survivors may not be friendly," John warned.

Bob, Tim and Mark loaded the car the same evening. For an added precaution, they put thirty gallons of gasoline in the trunk. Although from preliminary appearances there would be an adequate supply along the way, they were taking no chances on being stranded. The environment at present didn't seem hostile but there was no telling what they would find on their journey.

The next morning the Baileys arose early and by 7:00 a.m., Bob, Mark and Tim were on their way.

Mark drove while Bob and Tim studied a map of the area, trying to pick out the best route. They weren't sure whether they should try the interstate or the other highways and rural roads.

"Mark, take the next intersection to the right. We'll try to stay south of Winchester until we pass it and then angle back northeast toward Powell County," Bob instructed. "This looks like the best approach."

Small towns in all stages of destruction occasionally broke the monotony of the brown, sere countryside. In most of them, rioting mobs had taken their toll, pillaging and burning. Partially decayed bodies cluttered the streets and sidewalks. Many of the people remained outdoors during their final hours.

They received warning quite a while before reaching a bombed area when increased blast damage heralded a lifting needle on the Geiger counter. The contaminated area caused them to detour twenty miles to the south before they could turn back to the east.

Thirty miles farther on, they skirted another devastated area. Bob reached in the glove compartment and pulled out the map. "I believe I'll mark these craters. It may come in handy for future travels."

The bombed out cities hampered their travels. They left major arteries and took side roads to bypass them.

"I've been trying to think of something to say to describe

the sights of what we've been seeing today and the only thing I can come up with is 'dead'," Mark commented.

"That pretty well portrays it," Bob agreed. All those majestic buildings that dad helped build are nothing but twisted, burned out hulks.

They made frequent detours and removed debris from the roads in many places and used up most of the daylight hours. Although there was only a short distance to go, none of them relished the idea of driving at night.

"We'll hole up tonight and try again tomorrow." Bob stated.

"I'll be glad to get there," Tim remarked.

"So will I," Mark chimed in. "The only proof of other living people is to see them."

The next morning, they resumed their journey and at 9:15, entered Stanton. Their vehicle approached the center of town and turned north at the intersection. They headed up Morris Creek to the top of Morris Mountain.

"Park here Mark. This is the place where we're supposed to leave the car and walk." Bob instructed.

"I sure hope you got those instructions right," Tim said. "This is wild looking country to start walking in."

"According to the directions, we have five miles to go to get to their shelter. There should be a pretty good trail most of the way." Bob reported.

"Should we bring both guns?" Mark wanted to know.

"Yes, I don't expect to need them but you never know."

Bob took the lead and entered the trail which led them east along the ridge. He set a fast pace over the rugged terrain. The dead leaves had all fallen from the trees and were now underfoot. The dry leaves crunched loudly, signaling their presence to anybody who might be listening.

Hordes of insects swarmed about them. They constantly swatted and brushed their heads and necks.

"I'll sure be glad to get away from these flies!" Tim exclaimed, swatting vigorously.

An hour later they came to a fork in the trail.

"We'll rest here five minutes," Bob announced, looking around for a spot to sit.

Tim appeared relieved. Although he was toughening up, the fast pace was beginning to tell on him. He pulled his shirt up and formed a tent over his head.

Five minutes later, Bob led off on the trail that veered northeast and started down- hill. He traveled at a slower pace and began looking closely for any signs of life. Fifteen minutes later, they were stopped short by a loud, "Halt!"

Mark instinctively brought his rifle up and a screaming bullet kicked up dirt and rock ten feet in front of him.

"Drop those guns!" The voice spoke sharply from the concealment of some nearby rocks.

"Go ahead and drop it Mark," Bob advised, tossing his rifle down.

"Who are you?" The voice inquired.

Bob explained who they were and the purpose of their visit.

A tall figure, dressed in camouflage clothing, emerged cautiously from the rocks and approached them with a rifle at the ready. He studied them carefully and then relaxed, lowering the firearm.

"My name is Jim Mercer," he began. "My brother Alvin and I have our families in a shelter not too far from here. We were somewhat reluctant to broadcast our location but finally decided that it would be best. The ones of us who are left will have to work together."

"We're certainly glad to see you," Bob replied. "You are the first living thing we have seen, except insects. It appears that all domestic animals, wild animals and birds are all gone."

"Yes, we managed to keep a cow, two pigs and a few chickens but everything else is dead. We have scouted out the towns in the surrounding area and haven't found any other people or animals. We have noticed an abnormal number of flies, ants, bees, grasshoppers and all other types of insects. In fact, they are already quite a nuisance."

"Did all of your family survive?" Bob inquired.

Jim's face took on a more sober expression. "All of us that went to the shelter made it just fine. Our brother, two sisters and their families could have lived if they'd only listened. We had ample room and urged them to come, even up to the day of the bombing. They thought we were crazy or some kind of fanatic. Some of them finally made it to the shelter the day of the attack but too late. They were already riddled with radiation."

"I'm sorry to hear that," Bob sympathized. "This seems to be the general pattern of occurrences throughout the country. Newscasts state there will be several million survivors in the United States. They refer to information they received from the President's office. However, from what I've seen, I'm beginning to wonder. What about other people in Kentucky? Have you heard of any more?"

"Yes, we are in radio contact with a man in Harlan County. He knows of three other families besides his and there will probably be more. It's early yet for many people to be out of their shelters and Eastern Kentucky has quite a few mines and caves that could have been used."

"That doesn't sound like very many people," Tim commented.

"Come with me. I'll take you to meet my brother and our families."

Jim led the way on a narrow trail around the base of a cliff. Bob, Mark and Tim followed.

Twenty minutes later, he took them to a cleverly concealed cleft in the sheer limestone face.

"Just a minute," Jim said, walked over to a niche in the rock and pushed a concealed button four times. He waited a full minute and pushed it four times. After waiting another minute, he pushed it three more times.

"This is my signal to let Alvin know I'm coming so they won't blow us away," Jim explained, leading them on through the entrance.

Just inside, Jim paused and took a flashlight from a ledge. He turned it on and led them on under the mountain. The temperature dropped noticeably and a dank smell greeted them. They trudged slowly along a narrow, gravelly stream bed in single file. The ones in the back had difficulty seeing. Dislodged rocks generated echoes which bounced off the ragged walls.

"Just ahead, you'll need to get down on your hands and knees," Jim advised.

Jim stopped, went to his hands and knees and they followed suit. He preceded them through a hole leading from the corridor into a fairly large room. On the opposite side they saw another opening with a light shining through.

Upon entering the lighted area, the cave took on a lived-in appearance. Eight piles of bedding lay at intervals around the room, interspersed with boxes, two tables, chairs, and numerous other articles. Although fairly crowded, it was neat and orderly.

On the far side of the room a man stood, holding a rifle ready, and eyeing them warily.

"Alvin, here they are. They're from Breton, about fifteen miles north of Lexington. They don't know of any survivors in their area and didn't discover any others on their trip to find us," Jim wound down in a subdued voice.

Alvin's shoulders slumped perceptibly when he heard the news but straightened again immediately.

"So be it," he remarked grimly. "The country appears to be much worse than we imagined. If they hit Kentucky this hard, I can imagine what happened to the eastern states."

Jim made the introductions and Alvin shook their hands warmly.

"Follow me and I'll take you to the rest of our family." Alvin walked across the room to where it narrowed into a corridor and led them about 100 feet, taking them up, down, and around a faint trail through the rock-strewn cavern. His and Jim's flashlights lighted the way sufficiently for them to travel without too much tripping and stumbling. The cave widened and they entered another small chamber, dimly lit by a glow from another entrance on the far side. They could hear voices and laughter.

Alvin led them into a well lit large room where several curious faces, suddenly silent, stared at them.

They all stopped just inside and Alvin introduced Bob, Mark and Tim to his family.

Alvin's family consisted of his wife, Rhonda, seventeen year old Rachael, Herbert, sixteen, fourteen year old Pamela and his twelve year old son, David.

Bob, Mark and Tim smiled and nodded.

Alvin and Rhonda appeared to be in their late thirties.

Jim introduced his wife, Paula and their three children, Donald, Tiffany and Ron, twelve, ten and eight.

Bob guessed Jim and Paula to be in their early thirties.

Quite a hubbub followed the introduction while Alvin and Jim's families plied them with questions of the outside.

Bob looked at Alvin and Jim helplessly, not knowing how to answer their questions as they waited eagerly for their reply.

Alvin broke the news to their wives and children gently but their enthusiasm dwindled rapidly when they learned the horrible truth. Alvin tried to keep optimism in his voice, but how do you break the news gently that hundreds of millions of your fellow humans died?

Rhonda interrupted. "Let's get off that morbid subject. There's nothing we can say or do to change what happened. There will be a better time to discuss it."

Are you hungry?" Paula asked. "Could we get you something to eat or drink?"

"I'm hungry," Mark admitted.

"So am I," Tim agreed.

"No thanks," Bob declined. "I'll eat later."

"Rachael, you and Pamela get these young men something to eat and drink," Rhonda instructed.

Mark and Tim became engrossed with the two young ladies who enthusiastically prepared their refreshments.

During the meal, Tim experienced something akin to

love at first sight. Immediately after, he maneuvered Pamela off to one side and engaged her in earnest conversation. The quick, impish quirks of her mouth sent thrills all the way to his toes as she talked. Although not physically mature, her budding body promised only pleasant expectations for the future. It wasn't long until they had advanced to the hand holding stage.

Meanwhile, Mark and Rachael, an attractive teenager mature for her years, abandoned by the younger pair, sat at the table and pursued mature subjects related to the unknowns facing them. Not too far into their conversation, Mark related his new-found love with Kathy.

"Bob, would you like to see our control center?" Alvin suggested.

"Yes I would," Bob accepted.

Alvin and Jim led the way and Bob followed.

The equipment installed in the twelve foot square cubicle impressed Bob. They had a 500 watt short wave transmitter, two short wave receivers, AC-DC radio, radiation monitoring equipment and an alarm system.

"What do you use for power to run all this equipment?" Bob asked.

"We have a 5000 watt generator outside the cave. See this cable going out the hole in the top of this room? The generator sets on a shelf above us."

"What about your fuel supply?"

"That wasn't easy," Jim replied. "By using a different approach, we were able to haul it by jeep to a point a mile and a half from here. The rest of the way, we carried it."

"You must use quite a bit of fuel with all this equipment."

"You're right," Jim explained. We have used around 200

gallons and our reserves are down to about fifty. One thing that helped though, we operate off batteries most of the time and only use the generator to recharge them, or when we are operating the transmitter."

"You seem to know a lot about electronics," Bob said.

Jim laughed. "Fortunate for us, I owned an electronic outlet in Mount Sterling. Consequently, I not only had a good working knowledge of equipment, but also the materials were readily available at wholesale prices when I needed them, not that prices would have made any difference."

Alvin commented. "I was fortunate in that respect for I know absolutely nothing about radios and electronics."

"Why did you and Jim decide to move into a shelter? It's obvious you worked on this for a long time in advance of the bombing."

Alvin scratched his head reflectively. "You know, it was the strangest thing. About three or four weeks before the war started, Rhonda began having dreadful premonitions of danger. She became frantic with worry. After about a week, she came up with what I considered to be an entirely irrational request. She wanted me to build a fallout shelter!"

"At first, I refused and she almost went out of her mind. Her doctor said she was either going to have a nervous breakdown or possibly go crazy."

"I decided to humor her. I told her I would build us one and she immediately began to calm down."

"I tried to stall but she would again become agitated and the only thing that would calm her was positive, rapid progress toward building the thing. Jim, Paula and I had a long discussion and decided that we would build the shelter regardless. Whether we did or did not need it was immaterial if it would preserve her sanity. We went all out in preparing this place but even at that, the timing was close. We barely finished and got moved in before the bombs began falling." Alvin concluded.

"This sounds similar to what happened to our family. It was my father who had the premonitions. We seriously considered having him committed for observation. Needless to say, we're glad we didn't."

"Bob, what are your plans?" Jim asked.

"I'm not too sure yet," Bob replied. "We're planning a trip to the assembly point at Cave City right away. You probably know, the government has been urging consolidation but we have our doubts about it."

"So do we," Alvin replied. "There's no need to rush into a move."

"We have a spare radio transmitter if you'd like to take it back with you," Jim offered. "This way we could stay in touch and coordinate some of our activities."

"Good idea," Bob accepted. "I certainly wished for a way to answer while listening to your broadcasts."

"We would like for you to spend the night with us, or longer?" Alvin offered.

"Thanks for the invitation," Bob replied. "I would like to get a fairly early start in the morning though. Now that we know our way, we should be able to make it back to Breton in one day."

"Alvin, why don't you tell Rhonda and Paula our company will be spending the night. I'll take Bob on the remainder of the tour. He'll probably be interested in seeing our ventilation system, intruder alarms, water supply and some of the other gimmicks that we used to enhance our survival."

"Good idea. I'm sure Rachael and Pam will be glad to have someone their own age visiting us. The entire family stays depressed over losing so many friends and relatives. Sometimes our plight is almost more than reason can bare," he added soberly.

The Baileys and Mercers enjoyed a lively evening in each other's company. They all realized that tomorrow would bring separation and each of them would suffer a real loss at the parting. The casual associations of the past, taken for granted, were now a rare treat. Weeks could pass before each group could meet others.

"Do you have any current news from outside and the rest of the world?" Bob asked.

Alvin responded. "We're fortunate, having the type reception we've been getting. With our antenna on top of this mountain, we have several good sources. One of these happens to be a radio amateur in Switzerland in the Alps. We meet with him and get a good bit of the news coming out of Europe. We also have at least a dozen other good contacts, most of them here in the United States.

Much of the information we are getting is just rumors. It's impossible to know who or what to believe. We've been keeping notes on as much as we can to see if we can get some sort of correlation and reliability on what we hear. Some of what we are hearing is downright scary if it is true."

Bob replied, "Alvin, if you have the time and don't mind, I'd like to hear as much as you would like to tell. It could have a bearing on what we do in the future."

"I guess you're aware of what's been taking place overseas?" Bob asked.

"We have some sketchy information but not a lot. The

last we heard, the European Supreme Leader is tightening his control of Europe. Also, he was on the verge of making a pact with Israel." "To continue that little scenario," Alvin added, "Mikhail met with Colonel Abe Wolverstein, the Israeli Prime Minister on July the twentieth and they made the pact. European troops have moved into Israel in token numbers to symbolize the protection provided under the pact and serve warning on Russia and the Arabs to keep `hands off'."

"Another bit of news that filtered out has to do with the world famine. The nuclear winter stopped this year's crops in their tracks. Practically nothing got harvested before it hit. Now for a bit of irony. A lot of the food that's missing overseas is the grain that we would normally have shipped from our surpluses."

"We're also hearing of diseases sweeping the world. People in a weakened condition from radiation are especially vulnerable to starvation and disease."

"What about Russia?" Bob asked.

Alvin continued. "Russia has more or less been marking time since the war. The ruling Troika firmly controls Russia. They are extremely wary of the United States of Europe and don't seem to know yet how to deal with their new rival. Although Europe supposedly surrendered to Russia during the nuclear war, that fact became immediately ignored and forgotten."

"Have you heard anything out of China?"

"Not a lot. We did hear that China hit us with a few nukes, probably more to test their capability than for any other reason, and she may have sneaked in some on Russia. We're pretty sure that Russia stroked China with a few also."

"Do we have any better information on our own country?"

"Not really. Our ruling government has been putting out a lot of information but we believe it's mostly smoke. We're beginning to get a clearer picture of what actually happened. There's an information network made up mostly of ham radio operators and their stories sound plausible.

"The United States got wiped out - obliterated - for all practical purposes.

"How did that happen?" Bob asked.

"Remember the ABM treaty we made with the Russians years ago?"

"Yes."

"We honored it and the Russians didn't. They not only built their elaborate shelter systems, but also knocked down most of our missiles and planes before they got to their targets. We bloodied them but they came out of it in good shape. It's beginning to appear our population is possibly smaller now than it was with the thirteen colonies."

Bob experienced a feeling of shock, hearing the reality verbalized, although he had already suspected the truth. "This country is going to revert to a total wilderness then in a few short years."

"You're right," Alvin agreed. "That may not be all bad since our only hope for survival will be to hide if forces from this new world government decide to come after us."

"It seems to me the president's assembly idea stinks." Bob stated.

"You're right," Alvin nodded.

Alvin continued, "Bob, there's one thing you and your family may want to consider, Jim and I have talked it over with our family and we are seriously considering a move from here into the mountains of eastern Kentucky or into West Virginia. With the uncertainties of what we may encounter from roving bands, it may be safest to go into an almost inaccessible area where we can hide and also set up some kind of a defense."

Bob replied, "Alvin, what you say makes sense. We may have to revert back to a life style of the 1800's or early 1900's. I'll discuss this with our family and see if we may want to pursue that with you."

Alvin and Bob continued their conversation and speculation for another hour and then went to bed.

Late the next evening, Bob, Tim and Mark arrived back home, tired from their long and hard day's travel. The others were all anxiously awaiting their return.

Bob pulled their vehicle in next to the farmhouse and before they got out, John, Ellen, Jesse, Ruth, Karen and Kathy were already outside and at the car.

Ruth embraced Bob with unspoken fervor.

They were all talking at once.

John spoke loudly to get their attention. "Let's get on inside and away from all these pests. It's getting dark and the mosquitoes are absolutely terrible."

"The insects seem to be multiplying fast aren't they?" Mark observed.

"Yes," John agreed, "and you can expect them to get much worse."

"Why?" Tim asked.

"With the death of all the birds, frogs, lizards and other animals which normally preyed on insects, the ecology related to insect control no longer exists. Also, it's a scientific fact that insects can withstand much higher levels of radiation than humans."

"What effect will this have on our survival?" Mark asked the question uppermost in everyone's mind.

"There's really no way of telling," John answered. "We're going through a period of adjustment and hopefully, the insect population will reach an equilibrium that will be bearable."

"I can see already if they get much worse, we'll have to wear veils when we go outside," Jesse contributed.

"Since it is so cool outside, why are the mosquitoes out anyway?" Mark asked.

"I wish I could answer that," John responded. "We'll probably see several strange happenings before it's over."

"Are you ready for a rundown on our trip?" Bob offered after they settled into the living room chairs and sofas.

"Would you rather eat supper first?" Ellen suggested. "It's ready as soon as we set it on the table."

"We are pretty hungry." Tim answered.

Everybody laughed.

"That settles it; let's eat," John consented, "then we'll be more comfortable."

Following supper, Bob, Mark and Tim related their adventures and it was after 1:00 a.m. before they had fielded all the questions and satisfied curiosities. Bob went into more detail with Jesse and John about the possibility of joining up with the Mercers and moving into a more remote area.

Tim had been dozing and longed for bed and sleep by the time they broke up. His manly pride wouldn't let him leave sooner.

The Baileys retired on an optimistic note, keenly aware

their lives would be governed by the uncertainties and unknown factors in their future.

While Mark made the trip to Montgomery County, Ellen, Karen, Ruth and Kathy worked feverishly, preparing for the wedding. Small needs became major obstacles in the gathering of material, thread, and needles for the wedding dress. Unfortunately, they didn't have a sewing machine and ended up doing all the stitching by hand.

"I'm glad we have almost finished the dress. I've stuck myself a million times," Ruth moaned.

"You'll survive," Ellen laughed, finally sounding like her old self. "You may as well get used to it. There will probably be a lot more pricks when you start making all your clothes."

"Perish the thought, but I guess this is good training."

The dress making behind them, they used their exclusively female imaginations to help Kathy prepare for the great day, accompanied by quiet, intimate chatter, giggles, blushes, and then, moments of serious discussions. Kathy would even have a trousseau, and they topped it all off with a lingerie party.

While the women made all the other preparations, including decorations and food, John took his Bible and formulated a wedding ceremony. They carefully hid all the signs pointing to the coming event and avoided any mention of it when Mark, Tim, and Bob returned.

Saturday morning, Ellen cautioned the entire group, "I don't care what you do today, but this evening at six, I want all of you here for the wedding rehearsal."

Kathy wouldn't let Mark out of her sight all day and they spent hours off to themselves, talking about-whatever people in love talk about.

Before 6:00. John, with the help of Tim, built a fire in the fireplace to dispel the chill and gloomy appearance caused by the overcast sky. They cranked up the generator and provided light for the festive occasion.

The Baileys celebrated the upcoming marriage that evening with occasional lapses of memory blotting out their grim circumstances, and experienced authentic joy and happiness.

Kathy had her moments of dejection and it wasn't hard to understand what effect the absence of her mother and father must have at the special occasion of her wedding.

The festive atmosphere continued Sunday until 2:00 p.m. came and the time for the ceremony.

Karen and Jesse served as bridesmaid and groomsman. Bob gave away the bride. Ellen cried. John stood before them and led them through the ceremony which culminated in the exchange of rings, found in a Breton jewelry store. Kathy was breathtaking with her abundance of light brown hair swept up on top of her head, radiant face, wedding dress and veil, and misty blue eyes that excluded everything except Mark from her vision.

Mark, decked out in a light gray suit he confiscated in Breton, looked handsome and dashing.

Mark kissed the bride and the wedding was over.

Following the reception, Mark and Kathy left on their honeymoon, forty-eight hours of privacy in the fallout shelter which Karen and Jesse graciously made available.

Following the wedding, the Bailey clan concentrated on activities designed to enhance their survival and several days passed while they canvassed the surrounding area. Most of them concentrated on stockpiling food, gasoline, clothing, and items of equipment they felt would come in handy in the years ahead.

Bob spent his time installing the radio transmitter and within three days of their return, contacted the Mercers. He and Jim met on the twenty meter band each evening. They swapped news and ideas and discussed plans. These contacts were sometimes joyous occasions when members of both clans took turns chatting back and forth on the radio.

However, much of the news filtering in from the rest of the world contained deadly serious connotations. And also, it became impossible to separate fact from fiction; they could only take what they heard, and speculate.

Word of oppression, slavery, barbarism, murder and abuses from the cadres of the New World Government and regional governments became more persistent and ominous as the days passed.

If the Baileys and Mercers needed to relocate, it would need to be soon if they wished to get moved before winter.

## CHAPTER VII

# THE FIFTH SEAL IS OPEN

Matthew 24:9-13: "Then shall they deliver you up to be afflicted, and shall kill you: and ye shall be hated of all nations for my name's sake. And then shall many be offended, and shall betray one another, And shall hate one another. And many false prophets shall rise, and shall deceive many. And because iniquity shall abound, the love of many shall wax cold. But he that shall endure unto the end, the same shall be saved."

Revelation 6:9 -11: "And when he had opened the fifth seal, I saw under the alter the souls of them that were slain for the word of God, and for the testimony which they held: And they cried with a loud voice, saying, How long, O Lord, holy and true, dost thou not judge and avenge our blood on them that dwell on the earth? And white robes were given unto every one of them; and it was said unto them, that they should rest yet for a little season, until their fellow servants also and their brethren that it should be killed as they were, should be fulfilled."

The new world government, headquartered in Rome continued extending its tentacles out into the world and tightening control.

The United States of America was designated as region three.

Initially, the president of the United States and his government was designated as a provisional government until further notice. They were clearly warned that they were to do nothing without approval from the world government.

All occupants of the United States were to make contact with their designated registration point and register. A six month grace period would be allowed. Following the six months, all who were unregistered would be labeled as outlaws and fugitives and subject to punishment, including death.

Christians worldwide were branded as criminals until they came in, registered and denounced Jesus Christ and God. Failure to do so was punishable by life imprisonment or death. Those able to work would be imprisoned and used as slaves. Those unable to work would be executed.

Christianity was proclaimed the culprit of all the world's woes. The claim was that without Christianity there would now be world peace without all the destruction which occurred.

The new world government began conscripting able bodied citizens from Europe to function as their enforcers throughout the world. These, in turn, would move into the ten world regions and enlist people for that area to help maintain control.

As time passed, horrible tales of the mass executions and martyrdoms of Christians filtered in from around the world. There was no shortage of volunteers willing to join the execution cadres.

Christians were crying out to God, begging for relief from the horrible persecution and tribulation.

Many Christians, remembering that Jesus Christ had warned them that they would have joy, with tribulation, resigned themselves to the persecution knowing they would soon enjoy eternal life with their Lord in heaven.

The Baileys and their contacts made an easy choice to remain hidden for as long as possible. If they were eventually caught, then the choice was simple. Stand strong for their faith in Jesus Christ and God. Unless God intervened quickly, many millions more Christians would be slain.

The carnage from fallout continued around the world. Tens of millions would still die from radiation sickness although the greatest danger was over. Millions survived up to now because they had some protection from the fallout following the storm. Of these, many, not knowing, left their shelters too early and continued collecting radiation whose dosage kept building in their bodies and would eventually kill them.

Pestilence outbreaks among the radiation sick continued whittling away at the total world population and famine, soon to get worse because of the nuclear winter, waited in the wings with its scythe, ready to reach in and extract millions more from the land of the living and deposit them in the realm of the dead.

Regional governments around the world placed their governments in motion to assess the damage, regain their control over the people and take their place in the New World Order.

The great emerging powers included the United States of Europe, Russia and China. Canada, Brazil, Mexico and several other small countries were functioning but weren't significant world forces. They were being systematically conscripted into the ten regions as the World Government tightened its control.

An uneasy peace continued around the world with the United States of Europe, under their Supreme Ruler out in front. He wasn't losing any time in contacting Russia, China, and all the other nations, trying to enlist them peacefully, if possible.

Within his own boundaries of the U S of E, mechanisms were in place and in motion insuring loyalty and obedience from every man, woman and child. Microscopic stainless pellets with a magnetic core in the center, injected into the arm just above the wrist, formed a coded number in the flesh that would identify the individual until they died. The plan, in its infancy, met the usual amount of resistance. The benign Superleader decreed detention for those resisting the order, giving them time to reconsider.

"At least they don't have time to fool with us and that's good," Bob thought.

Bob briefed the rest of the family on all the latest. The news didn't have much impact on them for their immediate personal plight kept them fully occupied.

Jesse arrived home on the evening of August 23 after locating another supply of gasoline northeast of Winchester. He would leave again the next morning with his tank truck for a load.

Jesse slept late the next morning and when he walked into the kitchen, a female quartet greeted him singing "happy birthday". He stood there grinning until the song ended.

Karen embraced Jesse. "Happy birthday darling; we have a cake for you. I made it myself, with a little help.

"You can be thankful we didn't have to spend your birthday in the shelter," Ellen laughed. "The cake we had for you completely dried out, hard as a brick."

Following breakfast, Jesse enjoyed his birthday cake and then left on another gasoline scavenging trip.

On Monday, October 22, almost three months after their excursion east of Mount Sterling, John approached the family and suggested a second journey. "Boys, I hate to put you through the ordeal of another trip but we must decide soon whether we are to stay here or leave," John began.

"Father, I'd like to go this time," Jesse volunteered.

John studied Jesse thoughtfully. "You seem to have gained back most of your strength. The travel shouldn't hurt you, I wouldn't think."

"You don't mind, do you Karen?"

"That's an unfair question, Jesse. I mind, but not enough to keep you from going."

"What about Mark and me?" Tim asked.

"You and Mark can toss a coin. I want at least one of you here. There's a safety factor involved or you could both go."

"We understand," Mark replied.

"When should we leave?" Bob asked.

"The sooner the better," John advised.

"We could leave early in the morning," Bob offered.

"Go ahead and make your plans accordingly then," John agreed.

Early the next morning, Jesse, Bob and Tim climbed into the car and headed south. Mark had lost the toss, disguised his disappointment, and waited outside to see them off.

They started with a wide detour to the west of Breton and Lexington. Super highways and interstates were out of the question. Saboteurs felled key bridges and overpasses in the early hours of the war, making it impossible to drive over the interstates except for short distances. Bombed out cities further complicated their travel. They worked their way slowly and steadily southward.

It was obvious after a few hours they wouldn't make the trip in one day. One particularly frustrating point came when they tried to get across the Kentucky river. After a four hour delay they finally found the Clay's Ferry Bridge intact. They moved two wrecked cars and then made their way across. Toward nightfall, they began looking for a place to stay.

"I don't relish the idea of driving at night on these roads," Bob pointed out.

Jesse replied, "Neither do I. Can you imagine breezing along at sixty or seventy and go off into a five-hundred-foot-deep bomb crater?"

"I hope you find a good place for tonight," Tim said. "This car will be uncomfortable and cramped if we have to sleep in it."

"We'll stop at the first house that looks halfway decent," Bob assured.

They drove on another ten miles and found a place suitable for the night. Bob and Tim checked the house from one end to the other with their Geiger counter and then they concentrated on cleaning out their living quarters. The bedroom area, coated with dust, took an hour of sweeping, dusting and shaking out bedclothes before they finished. Luckily, they hadn't found any bodies.

As part of their preparations for the morrow, Jesse took

a towel and bucket of water to the car and began scrubbing the bugs off the windshield. They had already made three stops on the way down to clean it. Each time, they removed enough bugs to give them visibility but many remained. The windshield was unbelievably dirty; it took Jesse an hour to clean it.

The next morning, Jesse, Bob and Tim went on their way early and, at 10.00 a.m., they entered Cave City. On approaching the downtown area, they saw the usual aftermath of pillaging, but it appeared that most of the buildings were still intact. Luckily, no bomb fell close to the city.

They wended their way up and down the streets and finally located city hall. Their spirits fell when they pulled in to the parking lot of the vacant appearing building.

"Let's get out and stretch our legs," Bob suggested.

After they got out of the car, a figure appeared at the front entrance of the building and walked swiftly toward them. His face beamed and he approached with hand outstretched.

"Am I ever glad to see you. My name is Paul Landers," he informed them, shaking their hands.

With introductions over, Bob asked anxiously, "We're not the only survivors in this city are we?"

Paul laughed. "Oh no. There are several people in this area but quite scattered. Counting you three, we now have a head count of 347 in and around Cave City."

"What about doctors and medicine?" Bob asked.

"We're fortunate in that respect. We have two doctors and both of them are knowledgeable in pharmaceuticals. They are already practicing and share a common office two blocks down this street."

"How do you communicate with one another?"

"We've had our problems with that. We handle emergency communications and notification through a network of two way radios, radio receivers and runners. We have exercised our system a few times in practice and it works quite well."

"What about community activities? Do you ever see each other?" Jesse asked.

Paul replied, "At present, we meet each week on Thursdays at 7:00 p.m. to discuss the current news and for just plain fellowship. There's also a nondenominational religious service each Sunday morning at ten. They hold the Thursday meeting and Sunday Church services in the Cave City High School gymnasium."

"That's quite a switch," Bob commented. "Are all survivors members of the same religion?"

"I'm afraid not," Paul laughed. "We have quite a cross section of doctrines. Differences in belief have already surfaced and undergone discussion. It remains to be seen if they can work together or will splinter back into their former denominations."

"Do you have any news from other parts of the country?" Bob continued.

"Yes, I'm part of a radio communications network and receive updated statistics twice each week on latest population counts, radiation levels and other pertinent information. Believe it or not, we're receiving reports from all over the world. Most of it is pretty sketchy."

Paul continued, "So far we have a count of 12,850 for the United States. This figure is growing every day and I'm sure it will go much higher, at least to thirty-thousand."

"Why did so many people die?" Jesse asked.

Paul studied a few moments and then replied. "A

combination of factors entered into it but basically, a lack of shelter and lack of food, or in other words, no advance preparation."

"Where are most of the living people located?" Tim asked.

"We have a concentration here in the cave area of Kentucky and also around Carlsbad, New Mexico. Quite a few occupied the mines in Pennsylvania, West Virginia and Eastern Kentucky. In fact, just about every area with mines or caves has several survivors."

"What about the east coast?" Bob wondered.

"Survivors have been practically non-existent along the eastern seaboard. Some could have lived in those areas except for a wholesale usurpation of shelters by bands of bandits. In most cases, the bandits were already dying from radiation poisoning but were well enough to force their way into shelters and either slaughter or drive out the occupants. They not only didn't help themselves but also managed to doom any of the potential survivors. Many of the people with no radio or radiation monitoring equipment simply left their shelters too early and got too much exposure."

"You mean if there weren't caves or mines, all the people are dead?" Tim asked.

"Not exactly," Paul explained. "Quite a few survived east of the Rockies. Also, there are some pockets along the Pacific coast in northern California, Oregon and Washington." We also suspect there are quite a few in Montana, Idaho and the Dakotas but they aren't getting in touch."

"I don't know of any mines or caves along the west coast. Were there several shelters in that area?" Jesse questioned.

"No, the concentrations of people along the Rockies and west coast were due to the terrain and wind conditions."

"We have also heard about hundreds of submarine survivors," Paul added. "Many of them were out on patrol and remained submerged until the radioactivity subsided. Submarines in port at the time of the attack rescued several men, women and children and took them to sea."

"What about Alaska and Hawaii?" Bob asked.

"The figures I gave you does include Alaska and Hawaii. There are around six hundred reported so far in Hawaii and four hundred in Alaska."

"Do you have any figures for the rest of the world?" Bob probed.

"It appears that Sweden probably fared well, and Switzerland. They took their fallout shelters seriously several years ago and it paid off for them. We only have approximations but it looks as if their population will be in the hundreds of thousands or even millions. The bad news is that Russia fared much better than we did. It looks like millions of their people lived."

"Unless some of the other countries come up with some surprises, overpopulation in the world won't be a problem for a long time."

"Is the war over?" Bob asked.

"As far as we know, it isn't," Paul replied. "We have no way of knowing if there are other missiles, especially on submarines, that could be fired. For this reason, we remain dispersed and still have access to shelters. Our enemies would destroy the rest of us if they could."

"Only thirty thousand!" Tim exclaimed. "That doesn't sound like very many people!"

"You're right Tim. The original thirteen colonies had over three and a half million people. Before the war, there were hundreds of American cities with more than thirty thousand. Right now, with no more people than we have, this entire country will revert to a wilderness, except for a few small settlements."

"Do you have a breakdown on ages and sex?" Bob asked.

"No, we only have sketchy information on that. Right now it appears the majority will be men. The submarines accounted for quite a few."

"I hope there are some girls," Tim remarked anxiously.

Paul replied seriously, "What you have said would be funny ordinarily Tim, but under the circumstances, it's a matter of deep concern. We are entirely dependent on the women of child bearing age to populate the country. I'm afraid to guess at how many are left."

"Another uncertainty is the genetics effect of the radiation. We can expect a high mortality rate among newborn babies," Bob added somberly, thinking of the child Ruth carried.

"Yes," Paul spoke gloomily, "This world has about five hundred rough years ahead, if it survives at all."

"What about animals? Are there many left?" Jesse asked.

Paul replied, "Luckily, in some of the cave areas, people saved some cows, horses, pigs, chickens sheep, dogs and cats. I'm sorry to say, though, it appears that the country is completely devoid of birds, except bats. Unless some survived somewhere in the rest of the world, we're going to have real problems with insects. You can already see a large increase in their population."

"We saw some pigs, chickens and cows on one of our

trips before coming here. I hope we'll have enough for a new start." Tim said.

"Well, it's obvious that for several years, survival will demand full time attention," Paul commented.

"Paul, do you have a theory that would explain how we arrived at this sorry state?"

"Bob, hashing over that issue is like beating a dead horse but since you asked, I'll tell you what I think."

"Liberalism killed us, not that the conservative side of the issues was doing that much better. We elected one too many liberal administrations and during the cycle, history got us. As a nation of people, we had lost the tough fiber, the tough mindset that built this nation. There's a proverb that says, 'When a nation loses its vision, the people perish."

"We weren't tough enough to execute drug peddlers. We weren't tough enough to execute the heinous murderers. We weren't tough enough to boot the self - seeking, self -serving blood suckers who served themselves and big money interests out of Congress. We weren't tough enough to force the media to be honest and fair in their reporting. We weren't tough enough to balance the national debt. We were selling our children and grandchildren's heritage to the Japanese, Arabs, and others.

"We got what we asked for, no more and no less, and we ran out of time. Humanity has come full circle and now we're back to food-clothing-shelter, and survival."

"Paul, your views are similar to mine. We were living in a deadly environment with all those nuclear weapons stockpiled and just didn't have the wisdom to cope. Since we were a democracy, I can't really fault our leadership.

They basically followed our desires and we can only blame ourselves."

"I'm thankful we met you and got an update on all the latest news. We'll go ahead and scout the area and see what the potential is for us settling here."

Paul cautioned, "Be careful where you go. People are skittish and if you go to a place already occupied, you could get shot. We had a recent report of bandits attacking a group of survivors. In fact, on your way back home, you had better keep a close watch."

"Thanks for the advice."

Bob, Tim and Jesse spent the rest of the day reconnoitering Cave City and the surrounding countryside. They encountered three families during the course of their explorations. After cautiously checking them out, the families loosened up and exchanged news with them. Tim came away happy; he met four girls near his own age.

Bob and his brothers selected a nice two story house on the outskirts of Cave City and after some cleanup, ate their supper and settled down for the night.

The next day, Thursday, they explored and then went back to city hall for the meeting.

The crowds broke into groups after the business session and the meeting turned into a festive occasion. Clusters of people stood around and talked for three hours after the gathering adjourned. The people, hungry for companionship, left reluctantly in small groups later in the night.

Bob and his brothers stayed until only a few people remained. They knew that after tonight it could be quite a while before they saw humans again, other than their own family. Finally, after the last group broke up, they left and returned to their Cave City house to spend the night.

The next morning, Bob, Jesse and Tim left early. They were cheerful and somewhat optimistic on the journey to rejoin their family.

Spring in Kentucky didn't bring any encouragement and one year after the firestorm, nuclear winter remained with them. The exceptionally cold, dreary winter months had made them yearn for the warm summer days but this was not yet to be. They had spent a long winter, burned wood in the fireplace to stay warm, and for the most part stayed indoors, avoiding the harsh weather. Temperatures had dipped below zero several times and occasionally, snow piled up fifteen and twenty feet deep. Survival became uppermost in their planning and actions.

Frigid winter had kept the Baileys prisoners since the October snows made travel impossible. Radiation intensity at times became scary as more particles continued falling from the sky. Atmospheric conditions dictated when these times of fallout would occur.

Now that spring had come, the Baileys took to the outdoors even if it was chilly. The Baileys made wearing hats and carrying umbrellas a habit. Their intensive monitoring with the Geiger counter taught them that relatively "hot" particles could fall from the sky at any time. This would continue to be the case until the atmosphere cleared.

Jim Morris relayed an odd piece of news over the short wave radio that sounded ominous. The oceans started losing significant amounts of water with the onset of winter. It didn't take a lot of brains to figure out where the water went. The event posed a threatening, unanswerable question; what effect would the added accumulation of ice in and below the polar region have on the rest of the earth, and them?

The one bright spot in the otherwise bleak winter occurred on February the tenth when Ruth gave birth to their second child, a son whom they named Samuel. She and Bob knew the Lamaze method and the birth went smoothly. Ellen stayed in the background, supplied the needed utensils, water, materials, etc. and let Bob handle it. They felt uneasy for several days, not having a doctor and medicine available, but the baby thrived and grew.

Two weeks after Samuel's birth, Mark and Kathy shyly announced that Kathy was pregnant. The entire Bailey clan rejoiced, although apprehensive. Bob and Ruth began immediately teaching them Lamaze. They would need all the help they could get for future child births.

Karen and Jesse weren't faring too well. So far, Karen had suffered two miscarriages which left her seriously ill at each happening. They were afraid to try again and couldn't ignore the actuality of all the radiation they each received during the nuclear storm. Their chances of having a normal baby, if they were ever able to have one, was slim.

Naturally, gasoline became a treasured commodity. Jesse's stashes throughout the countryside kept them adequately supplied for the immediate future but long range, something would have to be done, such as alcohol, or find an oil well and collect the condensates.

After it warmed up in the spring, the Baileys began a serious, cautious, and systematic search for other survivors. They carefully screened each person they found, trying to determine their reliability. If in doubt, they never divulged their location. They scouted the countryside north to the

Ohio River, south to Cave City, west to Elizabethtown and east to Hazard. They couldn't, and didn't try, to contact everybody but took much of their census by the word of the ones they did contact. They could account for less than a thousand people by midsummer of the year following the nuclear firestorm.

They tried to get information on people that would spell out their individual qualifications and abilities. For example, they located school teachers, auto mechanics, two doctors, one lawyer, farmers, etc. Badly scattered, the people resource remained ineffectual. Only by grouping (and for the time being they didn't dare), could they take advantage of individual talents.

Several months more passed and news filtering in sounded better in some respects and worse in others.

The United States of Europe, under Mikhail Ivanovich, probably functioned better than any other nation in the world. However, the specter of famine stalked them and all other nations, with the exception of the United States whose population was so small; food hadn't yet become a problem.

The coalition calling itself the United States of Europe stretched its diplomatic tentacles to Africa and Asia, wooing other countries and tempting them to join the greatest federation ever to exist on the face of the earth. They claimed England, that empty island devoid of life, and also laid claim to the North American continent. Although radiation levels in the Continental United States prevented invasion from outside forces, restive nations established their claims, guaranteeing that in only a matter of time, invasion would come.

Arabs impatiently bade their time, waiting for

circumstances that would allow them to achieve their dream, eliminate Israel. However, the Supreme Ruler of the world government and of the United States of Europe, made it clear that this would never happen. He and Colonel Wolverstein continued to collaborate and maintain Israel's security. Both he and the Colonel, looking ahead, were already making plans to exploit the fertilizers in the Dead Sea, following the nuclear winter, and replenish their nation's food supplies.

Although skies were much lighter than a year ago, the nuclear winter wasn't over. Disappointed, the world would have to wait at least another year before crops could grow.

In the early fall, the Baileys asked for a meeting at Richmond of all interested parties to make plans. They knew that their time of isolationism would someday come to an end and all of their survival would probably depend upon a team effort. They set the date for September 10.

Kathy, eight months pregnant, couldn't travel so Ruth and Ellen and Ruth's two children remained with her.

John, Bob, Mark, Tim, Karen, and Jesse all traveled in the same vehicle to conserve fuel. They set out early on the tenth and discovered a large crowd at Richmond when they got there.

By 2:00 that afternoon, 650 people had gathered. They used the football field for assembly and started their meeting.

Different speakers took their turn in front of the group, stated their views and then relinquished the spot to the next speaker. Although they presented good information and ideas, the overall proceedings got pretty confusing. Finally, the assembly broke itself down into groups of ten who met and worked on the different issues.

The meeting lasted two more days. All the people in

attendance gleaned a wealth of information through the process, equally informed on all the details.

The overriding question had to do with assembly, looking to their future security and wellbeing. Realizing they would never be a military force or have the ability to defend themselves from one, they still recognized the security a group could offer, especially if the rumored marauding bands ever made it to their part of the country.

The group also resolved that recommendations coming from their deliberations weren't binding.

The assembly agreed to ultimately settle in Eastern Kentucky in the mountains of Harlan County and vicinity unless things changed. The mountainous country, multitudes of caves, old coal mines and natural defenses were some of the reasons for the decision. They hoped to make the move and be in place in time to plant spring crops if the nuclear winter allowed it. The lightening skies and warming temperatures offered some encouragement.

The Baileys and Mercers got together just as soon as they arrived at Richmond. The Mercers said they would probably remain at their cave, and for good reason, since they enjoyed a high degree of concealment and ideal living conditions. They encouraged the Baileys to take up residence near them so they could all work together.

Tim and Pamela highly favored that idea for they were renewing the friendship started a few months before when the Baileys first visited them.

A subdued group left the assembly and went back to their respective homes to set in motion plans decided upon during the meeting.

# CHAPTER VIII
# THE SIXTH SEAL IS OPEN

Revelation 6:12-17: "And I beheld when he had opened the sixth seal, and, lo, there was a great earthquake; and the sun became black as sackcloth of hair, and the moon became as blood; And the stars of heaven fell unto the earth, even as a fig tree casteth her untimely figs, when she is shaken of a mighty wind. And the heavens departed as a scroll when it is rolled together, and every mountain and island were moved out of their places.

And the kings of the earth, and the great men, and the rich men, and the chief captains, and the mighty men, and every bondsman, and every free man, hid themselves in the dens and in the rocks of the mountains; And said to the mountains and rocks, Fall on us, and hide us from the face of him that sitteth on the throne, and from the wrath of the Lamb: For the great day of his wrath is come; and who shall be able to stand?"

John 14:1-4: "Let not your heart be troubled: ye believe in God, believe also in me. In my father's house are many mansions. If it were not so, I would have told you. I go to prepare a place for you. And if I go to prepare a place for you, I will come again, and receive you unto myself, that where I am, there ye may be also. And whither I go ye know, and the way ye know."

Luke 21:25-28: "And there shall be signs in the sun, and in the moon, and in the stars; and upon the earth distress of nations, with perplexity; the sea and the waves roaring; Men's hearts failing them from fear, and for looking after those things which are coming on the earth: for the powers of heaven shall be shaken.

And then shall they see the Son of man coming in a cloud with great glory. And when these things begin to come to pass, then look up, and lift up your heads; for your redemption draweth nigh."

1 Thessalonians 4:16, 17: "For the Lord himself shall descend from the heaven with a shout, with the voice of the archangel, and with the trump of God; and the dead in Christ shall rise first: Then we which are alive and remain shall be caught up together with them in the clouds, to meet the Lord in the air: and so shall we ever be with the Lord."

1Corinthian 15:50-52: "Now this I say, brethren, that flesh and blood cannot inherit the kingdom of God; neither doth corruption inherit incorruption.

Behold, I shew you a mystery; We shall not all sleep, but we shall all be changed. In a moment, in the twinkling of an eye, at the last trump: for the trumpet shall sound, and the dead shall be raised incorruptible, and we shall all be changed."

A week after returning from Richmond, John and Ellen walked out of the house at 8:00 AM holding hands to take a stroll around the front yard. They often did this early in the morning just for the pleasure of quiet time in each other's company.

Helen asked, "John, what's different? Look at the sky. Look at the billowing white clouds. Look at the sun and the surrounding atmosphere. It's absolutely beautiful! It's surreal!"

John remarked, "Helen, wait right here. I'm going to get the rest of the family out here so they can enjoy the view."

Soon, John had the rest of the family out in the yard to enjoy the scene. Looking to the east, they could see a dove sitting on top of a statue of Jesus Christ in the Breton Memorial cemetery.

The earth began to tremble. The trembling soon became a shake. As the shaking increased, a rumbling noise could be heard and increased as the shaking increased.

Ruth pointed to the west. "The moon is turning red."

Jesse exclaimed. "Look at the sun. It is getting dark and it seems twilight is coming back."

As they watched, the moon became more blood-red and the sun became darker and darker.

The quaking of the earth became more violent. Terror began to steal upon them.

John spoke loudly to be heard above the increasing noise. "Let's all get in a circle and hold hands and pray. John prayed and praised God for the glory of God, the providence of God, and God's love for all his family and for sending Jesus Christ down to be their savior and in saving them all from the horrors that had come upon the earth in the past few months."

They all stood in a circle, holding hands, with heads bowed. John told them, "Look up and watch for Jesus!" They all looked up.

Suddenly, Jesus Christ appeared in the billowing clouds

in all His glory. The sky lit up in Shekinah Glory. All the surrounding earth stood out in brilliant relief.

The blood-red moon and the black sun could still be seen but had no effect on the surrounding light. The quaking and the noise subsided.

As they stood, holding hands and looking up, they heard the trumpet pealing out. They saw Jesus Christ coming down from the clouds and closer to the earth in power and great glory!

Looking to the east, they saw hundreds of transformed bodies rising from the graves and ascending into the sky, in the twinkling of an eye.

They immediately felt the change as their bodies transformed from corruptible to incorruptible and they rose in the twinkling of an eye and met Jesus Christ in the air!

AMEN and AMEN!

# EPILOGUE

Horrible events have devastated the world. The worst is yet to come. This is the beginning of the wrath of God and the wrath of the Lamb. Billions more will die.

Events prior to the opening of the sixth seal were equivalent to birth pains preceding a birth. Now the birthing has begun.

The opening of the sixth seal is probably not quite the mid-point of the seven years of tribulation. Likely, there's between four and five years left.

The war described is not the battle of Armageddon but is possibly related to the battle prophesied in Ezekiel, concerning the armies from the north and Middle East. (Gog and Magog)

All the destruction mentioned in this story is not the wrath of God. Up to this point, all the destruction and havoc has been Satan inspired and man-made with a prodding and manipulation by God.

The end of "The Church Age" has just occurred as Jesus Christ appeared in the clouds with a shout and the sound of the trumpet, and met His church as they were transformed and rose to meet Him.

There are no more Christians remaining on the earth.

"The Day of the Lord" which was prophesied many times in the bible has just begun as the moon turned the color of blood, the sun turned black and earthquakes begin to shake the earth.

The wrath of God and the wrath of the Lamb have begun and will get progressively worse until the culmination of the seven years of tribulation.

The beginning of the seven years began with the seven year peace treaty between the one world government and Israel.

The one world government materialized at the end of the nuclear war. The machinations of the government led by the anti-Christ and inspired by Satan, will continue to enslave the world, attack Israel and oppress and persecute the new Christians who are accepting Jesus Christ during the tribulation.

This satanic government and all the results from this are running in tandem with the outpouring of the wrath of God which is described in the book of Revelation.

The end, culminating in the return of Jesus Christ and the battle of Armageddon are inexorable and fast approaching.

Many scholars have pored over the intriguing and cryptic message Jesus Christ gave to John the Apostle on the Isle of Patmos. Many books have been written. All we know for sure is, it's coming and we don't know when.

God will continue to extend his offer of salvation to the peoples remaining on the earth. Most will refuse, having believed the great delusion put forth by Satan and the anti- Christ. Most of them will have taken the mark of the beast.

Life on earth will become much worse as Jesus Christ comes down to wage war against His enemies and God's enemies until they are totally defeated and destroyed.

Then, Jesus Christ, the Lamb of God who took away the sins of the world, who has now taken on the role of the Lion of Judah, will rule the world with a rod of iron for a thousand years.

Printed in the United States
By Bookmasters